DARK WITCH

RESURRECTION

THE CHILDREN OF THE GODS
BOOK EIGHTY-FIVE

I. T. LUCAS

Dark Witch: Resurrection **is a work of fiction!** Names, characters, places, and incidents are products of the author's imagination or are used fictitiously and are not to be construed as real. Any similarity to actual persons, organizations, and/or events is purely coincidental.

Copyright © 2024 by I. T. Lucas

All rights reserved.

No part of this book may be reproduced in any form or by any electronic or mechanical means, including information storage and retrieval systems, without written permission from the author, except for the use of brief quotations in a book review.

Published by Evening Star Press, LLC.

EveningStarPress.com

ISBN: 978-1-962067-45-4

1

KIAN

Kian surveyed the unusual group of people he'd assembled in his office and wondered if he was overdoing it. After all, the royal twins were little more than emaciated corpses and were in no state to offer resistance or cause any trouble.

Still, after all the warnings about how powerful and dangerous the twins were, Kian wasn't taking any chances. If the Eternal King feared them, he must have a good reason for it.

Or maybe not.

The king might have been paranoid, which was very likely given the lengths he was willing to go to, to keep his throne. It could also be that the paranoia was genetic, and if so, Kian might have inherited the trait from his great-grandfather.

The thought was so amusing in a macabre way that a soft chuckle escaped Kian's throat.

"What's so funny?" Bridget asked.

"The role genes play in shaping who we are." He waved a dismissive hand. "Don't mind me. It's not important."

The doctor leaned back in her chair. "We have nothing better to do while we wait for William to arrive and Anandur to return with the coffees and pastries, so you might as well tell me."

Kian let out a sigh. "I thought I might have inherited my paranoia from the Eternal King. I wouldn't have minded inheriting his brilliance, his charm, and his leadership skills, but the flip side of that is megalomania and disregard for the sanctity of life, and I'm grateful that I didn't inherit those traits."

Bridget's eyes softened. "You are an excellent leader, Kian. We all tease you about your paranoia, but the truth is that we are glad you are so diligent about protecting us."

He dipped his head. "Thank you."

She smiled. "That being said, I don't think we all need to wear compulsion-filtering earpieces on day one. The twins will not wake up from stasis and immediately try to compel everyone to obey them."

"They might."

That was why they were waiting for William to bring more devices for those who still didn't have them and needed instructions. That included Bridget, Merlin, and Gertrude, the medical team tasked with reviving the twins from stasis.

Jade had her pair, but the four hybrids she had chosen to accompany her needed filtering earpieces of their own.

Her task was to provide familiarity and security.

The twins didn't know her personally, but they would find her Kra-ell features familiar and understand her language. Not so with the hybrids, who looked different, and Kian wondered about Jade's choice.

She could have selected some of the older pureblooded males, those who had arrived on the settler ship with her and knew the old customs, but they had been sentenced to community service, so she'd probably decided that taking them out of the village wasn't a smart move. The purebloaded females could have also been a good choice. They knew the Kra-ell customs as well, and some of them were skilled warriors, so they could have provided protection if necessary.

The younger pureblooded Kra-ell who had been born on Earth were not familiar with the Kra-ell traditions, and their mastery of the language was probably only so-so, but the hybrids were no better.

Had she chosen them because she trusted them more or because they were easier to control?

Or maybe...

When the answer suddenly occurred to him, Kian realized Jade's choice was brilliant. The hybrid Kra-ell were half human, and therefore resembled how the twins probably looked. Showing the twins people who were hybrids like them and who were not reviled by their pureblooded companions was an excellent and expeditious way to assure the twins that they were safe and welcome.

Still, her brilliant choice might miss the mark simply because the intended beneficiaries would not be aware enough to realize what they were seeing.

It would take weeks or even months for the twins' bodies to regenerate to full strength, and their minds might take even longer to recuperate.

There was also the issue of the dead Kra-ell, who needed proper funeral ceremonies, but that wouldn't happen immediately upon their arrival either. Jade would have to return and bring along purebloods who knew the Kra-ell prayers to send the souls of their dead to the fields of the brave, or whatever they called their afterlife.

"I'm a little worried," Merlin said. "Hildegard is an experienced nurse, but I'm uncomfortable leaving her alone in charge of the village clinic." He turned to Bridget. "One of us should stay behind, and the other should take both nurses to the keep."

Bridget regarded him with a smile. "The only ones who might need our help are the humans, and I don't expect any emergencies that Hildegard can't triage in our short absence."

Merlin shook his head. "The village is isolated, and if, Fates forbid, anything serious happens, it might take us over an hour to get back here."

"Relax." Bridget put a hand on his shoulder. "Nothing will happen while we are gone for a couple of hours."

"It's going to take much longer than that," Merlin grumbled. "It's not like we're going to throw some fresh water on the twins and leave. If it was that easy, Anandur could do it by himself. We must monitor them until they stabilize and intervene if they become distressed."

Bridget nodded. "Just in case, we should revive them one at a time."

"I agree a hundred percent." Merlin leaned back in his chair. "And you can handle it on your own, so I can stay here in case any humans need medical attention."

It seemed to Kian that Merlin didn't want to leave the village for some reason, or maybe he had a problem with reviving people from stasis, or maybe his problem was just with reviving the royal twins. Whatever his issue was, he wasn't wriggling out of it.

Kian leaned forward and squared his gaze at Merlin. "I need you there. You are our expert on tracker removal after performing dozens of these procedures on the Kra-ell. There is every reason to suspect that the twins have trackers implanted in their bodies, and we cannot risk them being activated when the twins are revived. It is critical to remove them while their bodies are still at minimal functioning, so the trackers don't go online and alert the Eternal King. It is crucial to hide their survival from him."

For a second or so, Merlin looked like he was searching for a rebuttal, but then he nodded his agreement.

Gertrude frowned. "Will we be able to move them into the scanner, though? I thought their condition was so bad that Julian didn't want to even remove them from the pods before they were brought to the clinic."

Kian nodded. "William rigged up a hand scanner that we hope will be sensitive enough to find the trackers while the twins remain in their stasis chambers. He will explain when he gets here."

2

KIAN

"Sorry I'm late." William rushed into the office with a large bag dangling from his fingers. "I had to wait for the earpieces to be tested. They were fresh off the assembly line."

Merlin cocked a brow. "You have an assembly line?"

"Of course." William pulled out a chair and sat down. "How do you think we put together all these gadgets you all love?"

The doctor shrugged. "I thought one person did everything from start to finish."

"It's less efficient that way." William reached into his bag. "But we do that when we're working on a one-of-a-kind like this beauty." He pulled out a device very similar to the wands used by airport security to scan individuals manually. "This portable tracker scanner is just as efficient as the big machines we used on the

Kra-ell. I calibrated this one for the dimensions of the Anumatian trackers and their X-ray signature."

"When did you do that?" Merlin eyed the device suspiciously.

"Right after the gods arrived, they told us they were looking for the other Kra-ell pods. I figured that we may again find ourselves needing to look for these implanted trackers and may not have a CT machine available." He chuckled. "I didn't expect to have to put this wand to the test so soon."

Looking closely at the device William handed him, Merlin still seemed skeptical. "Won't the stasis chamber interfere with the device's readouts?"

William shook his head. "The wand is programmed to look for the specific trackers we found. It will ignore anything else, even if made from the same material."

Kian sighed. "Scanning them in the stasis chamber is not ideal, let alone performing any procedure on them if trackers are found. In their condition, that may prove fatal, but the trackers going live poses an existential risk not only to the clan but possibly to the entire population of Earth. It is not a risk I'm willing to take to save the twins."

He wasn't being paranoid or dramatic for effect. The Eternal King would not allow such a potential risk to his reign to continue.

For a long moment, no one spoke, and when the door opened and Anandur walked in with trays of coffee and bags of pastries, there was a collective sigh of relief.

"It's a madhouse down at the café," Anandur said as he put the trays on the conference table. "Wonder hopes the new human arriving in the village this afternoon will apply for a job. They need help desperately." He put down the paper bag and started pulling out wrapped pastries.

"Who is the human?" Merlin asked.

"She is from Igor's former compound," Anandur said. "You've probably seen her around during the cruise. The server with the blue hair and the piercings. She and Peter got close, and she asked to be transferred to the village."

Merlin's face split into a huge grin. "I know who you are talking about. Marina is lovely. I'm so glad that they are going to live here."

Kian had approved Marina's transfer because he believed the Fates must have brought her and Peter together for a reason, although he couldn't fathom what that reason might be.

Unions between immortals and humans were a prescription for heartache, and Kian knew that better than most.

In his youth, he had fallen in love with a mortal, married her against his mother's wishes, and had a daughter with her.

That story hadn't ended well, but maybe Peter's would.

Kian groaned. "I never expected so many humans to be living in the village."

"We don't have all that many," Bridget said. "Including the newcomer, there will be nine people in total."

Kian frowned. "Are you counting Karen's kids and Lisa in that?"

"No, of course not." Bridget tore a piece of her pastry and put it in her mouth.

"Then it's five more." Kian lifted his hand, fingers splayed. "That brings the total to fourteen."

Kian glanced at his watch. "We should head to the parking garage in a few minutes."

"Did they land yet?" Jade asked.

"No, but they are about to."

The time it took to get from the village to the keep was about the same as from the clan's airstrip to the keep, so as soon as the two planes carrying the Tibetan team and the stasis chambers landed, he and his group should head out.

Jade glanced at her watch. "Weren't they supposed to arrive almost an hour ago?"

Kian nodded. "They hit a bit of a snag on the way, something about avoiding turbulence, so they were delayed. But they should be landing at the airstrip any minute now. Okidu and Onidu are there to meet them and help transport the team, the equipment, and the stasis chambers to the keep."

"I remember when we revived Dalhu from stasis," Anandur said. "The dude was only entombed for a week, and he still looked like death warmed over when we opened the sarcophagus. I can't even imagine what state the twins are in." He shivered, but it was more of an act than an involuntary response.

Kian let out a soft chuckle. "You don't have to imagine. Just stroll down to the catacombs and look at the Doomers stashed away there. That should give you a pretty good idea."

None of the Doomers they had collected over the years had spent more than a couple of centuries in the clan catacombs, though, so they were probably in a much better state than the twins.

Up until recently, Annani had disallowed executing captured Doomers, and they had been forced to put them in stasis and take care of the bodies because of his mother's naive belief that someday they could be redeemed. But after what they discovered in Acapulco and the atrocities that the Doomers had the cartel commit, she had finally changed her mind.

Kian didn't know why it had taken her so long.

Doomers had been committing terrible atrocities throughout human history. But the truth was that it had been a long time since they had done something so evil, and his mother had probably thought that those days were over, never to return. It must have been a shock for her to realize that their cruelty and barbarism were still just as present.

"Wonder told me about what she looked like when she woke up from stasis after five thousand years," Anandur said. "She was a walking skeleton."

"I'm surprised she could walk at all," Bridget said.

Anandur puffed out his chest. "My Wonder is a warrior. She's unstoppable."

Bridget nodded. "She is, but don't forget that the twins have been in stasis for seven thousand years without the benefit of being able to absorb nutrients from the earth like Wonder could. They are probably much worse off."

Kian reached into his pocket, his fingers brushing against the smooth, metallic surface of the compulsion-filtering devices. "Should we test the new earpieces?" He looked at William. "I'm curious about the new Kra-ell translation feature."

"Sure." Jade pulled hers out. "I tested mine with Phinas, and they worked beautifully." She nodded at William. "These will save me a lot of time translating for everyone else and make wearing them less awkward." She turned to Kian. "We don't even need to tell the twins about the compulsion-filtering feature of the devices. They will assume we are wearing them for their translation capabilities alone."

Kian shook his head. "They will figure it out eventually, and then they will not trust us. I'd rather be upfront about it." He smiled coldly. "That way, they will know not to try anything. But we can wait until they get better before telling them."

His mind flashed back to Igor and the moment when the powerful Kra-ell had held him at his mercy, his will subsumed by the force of the pureblood's compulsion. If Jade hadn't been there, and if she hadn't acted with such decisiveness and courage, Kian shuddered to think what might have happened.

He shook off the disturbing memory and straightened his shoulders. "Even though it is unlikely that the twins will pose a threat to us in their current state, we need to take the necessary precautions and ensure our safety, which means never forgetting to wear the earpieces while around them." He looked pointedly at Jade. "But we must also remember that they are my mother's half-brother and sister and are most likely not our enemies. We should treat them with kindness, care, and vigilance."

3

JASMINE

Jasmine squirmed in her seat as the bus driver navigated the spiral drive's sharp turns down into the keep's bowels.

How deep was it?

They had already passed several parking levels, and there still seemed to be no end to the downward drive. The bus was air-conditioned, yet she could feel it getting colder the deeper they went.

Imagining the layers of earth above them made her feel claustrophobic, and she instinctively lifted her hand to reach for Edgar's, but she fought the urge and put her hand back in her lap. He wouldn't deny her, but it would be cruel for her to do that.

They were no longer together as a couple, and she needed to respect the new boundaries of their tenuous friendship.

Behind them, the large truck that carried the eighteen Kra-ell stasis chambers trundled along, forced to make the same sharp turns as the bus while somehow avoiding scraping against the concrete walls.

Thankfully, the twins' stasis chambers were on the bus, secured with ropes in the back, with Julian and Ella watching over them.

When they finally reached the bottom, the bus driver stopped in front of a gate, and as it slid to the side, he drove through and parked.

The place was nearly empty, with only a few cars parked in a row. The truck followed inside and stopped next to the bus.

"Have you been here before?" Jasmine asked Edgar.

"Of course. This is the clan's private parking level."

Despite the breakup, Edgar was doing his best to be not only cordial to her but also friendly, and she appreciated his effort.

It had been a difficult conversation, a painful admission of the truth that had been staring them both in the face for longer than either cared to admit. Their relationship had run its course. The spark that had once burned between them had faded, leaving behind only the dying embers of what might have been.

They still cared for each other, but they both knew that they were not meant to be. They had been good together, but it was more of a friends-with-benefits arrangement than the love she'd witnessed between Margo and Negal and the other couples who had accompanied them to Tibet.

After witnessing their eternal and all-consuming love, Jasmine wasn't willing to settle for anything less.

Still, Edgar had been hurt by her words, and the pain she'd seen in his eyes had made her heart ache, but to his credit, he had been more gracious and understanding than she had thought he would be.

"I'm not going to pretend that I'm not disappointed," he had told her. "But I get it. We had a good run, and I don't regret it." He'd offered her his hand. "I'm all for staying friends if you are up for it."

Jasmine had felt a rush of relief at his words. She would love for them to move forward as friends without bitterness or resentment.

"Of course, I am." She'd put her hand in his. "You are a great guy, and I care about you. I will keep my fingers crossed and light candles to hasten your truelove mate's arrival."

Edgar had chuckled at that, a glimmer of his old humor returning to his eyes. "I hope you will do that in reverse order. Light the candles first and cross your fingers later."

When she'd laughed, he'd continued, "And what about you? Is Prince Charming your truelove mate, the other half of your eternal soul?"

Jasmine had shrugged, a flutter of uncertainty and anticipation mingling in her gut. "Maybe. It's also possible that he'll take one look at me and run screaming in the other direction."

Edgar had laughed and shaken his head. "That's very unlikely. You are a beautiful and desirable woman."

Jasmine knew she was attractive, but the prince was not from Earth, and what he considered desirable might be very different from who and what she was. Maybe he was into Amazonian warrior women who could wield a sword and jump forty feet in the air.

In her fantasies, though, the prince opened his eyes for the first time after seven thousand years, took one look at her, and fell in love with her on the spot. But that was so silly that she felt embarrassed even thinking it.

The poor guy was barely alive, and if he managed to open his eyes at all, the first person he'd see would be the doctor, and the first thought that would cross his mind was to try to understand where he was and when.

She felt sorry for all he had lost while asleep in stasis.

"You know…" Edgar had leaned closer to her. "There is a chance that the prince isn't into women. In which case, I'd say you dodged a bullet."

Jasmine had laughed at that, but it wasn't all that funny.

The prince had been consecrated into the priesthood, and Kra-ell priests were celibate. He might not be into anyone other than the deity he worshiped.

4

EDGAR

"I'm heading up to the penthouse for a proper shower." Edgar leaned over to kiss Jasmine's cheek, remembering at the last moment that it was no longer appropriate.

In some human cultures, it was common for everyone to kiss each other in greeting and farewell, but Edgar wasn't comfortable doing it.

"Okay." Jasmine smiled at him, and it wasn't fake. There was genuine affection there, which made it even worse. "I'll see you later, right? You're not leaving yet."

She wasn't getting rid of him that easily. "No, not yet. I'll wait for you." He forced a smile. "We still need to have an end-of-mission party."

"Of course." The softness in her eyes was slaying him.

Couldn't she be more of a bitch about it so he could rage at her?

Turning on his heel, Edgar stalked through the halls of the keep, heading to the freight elevator in the back so he wouldn't be in the way while Jade's crew of hybrids carried the stasis chambers from the truck to the catacombs.

The problem was that the service elevator didn't go to the penthouse, and he had to get out at the lobby level and switch to the one that did.

Waving at the guards, he called for the penthouse's dedicated elevator, and when the doors opened, he was greeted by soft instrumental music playing on the hidden speakers. Regrettably, it wasn't loud enough to drown out Jasmine's voice in his head. The conversation they'd had on the plane was still replaying in his mind in a relentless loop of anger and regret.

She had dumped him.

Edgar had never been dumped before.

He had always been the one who walked away, and it hurt to be on the receiving end of the boot. It was a bitter pill to swallow, a jagged shard of glass that lodged in his throat and refused to move no matter how much logic he tried to wash it down with.

He knew he should be happy for Jasmine and respect her wishes like the good friend he had promised to be. But the green-eyed monster of jealousy had sunk its claws deep into his soul, poisoning his thoughts and twisting his emotions until he could barely recognize himself.

She was right that they both deserved better and that his truelove mate was waiting for him somewhere, but knowing and accepting were two different things.

As he reached the penthouse, Edgar slammed the door behind him with a satisfying bang, the sound echoing through the empty rooms, a hollow and mocking reminder that he was once again on his own.

It had been nice to be part of a couple, to have someone to return to at the end of the day, someone he'd thought belonged to him. And it wasn't about being a possessive asshole. For the short time they had been together, Edgar believed that he also belonged to Jasmine.

Except, she didn't want him.

Stripping off his clothes, he left a trail of discarded garments in his wake as he stalked toward the bathroom. The shower beckoned with a promise of a powerful stream of hot water and a good soap that might wash away the stain of failure and inadequacy.

But even as he stood beneath the scalding spray, Edgar couldn't escape the anger that felt like a corrosive acid in his veins.

If not for that damn corpse of a prince, Jasmine would still be his.

He had done his best for her. He had been there for her every step of the way, and they had been great in bed together. What more could that alien prince give her?

Nothing.

Even if he woke up from his stasis with his brain intact, the prince and Jasmine had nothing in common, nothing to talk about, nothing to share. How could she hope to love the half-god, half-Kra-ell alien?

Better yet, how could she hope that he would love her?

Or perhaps love didn't matter to her?

Jasmine was obsessed with royalty so much that she didn't even care that her royal was not the same species as her, which painted her as shallow and stupid.

The thing was, though, she was neither of those things. She was just misguided and blindsided.

As he stepped out of the shower, Edgar felt a flicker of something dark kindle in his chest. It was a feeling he had never experienced before, a burning need to lash out, to hurt and destroy, and make someone else feel the same pain and turmoil that was tearing him apart from the inside out.

He knew it was wrong and that it went against everything he had ever believed in, every code of honor and decency that had guided his life until this moment. But the jealousy was like cancer, eating away at his reason and his restraint until there was nothing left but a raw, bleeding wound that refused to heal.

"Take a breath," he commanded himself. "You are not going to hurt anyone."

Edgar toweled off, pulled on a fresh set of clothes, and began to plot.

He wouldn't do anything stupid, but there was no law against competing for the affection of a female and using any means considered fair play. He would find ways to undermine the prince and expose him as the dangerous alien freak he surely was.

There was a good reason for Kian to demand that they all wear compulsion-filtering earpieces around the twins. They were rumored to be incredibly powerful and dangerous.

Jasmine was just a fragile human, and she had no business being anywhere near the powerful alien creatures. She might not realize that, but she needed him to protect her.

5

JASMINE

Jasmine observed the wide, industrial-style corridor as she followed Negal and Dagor, who were carrying the prince's stasis chamber.

The bowels of the keep looked very different than the top portion, and not only because they were underground—there were no windows ,and the only light was artificial. No interior decorator had bothered to spruce up the space, and everything was utilitarian. There were naked concrete floors, walls made from blocks painted some off-white, and no pictures or plants in sight.

"I need coffee." Frankie stopped in front of the open doors of a huge commercial kitchen. "Do you think they have the stuff to make it here?"

"They do," Gabi said. "Follow me."

As Margo joined the two, Ella fell in step with Jasmine. "I wonder if the stasis chambers could hover when they were still working. It doesn't seem right that such advanced technology needs to be carried."

If self-driving cars were a reality on Earth, which was primitive compared to the planet of the gods, then the stasis chambers could probably drive themselves too.

Jasmine tried to imagine them hovering into the pod, perhaps guided by a technician or maybe self-guiding. The latter made more sense, given the advanced technology of the gods.

"Over here." Bridget waved Negal and Dagor into the clinic and then straight into one of the patients' rooms. "Put it right here on the floor."

The hospital bed had been shoved against the wall to make room for the stasis chamber, and as the two gods carried it inside and lowered it to the floor, it took up most of the floor space in the room. There were about two feet left on each side, so the doctor and the nurse could attend to the patient while he was still inside his chamber.

There was no room left for observers, though, and Jasmine hated having to stay out in the waiting room.

"Where do you want the princess?" Aru asked as he and Julian arrived with the other stasis pod.

"The next room!" Bridget called out. "It's ready for her."

Jasmine moved to stand against the wall to let them through, and when they cleared the waiting room, Kian walked in.

"Hello, Jasmine." Kian offered her his hand. "I want to thank you in person for helping us find the pod. It wouldn't have been possible without you."

"I'm glad that I was able to help." She put her hand in his and let him shake it. "I just have one favor to ask in return."

It was bold, but she had rehearsed the request for hours.

Kian let go of her hand. "What is it?"

"I want to be present when the prince is revived. The cards foretold his arrival in my life for months, and I'm eager to meet him."

Kian nodded. "I have no problem with that, but you might. He's not looking pretty at this time. Wouldn't it be better to wait until he looks less corpse-like and has some flesh on his bones?"

Jasmine swallowed. "I can't. I need to be here when he opens his eyes." She put a hand over her chest. "I feel it here that it's the right thing for me to do."

"As you wish," Kian said. "Don't say that I didn't warn you, though."

Behind him, the tall redheaded Guardian nodded. "I've seen a dude wake up from stasis once, and it turned my stomach. It's nasty, and I'm not talking just about the looks. The stink is almost worse."

Jasmine grimaced. "Thanks for the warning. I'll make sure not to breathe through my nose."

Kian walked into the first patient room, where Bridget was still fussing around the prince. "Don't do anything yet. I need Merlin to scan them first. In the meantime, Aru and I also need to discuss a few things." Jasmine couldn't see the doctor because Kian was blocking the entrance to the room, but the silence that followed was telling.

"They don't have much time, Kian," Bridget said. "I can't even hook them up to monitoring equipment because their skin is frail, and it will break if I try to attach anything to it. The sooner we douse them with pure water, the better."

Why was it so important to use pure water?

Jasmine looked around until she located the two containers each with twelve one-liter bottles of mountain spring water. That was all that was needed to revive two ancient beings from stasis?

Surely, they had more containers stacked up somewhere?

"Shouldn't you do that in the operating room?" Kian asked the doctors.

"It won't make a difference," Julian said. "We are not operating on them, and we have all we need in the patient rooms." He ran his fingers through his shoulder-length tawny hair. "I should shower and change first, though." He looked at Kian and then shifted his gaze to Aru. "When will you be ready?"

"That depends on the results of our talk." Aru looked at Kian. "Can we talk in your office?"

"Of course."

What was that all about? What did Aru have to discuss with Kian, and did it have anything to do with the prince?

Jasmine had a feeling that it did.

When the two left, Ella pushed away from the wall. "Coffee?" she asked Jasmine. "I'm sure Frankie has a fresh pot by now."

Julian had ducked somewhere inside the clinic, probably to shower and put on scrubs, but Bridget and the nurse could take care of the twins. No danger lurked down in the depths of the keep, and Jasmine felt it was safe to leave her prince in the clan doctors' capable hands.

The only thing that made her uneasy was the conversation between Aru and Kian, but it wasn't as if she could find Kian's office and eavesdrop.

"I would love some."

6

KIAN

As Kian led Aru to his office, curiosity gnawed at him, but he held off asking the god what he wanted to talk about until they were inside, and he closed the door behind them.

He moved to lean against the edge of the conference table, crossing his arms over his chest as he fixed Aru with a steady gaze. "Let me guess. This has to do with your queen."

"Good guess." Aru pulled out one of the chairs and sat down. "We can't let the Eternal King know the twins survived. The best way to go about it is for me to report that everyone in the pod we found was dead. The problem is proving that to him, and before you suggest it, let me assure you that computer manipulation won't work with Anumatian technology. They'll instantly see through any digital or computer tricks."

"I wasn't about to suggest that. I know better." Kian pulled out a chair and sat next to Aru. "So, what's your idea?"

"It's not mine. It's the queen's. She suggests that we fake a funeral pyre for them like we intend to do for the Kra-ell, but I have no idea how we can do that without actually incinerating them."

Kian drummed his fingers on the conference table. "I wouldn't know the first thing about faking a funeral pyre, but I can ask our media expert for help. After all, they were doing that in movies long before computers and digital manipulation were a thing."

Aru nodded. "That's good. There is another problem that we need to take into consideration. The twins are emaciated, while the Kra-ell bodies are perfectly preserved. The difference is self-explanatory. Being half gods, the twins could enter stasis unaided, while the Kra-ell did not, and that's why their bodies consumed themselves to preserve basic function. Anyone on Anumati will figure it out at a glance."

Trying to figure out a solution to a seemingly unsolvable problem, Kian was silent for a long moment, his brow furrowed in concentration as he turned it over in his mind. Perhaps he should call Turner and Kalugal and ask them for ideas. After all, the queen wasn't the only one who knew that the Eternal King must never find out that the twins were alive, and he could ask their advice without mentioning her.

A thought, or rather a memory, was trying to push itself to the forefront of his mind—something about faking death.

Then it hit him. "I know what we can do. We will wait until the twins have recovered from their stasis so they look as whole as the Kra-ell, and then Bridget will administer a drug that will slow their vitals to a crawl even more so than stasis and make them appear dead to even the most advanced scanners. Once you record their lack of vitals, she will administer the antidote and revive them."

Aru's eyes widened. "If she can do that, it would be perfect. We can forgo recording the funeral pyres altogether. After all, no one expects us to give the Kra-ell their proper funeral rites." He tilted his head with a frown. "Did you base your idea on anything concrete, or was it only a hypothesis?"

"We've done something like that in the past." Kian pushed to his feet and motioned for Aru to follow him. "We needed to infiltrate the Doomers' island. The problem was that getting in was easy, but getting out was impossible. The plan was for our operative to fake her own death by administering a drug, getting out of there in a casket, and then being revived. In the end, her escape happened differently, but Bridget tried the method on her, and it worked."

"Who was your operative?" Aru asked.

Kian smiled. "Carol. Lokan's mate."

The god gasped. "That sweet little angel infiltrated the Doomers' island alone?"

"She did," Kian said. "Don't let her delicate appearance fool you. She's the gutsiest and most resilient person I know."

They strode down the hall together, their footsteps echoing off the concrete walls.

As they entered the clinic, Kian caught sight of Bridget, her red hair pulled back in a ponytail. She stood still next to the prince's open stasis chamber, partially obscuring Merlin while observing him scanning the prince.

"I need a word with you," Kian said. "Can we talk in your office?"

"Of course." She cast one last look at the emaciated figure and then at Merlin. "If you need my help to maneuver the prince carefully, let me know."

Merlin remained focused on the prince. "I think I got it, but thank you, I will." Kian walked toward the doctor's office. "Merlin seems to have it in hand; I just hope there are no trackers we need to cut out of them in their condition."

"Why haven't you sent Jasmine away?" Bridget grumbled, redirecting her frustration to another subject. "There is no need for her to be hanging around the clinic."

"I owe her." Kian opened the door. "Without her, we would have never found them. Besides, do you really want to stand in the way of the Fates' plan?"

"Good point." Bridget walked around the desk and sat behind it. "So, what's going on? What did you want to talk to me about?"

After Kian explained his idea, she was silent for a long moment, her lips pursed in thought.

"Carol was an immortal," she said at last. "I knew her physiology inside and out. But these twins are half Kra-ell, half god, and I'm not as sure that I can predict how their bodies will react to the drugs. The Kra-ell get tipsy from painkillers, so obviously, their chemistry is a little different than ours. Also, it will take a long time for the twins to regain their health, and I won't be able to experiment on them until they are back to full strength."

Kian turned to Aru. "It's your call. How long can you wait before reporting to your commander?"

The god closed his eyes for a moment. "As long as I want, but within reason. I can tell him that the mission to Tibet failed, and that we are back in Los Angeles to investigate another lead. Once we have a good plan, I will schedule another expedition to Tibet and report my findings then." He rubbed a hand over his jaw. "I need to tell Dagor to erase his recordings. Thankfully, we had the foresight to record with an offline device."

Kian canted his head. "You must have subconsciously known that you would need to delay the report."

"I guess I did." Aru turned to Bridget. "So, what's next, doctor?"

"As soon as Merlin is done, we will start reviving one of them and then the other. I don't want to risk doing it to them both at once."

7

JASMINE

"I need to get back." Jasmine pushed to her feet.

Gabi looked at her. "What's your rush?"

"I'm afraid they will start without me. I want to be there when the prince opens his eyes."

Jasmine wanted to be the first one he saw when he opened his eyes and for the connection between them to be powerful and immediate. It was a silly fantasy that was as anchored in reality as driftwood on a stormy sea, but she didn't want to miss the prince's resurrection on the one-in-a-million chance that it might happen.

Ella put her coffee mug down on the industrial kitchen counter. "Perhaps it's better that they do that without you. When you see what he looks like, you might faint, and they will need to attend to you instead of focusing on the prince."

As her imagination supplied vivid images of what the prince might look like, bile rose in Jasmine's throat. Zombies and ghosts looked better, but whatever. She would hold it together, and if she felt faint, she would walk away so no one would have to take care of her.

"I'll be fine." She took her empty coffee mug, carried it to the sink, and rinsed it. "Are you going to be here?" she asked.

Margo regarded her with worried eyes. "I wanted to go up to the penthouse and shower, but I'm afraid to leave you here alone. You might need someone to hold your hand during the resurrection."

Tears stung the back of Jasmine's eyes as the full impact of Margo's words hit her. She no longer had Edgar to lean on in a time of need, so Margo was offering herself.

With a sigh, she walked over to her friend and wrapped her arms around her. "You are a good friend, Margo. Thank you for having my back, but have you seen the clinic? There is not enough room for everyone who needs to be there to stand, and Kian is doing me a favor by allowing me to witness the revival. As much as I would love to have you there to hold my hand, you can't be there. It would be best if you went up, got a decent shower, and ate something. Come to think of it, you can order delivery from that Chinese restaurant we all love."

"I like the sound of that." Gabi rubbed her tummy. "I'll take care of the delivery." She rose to her feet and took the rest of the cups to the sink.

They parted in front of the clinic, and as her friends continued to the elevators, Jasmine pushed the door open and entered the waiting room, where five imposing people were standing outside the prince's room.

She had no trouble guessing who they were.

The imposing female was, without a doubt, Jade, the Kra-ell leader Jasmine had heard so much about. The four males with her were probably her guards. They did not look purely Kra-ell like their leader, though, and could be mistaken for tall and slim Eurasian men.

Still, even though Jade was a pureblooded Kra-ell, and her eyes were indeed larger than normal and her waist was unnaturally slim, she was not weird looking. She was quite beautiful in an otherworldly and intimidating kind of way.

The female radiated dominance like the most alpha of males, and it was curiously attractive even though Jasmine had never been on the fence about her sexuality. She had always been a hetero through and through, but there was something about Jade that made her pulse quicken a little.

Feeling her gaze, Jade turned and looked at her. "You must be Jasmine." She crossed the few feet between them and offered Jasmine her hand. "I'm Jade."

She didn't smile, but Jasmine did as she took her hand. "I know. I've heard a lot about you."

As she'd expected, the female's handshake was firm and brief. "Same here." Jade lifted her hand and pushed Jasmine's hair aside to expose her ear. "You should put in your earpieces."

"I'll do that when they start." Jasmine glanced at the door to the prince's room. "Are they about to?"

"Not yet, but soon. Did Kian tell you about the latest upgrade to the earpieces?"

Jasmine shook her head.

"They can translate Kra-ell to English and the other way around. If he speaks, you'll be able to understand him. Regrettably, we can't put earpieces on him yet until he has ears, so I'll have to translate things for him."

As bile rose in her throat again, Jasmine swallowed. The prince had no ears?

Shaking off the disturbing visual, she changed the subject. "Everyone refers to the prince and princess as the royal twins. Do they have names?"

"I don't know what they are," Jade admitted. "Priestesses were always referred to as holy mothers, and there were no male priests before the prince. When we left on the settler ship, the twins were still acolytes, and therefore, they were called holy sister and brother in training."

Jasmine nodded, a pang of sympathy welling up in her chest. To have one's identity reduced to a title, to be known only by the role one was meant to play, seemed like a lonely and isolated existence.

Her heart ached for the twins and all they must have endured.

As the door to Bridget's office opened, Kian, Aru, and the doctor stepped out. Kian nodded at Jade and then shifted his gaze to Jasmine.

"Are you sure that you want to witness the resurrection?"

Swallowing again, she nodded. "I am."

8

ARU

Aru approved of Kian's decision and Jasmine's gumption. She had more than earned the right to be there for her prince's revival.

Bridget grimaced. "There is very little room around the stasis chamber."

"I can stay outside," Aru said. "If you leave the door open, that is. I still want to witness this."

Behind him, Negal and Dagor also said they were happy to stay out of the room provided the door was open.

They and Jade's crew had finished transporting the stasis chambers carrying the dead Kra-ell to the catacombs, and even though they had wiped the chambers clean as much as possible before loading them onto the planes, some dust had remained and found its way onto the males' clothing.

Perhaps it wasn't the best idea for them to be so close to the corpse-like fragile prince while he was being revived. With almost no blood in his veins and organs that were a hair away from failing, he might not be able to fight off pathogens in the same way a healthy god or immortal could.

Curiously, Kalugal had opted out of witnessing the momentous event and had gone home, so there was one less person to crowd the packed waiting room.

"I can stay outside as well." Kian turned to Jasmine. "Just remember to keep your earpieces in."

She nodded, her fingers trembling slightly as she pulled the devices out of her jeans pocket and inserted them into her ears. Around her, the others did the same.

Just as she was done adjusting the earpieces, Merlin stepped out of the room and seemed startled at the crowd outside the door.

"If this device is as effective as William assures us it is, the prince had no trackers implanted in him."

Jade nodded. "That makes perfect sense to me. The twins were never supposed to be on the settlers' ship. They were snuck on board covertly minutes before the last pods were sealed. It is extremely unlikely that someone managed to put trackers in them during that time."

Looking at Merlin, Kian tilted his head toward the

princess's room. "Just to make sure, please scan the princess as carefully as well."

"I need to be in the room when you revive the prince," Jade said. "He might recognize me from my time serving in the queen's guard." She turned to Aru. "You and the other gods should stay out of his line of sight."

Aru glanced at the petite redheaded doctor. She was almost beautiful enough to pass for a goddess, but not quite. Would the prince think that she was one?

The settlers knew about humans, so he might assume that, and the same was true for Jasmine.

Bridget pursed her lips. "I doubt he will be cognizant enough to evaluate what he's seeing, but I agree that Jade's face will be the least disturbing to him." She looked to her son, who was waiting with a bottle of mountain spring water in each hand. "Get in position, Julian."

Behind him were Jade's hybrids, each holding two bottles, ready to hand them to Julian when needed.

That was enough water to revive several people from stasis, but Aru said nothing. Perhaps the prince's fragile state necessitated more than usual.

As Julian stepped forward, Bridget motioned for Jasmine to get in and stand next to the wall.

Aru expected Julian to pour the first bottle over the prince, but after removing the cap, the young doctor handed it to his mother. "His bones are so brittle and fragile that I'm afraid a strong stream of water might crumble him."

Bridget nodded. "I'll start at his feet and go up. If they fall off, he can regrow them."

Jasmine swallowed hard, her heartbeat so loud that Aru heard it from his position by the door. She wasn't looking at the stasis chamber and the body inside. Instead, her eyes were fixed on Bridget's face.

He wondered if her courage had left her, and she was afraid to see what state the royal was in.

"Here goes," Kian murmured next to him, the low tone sounding even odder through the earpieces.

Aru fought the impulse to adjust the devices. It wouldn't help and would only reduce their effectiveness.

Taking a deep breath, Bridget lifted the bottle and drizzled a few drops over the prince's withered feet.

Aru had seen a baptism on television once, and what Bridget was doing reminded him of the ritual cleansing that was supposed to wash away the sins and sorrows of the past.

When the feet remained intact, Bridget got bolder and sprinkled more water over the parchment-like gray skin.

As the minutes ticked by, the silence was tense, and the

only sounds were the steady drip of water, the rasp of everyone's breathing, and their various heartbeats.

Aru tried to ignore all that background noise and focus on the prince, but there was no sign of life in his body, not even a flicker.

He couldn't be dead.

Julian had been monitoring the infrequent heartbeats of the twins, and he would have known if time had run out for the royal.

Still, too much time seemed to have passed since the last heartbeat Aru had heard.

Had he missed one?

Yeah, that was more likely than the doctors not being aware of the prince's passing.

The twins' death would solve many problems, but Aru couldn't bring himself to wish for that. That being said, he wouldn't pray for their survival either.

9

JASMINE

It wasn't working, Jasmine realized with a sickening lurch of dread.

She felt her heart sink, a leaden weight settling in her chest as she watched the scene unfold. She still hadn't looked directly at the prince, afraid of what she would see, but the tense silence and Bridget's pinched expression spoke loud and clear.

Was he dead?

Was his body so depleted that it had crossed the point of no return and couldn't pull itself out of stasis?

Bridget was being very careful. She wasn't filling the stasis chamber with water like Jasmine had imagined she would, turning it into a bathtub. Instead, she was dripping it over the prince, and she wasn't done even with the first bottle Julian had handed her.

When the doctor reached for the second water bottle, Jasmine bit her lower lip to refrain from telling her it wouldn't work like that. She needed to fill the thing so it would cover the prince, leaving only his nose exposed so he could breathe.

But what did she know?

Jasmine had no medical training and knew next to nothing about immortals, gods, or the Kra-ell. Their bodies probably worked very differently from humans, and Bridget had a lot of experience getting people out of stasis.

Closing her eyes for a long moment, Jasmine gave herself another pep talk about not being a chicken, and not wanting to draw attention to herself, she took in a slow, shallow breath.

She turned her head down so that when she opened her eyes, they would be trained straight on the prince, caught her lower lip between her teeth to stop herself from uttering any sound, and started counting.

One, two, three…

She opened her eyes, and a sob lodged in her throat.

Just as Julian had warned her, the prince was in a horrible state, but he didn't look like a zombie, ghost, or corpse.

Well, he did look a little like a corpse, but mostly, he looked like a victim of starvation, and Jasmine hoped that he hadn't been aware of any of it and hadn't suffered.

What surprised her the most was that his clothing was intact. She'd expected something like what she'd seen on mummies—deteriorating scraps of robing or nothing except a loincloth. Instead, the prince was wearing a uniform of some sort, and even though it had probably been form-fitting when he had entered the stasis chamber, it was now loose around his emaciated body, the dark gray fabric clinging to his protruding ribs.

How had it survived for seven thousand years?

If the Kra-ell had survived intact in their chambers, it shouldn't surprise her that their clothing also had. She hadn't looked into the other stasis chambers because they had been transported from the pod to the catacombs locked, but it made sense. The only reason the twins' bodies were in such a horrid state was that they had consumed themselves to keep alive.

When Bridget reached the prince's face, she dripped a few drops on his forehead, eyelids, lips, and cheeks and then repeated the process with infinite patience and care.

Jasmine longed to spread the moisture with her fingers, to see the prince's skin turn pink, but she wouldn't have done that even if she wasn't such a coward. His skin was so fragile that it would probably disintegrate when touched, which was why Bridget was going so slowly.

But wasn't he supposed to be showing some signs of life already?

Jasmine was about to shift her gaze to Kian and check his expression to see if he was worried when a barely-there twitch of the prince's eyelids froze her in place.

She sucked in a breath, and so did everyone else, which meant that she hadn't imagined it.

And there it was again. A flicker of movement, so subtle and fleeting that it could have easily been missed if she wasn't so focused on the prince's face.

A twitch of an eyelid, a flutter of lashes against a sunken cheek.

And then, with a hoarse, rasping gasp, the prince's eyes opened, a sliver of shocking blue amidst the ruin of his face.

For a long moment, he just stared, his gaze unfocused and glassy as he blinked once, twice, but then the haze seemed to clear, and awareness shone from those incredible eyes as he looked straight at her, his gaze locking on to hers with an intensity that stole her breath away.

It was just as she had dreamt it. Hers was the first face he saw when he opened his eyes.

A rush of emotion washed over Jasmine, a tidal wave of joy, relief, and awe at the sight of him alive and awake. It was a miracle, a gift from the Mother of All Life.

The prince's lips parted, a soft, rasping sound escaping his throat as he tried to speak, but the effort was too much, his weakened body failing him, and his eyes fluttered closed once more.

"He's alive," Julian murmured.

"Of course, he is," Bridget said.

"Shouldn't we put an IV in him and feed him intravenously?" Julian asked.

She shook her head. "We don't know if he is more god than Kra-ell or the other way around. He might need blood to survive."

Blood?

Ella hadn't mentioned anything about blood.

Were the Kra-ell vampires?

10

KIAN

Kian let out a relieved breath. The Prince had woken up, even if only for a split second.

"Is that normal?" he asked Bridget. "Wasn't he supposed to revive?"

"Dalhu did," Anandur said. "And so did Wonder. As soon as water touched her body, she was awake and didn't lose consciousness since. Well, except for fainting when she saw the Clan Mother."

"Maybe it's his clothing," Jasmine said. "What if it's preventing the water from touching his body?"

Kian opened his mouth to reprimand her for butting in about something she had no clue about, but Bridget's frown stopped him.

"You might be onto something." The doctor put the bottle of water aside, leaned over the prince, and gently peeled back the sleeve of his uniform. "His skin is completely dry underneath." She chuckled. "I'm so embarrassed." She looked up at Jasmine. "It didn't occur to me that his clothing was water resistant because it shouldn't be. Not for a god and not for an immortal. But for a Kra-ell, it didn't matter because the Kra-ell relied on stasis chambers to sustain them."

Julian nodded. "We need to cut it off him, and that scares the crap out of me."

His mother smiled indulgently. "I'll do that. During my residency, I had to remove clothing from burn victims. They were in a much worse state than our prince." She straightened to her full five feet and two inches. "I need everyone to leave while I do this. First, to preserve the prince's dignity, we shouldn't expose him in front of an audience. And secondly, this is going to be a delicate operation, and I want to be able to concentrate on my patient."

Kian nodded. "We can wait in the waiting room."

Bridget shook her head. "This is going to take a long time, and I don't expect him to wake up even after we've soaked his naked body." She let out a breath. "I'll call you if there is any change in his state."

"I need to stay," Jade said. "If he wakes up and can't understand what you are saying, he might freak out. You need someone who speaks Kra-ell."

Bridget hesitated. "I wish the translating earpieces came with a speaker. That would solve the language barrier problem."

"William is working on a device," Kian said. "He told me it should be ready in a day or two."

Jade shook her head. "A translating device is not good enough. The prince will wake up in a different world than the one he left and not the one he expected to arrive at. He is going to be confused and frightened. Seeing a familiar face and hearing his mother tongue will go a long way to make his awakening smoother."

"True." Bridget waved Jasmine and Jade out. "You can stay in the waiting room. I'll call you if he wakes up."

"Should I also stay in the waiting room?" Jasmine asked.

"You should go up to the penthouse, shower, and get something to eat."

Jasmine put a hand on her stomach. "I'm too anxious to eat. I want to make sure that he's okay first."

The exasperated look on Bridget's face had Kian moving toward Jasmine and taking her elbow. "Come. Let's give the doctors room to breathe. They don't function well when people are hovering over them."

Behind Jasmine, Bridget mouthed, "Thank you."

The three gods followed as he led the woman out of the clinic and toward the elevators.

He stopped outside the clinic door and waited for the hybrid Kra-ell, Anandur, and Brundar to join them.

"I'm going to escort Jasmine to the penthouse," he told his bodyguards. "Can you take these men to the kitchen for a bite to eat? You can order a delivery from one of the local restaurants."

Brundar grimaced, but Anandur spoke up. "We are not supposed to leave your side. We should accompany you to the penthouse."

Kian let out a long sigh. "I'm only going to be gone a minute, and then I'll join you in the kitchen."

Anandur still didn't look happy, but he nodded. "If you are not back in five minutes, we are coming up."

As the two groups continued in opposite directions, Aru fell in step with Jasmine. "Good call about the clothing," he said. "I should have thought about that."

She seemed embarrassed by the compliment. "Did you wear the same uniform during your interstellar travels?"

He nodded, pushing his hands into his pockets. "Very similar, but not the same. The gods supplied the settler ship, the pods, the stasis chambers, and everything else. The Kra-ell were not technologically advanced back then and are still not today. It's just not in their culture. They are what humans would call naturalists. They prefer a nomadic lifestyle and keeping things simple. The ship that brought me here was much more advanced, and our uniforms were made from a material different from what the prince was wearing. I wonder if everyone wore that back then or if it was chosen specifically for the Kra-ell."

As the elevator doors opened and they all stepped inside, Jasmine leaned against the mirrored wall. "Why don't the Kra-ell embrace technology?"

Aru shrugged. "There are many reasons, but the most important is cultural."

Kian knew that the explanation was more complex than that, but Aru probably reasoned that this wasn't a good time for Jasmine to get a lesson about Anumati politics and the class system.

11

JASMINE

As Jasmine walked into the penthouse, her heart was still racing with the adrenaline and emotion of the past few hours. The prince's awakening had been fleeting but still left her shaken.

She couldn't believe that she had been the only one who had thought about the clothing being a problem. It should have made her feel smart, and it did, but only a little. Sometimes, an uninformed outsider saw things more clearly than the experts.

Thankfully, Kian parted with Aru and the other gods at the door and headed back down to the clinic, or rather the kitchen where his bodyguards and Jade's crew were waiting. She needed a respite, and he wasn't an easy guy to relax around.

"You are just in time." Margo waved them over to the massive coffee table that was covered with boxes from their favorite Chinese restaurant. "The delivery arrived a few minutes ago, and everything is still hot. Come and dig in."

"We really should move to the dining room," Jasmine grumbled before finding a spot on the carpet beside Ella. "And I need to shower, but I'm hungry, and I also need to talk to you." She glared at Ella.

"What did I do?"

Frankie lifted a hand. "Before anyone says another word, I need to know what's happening with the twins. Were they revived?"

"Bridget is working on the prince," Aru said. "He opened his eyes briefly, tried to say something, and went under again. Bridget won't start on the princess until she has him stabilized."

Everyone's mood seemed to plummet at the news.

"Is he going to be okay?" Margo asked.

Jasmine's throat felt too tight to answer, so all she could do was shrug and fold in upon herself.

"He will be," Aru said with more conviction than Jasmine felt. "Bridget and Julian are cutting away his clothing so the water can touch all of his skin. Bridget kicked us out to preserve his privacy, and she will let us know when and if he wakes up."

"Jade stayed in the clinic in case she was needed," Jasmine said quietly. "Being a Kra-ell, she would look familiar to him and can speak his language." She cast Ella another baleful look.

"What?" Ella asked.

"Never mind." Jasmine took the paper plate Margo was handing her and a pair of chopsticks. "I'm hungry." She reached for one of the boxes and opened it.

"The doctors might decide to put him in an induced coma to help him heal," Margo said. "When Mia's heart gave out and the doctors were fighting for her life, that was what they did."

"Makes sense," Ella said. "Especially since her heart was probably operating at a fraction of the capacity it should have been."

Frankie nodded. "It was such a horrible period in our lives. It changed me."

"Me too." Margo sighed. "But it changed us in different ways. I lost my naive belief that everything would be okay and that I was invincible because I was young, and you decided to throw caution to the wind and live every day as if it were your last."

"True." Frankie popped a piece of orange chicken into her mouth, chewed it, and swallowed. "My way was better because I was having fun."

Margo waved a dismissive hand at Frankie before turning to Jasmine. "You said that the prince was trying to say something. Did Jade understand any of it?"

Jasmine shook her head. "It was just a croak." She closed her eyes and tried to recall every detail of those precious seconds he'd been awake. "His eyes are the most amazing shade of blue. I've never seen eyes like that. And he looked right at me." She lifted her gaze to Aru. "Did you see that? Or was it my imagination?"

"He looked at you," Aru confirmed. "It was mostly a glazed-over look without seeing, but there was some momentary awareness in his gaze." He smiled at her. "You should be glad that his eyes are shaped like a god's and not like a Kra-ell's."

She hadn't thought of that, but it was a good point, and she was relieved that he looked more human than she had expected. The rest of the physical differences didn't bother her as much, except his dietary preferences.

She turned to Ella. "When you told me about the Kra-ell, you forgot to mention one significant detail."

Ella frowned. "I told you about their huge black eyes, but the prince apparently doesn't have them."

"You told me about that, but you didn't tell me about something much more important than the shape of their eyes. They are freaking vampires! They live on blood, Ella! Don't you think it should have been the first thing to mention?"

Ella didn't even look guilty as she shrugged. "You are making too big of a deal about something that is not all that important. They drink from animals, and they don't kill when they drink. It's all very sustainable."

The chuckle that bubbled up from Jasmine's throat sounded manic. "Sustainable? Are you freaking serious? They drink blood!"

"So what? What's the big deal? You drink milk and eat animal flesh, and they drink its blood. They prefer it fresh, that's true, but they can live on frozen store-bought blood, too." She leaned back and looked at Jasmine down her nose. "You didn't seem to have a problem with Edgar's fangs."

"That's because he doesn't drink blood." It dawned on her that she hadn't seen him or even noticed his absence. "Where is Edgar, by the way? Did he leave?"

Ella shrugged. "I didn't see him when we got here. He must have decided to return to the village."

A pang of unease coursed through Jasmine. "He said he would wait for me to return. He also said that we need to celebrate the successful completion of the mission."

"Maybe he went underground to look for you," Frankie said.

"Maybe." Jasmine lifted a piece of broccoli with her chopsticks. "I hope he will return when he doesn't find me."

The truth was that she missed him and felt a little lost without him.

Well, a lot lost.

What would happen to her now? Would she go back to her apartment and her customer service job? Was she still in danger from the Modanas and their cohorts?

Who would induce her godly genes?

Would it be the prince?

As she remembered what he looked like, a shiver ran down Jasmine's spine, and not the pleasant type. It could be months before he was in any state to be intimate with a woman, and then he might remember that he was a celibate priest and not give her the time of day.

Would she have to find another immortal to do the honors?

Mother of All Life, what a mess. Maybe she shouldn't have ended things with Edgar so soon. She could have waited until they were back in the penthouse and had unprotected sex with him.

It wouldn't have been such a great hardship, but it wouldn't have been fair to him unless he was willing to be just the venom donor and didn't expect anything else.

They ate silently for the next few moments, and then Margo put her plate down. "So, what happens now?" Her voice cut through the haze of Jasmine's thoughts like a beacon in the fog. "I mean, we found the twins, we brought them back to the keep. What's the next step?"

Jasmine shrugged. "I honestly have no idea. I feel like a ship adrift in the ocean. I don't know what I'm supposed to do next."

Gabi put her plate down and wiped her mouth with a napkin. "I don't know about you, but I'm glad to be back. I thought we'd be trekking through those mountains for months, freezing our asses off and battling altitude sickness. Thanks to Jasmine, the mission was over much sooner than I expected."

12

MARINA

The day Marina had been simultaneously dreading and eagerly anticipating had finally arrived.

It was time to leave Safe Haven and part with her friends, her family, and the place that had been her temporary sanctuary after her people's liberation from near slavery in Igor's compound and the oppressive rule of the Kra-ell.

The irony wasn't lost on her.

She was willingly moving to a place where her former masters had chosen to reside, and although they weren't in charge there, she couldn't help the apprehension that gripped her at the prospect of facing them again.

Not all had been cruel, but they had all acted superior, looking upon her and the other humans in the compound as less worthy. After a lifetime of believing that was true, she would have a hard time interacting with them without feeling inferior again.

In the immortals' village, the immortals were naturally at the top of the hierarchy, with the Kra-ell below them, and as usual, humans were last. The difference was that the Kra-ell were in-your-face kind of people who never tried to hide how they felt, while the immortals did their best to appear inclusive and respectful but probably felt the same as the Kra-ell.

What if she was making a huge mistake by moving there? Perhaps she should have convinced Peter to stay with her in Safe Haven, where humans were the majority.

Stop it, Marina commanded.

If she didn't like it in the village, she could always return to Safe Haven, and Peter would come with her because he loved her.

Standing in the parking lot of the main lodge, her belongings packed into a single duffle bag at her feet, she watched as the new team of Guardians spilled out of the rented SUV and exchanged greetings with the departing team.

When they embraced and clapped each other on the back, the sound reverberated from the walls enclosing the parking lot, and their male voices were made more boisterous because of the echo amplifying the sound.

Marina saw Larissa rushing to her from the corner of her eye even though they had already said their goodbyes. Her eyes red-rimmed and her face streaked with tears, she pulled Marina into a fierce, desperate hug. "I'm going to miss you so much," she whispered, her voice choked with emotion. "Promise that you'll call every day."

Marina fought back tears as she held Larissa in her arms. "Of course, I will. At least twice a day." She pulled back a little to look into Larissa's tear-stained face. "You can move to the village, too. It's not as difficult to transfer there as we thought. All you have to do is fill out a request form or have Eleanor fill it out for you and sign it. Plenty of jobs exist, and they need people to fill them."

"I can't." Larissa rubbed a hand over her face, wiping off the tears. "I don't want to live with the Kra-ell again and not with the immortals either. I want to be among humans." She grimaced. "I've had enough immortals to last me a lifetime."

Larissa was still in the process of getting over her very short relationship with Jay, and as a result she was sour on all immortals.

"I get it." Marina took her friend's hand and gave it a gentle squeeze. "You need to do what's right for you, staying in Safe Haven and dating human guys."

"Yeah." Larissa let out a watery chuckle, a spark of mischief dancing in her eyes despite the sadness that still clouded them. "I've had enough of immortals, but I'm not going to lie. I will miss the sex and the venom-induced trips." She sighed. "Perhaps I shouldn't be so harsh and give moving to the village some more thought."

They both knew it was nothing more than a joke, a bit of gallows humor to lighten the mood. Larissa's heart was set on staying in Safe Haven and finding a nice human guy to settle down with and have kids.

"You do that," Marina said.

"Right now, I'm still too mad at Jay to even think about it," Larissa admitted in a whisper.

"Why are you so angry at him?" Marina blurted out the question she hadn't dared ask before. "Did he make you any promises? Did he ever lead you to believe it could be more than just a bit of fun?"

Larissa shook her head. "No," she admitted, her voice barely above a whisper. "Jay was upfront about what it was, but I let myself get carried away and yearned for something that I knew wasn't on the table." Her chin wobbled. "Seeing you and Peter and how happy you are together made me hopeful. You two started the same way as Jay and I, so I thought things with Jay might also grow into more."

Marina pulled her into another hug, holding her close as if she could absorb some of her pain. "I'm sorry," she murmured. "I wish I could wave a magic wand and give you the happy ending you deserve."

Taking a deep breath, Larissa pulled out of Marina's arms. "I deserve better than Jay, that's for sure. I deserve someone who will love me and feel lucky for having snagged a rare find like me." She smoothed her hands over her ample curves. "Because I am worth it."

"Yes, you are." Marina grinned. "You are a goddess."

"That's right." Larissa took another fortifying breath.

A gentle hand on Marina's shoulder made her look up, her gaze meeting Peter's warm eyes.

"It's time to go, love," he said.

Marina nodded and turned back to Larissa. "I'll come visit as often as I can. I don't know the rules in the village, but I'm sure I can come back here with Peter. And maybe you'll change your mind and stay with me for a while."

Larissa smiled. "Come back as soon as you can. And call me when your plane lands so I know you are safe and call me again when you get to the village. I want to hear all about it in detail."

With one last fierce hug, Marina followed Peter to the waiting SUV. The three other Guardians returning to the village with them were already seated, two in the front and one in the back, leaving the middle seat for her and Peter.

After he'd loaded their things into the trunk, he got in, sat down, and wrapped his arm around her. "Have you ever flown in a private jet?"

"Yes. We were picked up from Greenland by private charter planes."

"That's not the same as flying in a luxury executive jet. You are in for a treat." He smiled. "Usually, Charlie flies the teams to and from Safe Haven in the larger and less fancy plane, but he and that plane were needed for another mission, so the jet is being piloted by Eric, the clan's standby pilot."

Marina felt a twinge of apprehension. "Is he any good?"

"He's excellent. Eric served in the Air Force for many years. After getting discharged, he started a private charter-jet business and did that for a while, so he has thousands of flight hours under his belt. You have nothing to worry about."

13

JASMINE

The meal was over, the table was clean, and the leftovers were stored in the fridge, but there was still no sign of Edgar.

Jasmine had thought about calling him, but that wasn't smart. She shouldn't cling to their relationship and rely on him when she'd been the one who had ended things between them.

It wasn't fair to Edgar; she wasn't the type of woman who took advantage of a man's attraction to her.

A small, insidious voice in the back of her head whispered, *why not?* Women did that all the time, especially those the goddess had gifted with good looks and charm.

The truth was that Jasmine wasn't a saint, and she'd used her assets to her advantage in the past, but it had always been with men who saw her as an object of desire, not those who had genuine feelings for her.

Like Edgar.

"Coffee is served, *mesdames et messieurs*." Frankie put the tray down on the coffee table. "Help yourselves."

Gabi leaned back against the plush cushions of the couch, her expression thoughtful as she gazed out the window at the sprawling city below. "Aru and I will probably stay here for a while. My clients are okay with me working remotely, and I even did that from Tibet, but it was a hassle because of the time difference. It's going to be a breeze doing it from here."

"What about you?" Jasmine asked Aru. "What are you going to do now?"

The god looked unsure. "We need to evaluate the equipment we salvaged from the pod. I hope William can help us with that. I also need to figure out our next move." He sighed. "Given the state of the pod we found, I don't have much hope of finding any other pods with living Kra-ell inside. Still, we need to find them and ensure that they don't fall into the hands of humans."

Jasmine felt a pang of sorrow at the thought of all the lives that had been lost and all the hopes and dreams that had been lost with them.

Gabi smiled with a mischievous glint in her eyes as she turned to Frankie and Margo. "You two can finally come to the village and start working as beta testers for Perfect Match."

"That's right." Frankie clapped her hands. "By the way, Mia and Toven are coming over, and they are picking up champagne to celebrate with us. Mia is over the moon that we are back so soon. She expected this to take months."

Jasmine envied what they had so much.

They had all already found their forever mates, had transitioned into immortality, and knew what their future held. At the same time, she was stuck in limbo with nothing more than vague readings from her tarot cards and promises that might or might not come true.

"Do you think I could come see the village?" she asked. "I'd love to see it, and maybe they can find a spot for me on the Perfect Match team."

"I'm not sure," Gabi admitted. "It's not really up to me. Kian will have to make that call." She glanced at the others, a shadow of uncertainty passing over her face. "I hope Kian will be okay with us staying in his penthouse. If not, we will have to look for a place to rent."

"I'm sure Kian will let you stay here," Ella said.

"Yeah, I think he will, but we should ask and not just assume that we can stay." Gabi cocked her head to the side, a curious expression stealing over her features. "Speaking of decisions…" She pinned Jasmine with a questioning look. "I understand that you and Edgar have shifted into the friend zone. Is it friends with benefits?"

Jasmine chuckled. "Before, it was. Now it's only friends. Why?"

Gabi shrugged. "I was just thinking about your induction and who will do it."

Margo shook her head. "Couldn't you have waited a few more days? Now you will have to find someone else to do it."

Jasmine had been thinking the same thing only moments ago, so she shouldn't get angry at Margo for suggesting that she would have been better off using Edgar and discarding him when she got what she needed from him.

"Edgar was fun to be with, and I'll always care about him as a friend, but things just fizzled out between us, and there was no point in dragging it out. It wouldn't have been fair to him if I just used him to induce my transition."

Negal nodded his approval, and Dagor did too.

"You did the right thing," Negal said. "Edgar might be hurting right now, but it would have been much worse if he felt used."

Tears prickled the backs of Jasmine's eyes. "He's a good guy, and he deserves someone who can give him her whole heart and looks at him like he hung the moon and stars for her."

Frankie sighed, a wistful expression stealing over her

face. "I just hope your prince will feel that way about you once he wakes up and gets to know you."

"There is no guarantee of that." Gabi winced. "The guy is a celibate priest."

"Was," Jasmine said. "The twins' mother consecrated them to the priesthood to hide them from their people because they looked hybrid, and it was crucial that no one found out. They didn't join out of religious convictions or the wish to serve their people through their spiritual journey. It was just the part they were forced to play."

Jasmine wasn't sure who she was trying to convince, herself or Gabi.

"Still, even if he has no qualms about dropping his celibacy, he might take one look at me and run screaming in the opposite direction."

She'd said that as a joke, but Gabi wasn't smiling.

"There might be another problem," she said. "It is not a foregone conclusion that the prince could induce your transition at all. The Kra-ell don't have that ability. Only the gods and immortals do. Let's hope the prince's venom is as potent as the gods' or the immortals'."

Jasmine nodded as fear and hope mingled in her gut. Gabi was right, and there were no guarantees about anything, but even as doubts and uncertainties coursed through her like a gathering storm, deep down, she knew everything would be okay.

Whether the prince could induce her transition or not, she had to believe he was her destiny, the other half of her soul.

14

THE PRINCE

He was dreaming, his mind a swirling maelstrom of fragmented images and half-formed thoughts he couldn't grasp the threads of, but one image pierced through the fog of confusion, clear as if it was seared into his mind's eye—luminous eyes staring into his as if their owner knew him, knew who he was while he did not.

Could she tell him his name?

Was she the Mother of All Life?

Oh, that was a cohesive thought. A memory. He remembered the Mother. All was not lost.

Had the Mother come to escort him to the fields of the brave?

No. He did not deserve entry.

He had failed.

At what?

He could not remember but felt the failure like a crushing weight on his chest.

If she was the Mother, she came to escort him to the valley of the shamed.

But if she was not the Mother, who was she?

The question echoed through his mind like a relentless drumbeat. It drowned out all other thought fragments.

Who was she?

Who was she?

Who was he?

He had no name, no sense of who or what he had been before the awakening inside a dream. The very concept of identity seemed to slip through his grasp like water through his fingers, leaving him adrift in a sea of uncertainty.

Perhaps he was dead and no longer possessing a separate identity. Maybe he was a part of a larger whole.

Voices murmured around him, hushed and urgent, but their words were little more than a garbled hum to his ears.

Did hearing spoken language mean that he was not dead? In the afterlife, talking was unnecessary because everyone was connected, and thoughts floated on the ether like sparks of light.

Where had that idea and the imagery come from?

A memory tickled his mind, but it was like trying to hold on to a tendril of smoke.

It was no use.

He did not know.

He strained to make out the meaning of the words spoken next to him, to latch on to some scrap of context that might help him piece together the shattered fragments of his reality, but it was no use. The harder he tried to focus, the more the sounds seemed to slip away, fading into the distance like a half-remembered dream.

He tried to open his eyes, to force his way back to the waking world and the answers that surely awaited him there, but his eyelids refused to move. He felt as if they were weighted down by some invisible force that he lacked the strength to overcome.

Panic began to rise in his chest, a clawing, desperate thing that threatened to consume the precarious connection to his consciousness.

Concentrating, he tried to feel anything, but even though his mind did not register any sensations, he still felt a connection to a physical form. Was it an illusion? Or was he trapped, a prisoner in his own unresponsive body?

As fear threatened to overwhelm him, the sense of failure from before reemerged, forcing the fear for himself to a secondary position in his barely functioning mind. It wasn't for himself that he feared but for another.

For her.

Sister.

The realization hit him like a bolt of lightning, a sudden, blinding flash of clarity that cut through the haze of confusion like a knife. He had a sister whose face he could not conjure and whose name danced just beyond the reach of his fractured memory. But he knew with a certainty that defied explanation that he had failed her.

He had vowed to keep her safe, but his promise had been worthless. It had shattered like glass upon the ground.

He had a sacred duty that superseded all others, and he had failed. He failed her, himself, and whoever had entrusted him with his sister's safety.

He wanted to scream, to plead with the Mother to give him another chance to fulfill his duty, but his voice remained locked within his chest, a silent, impotent cry of anguish that echoed only in the confines of his mind.

Despair washed over him in waves, a cold, numbing tide that sapped what little strength he had and left him feeling hollow and utterly alone. He had no idea where he was, no concept of how much time had passed since he had last drawn breath. All he knew was the pain of the all-consuming guilt that gnawed at his soul.

As consciousness began to fade again, he clung to the one scrap of memory that remained, the one thing that tethered him to a world he no longer understood. A pair of intense golden eyes staring into his own with hope and some other emotion he couldn't decipher.

Whoever she was, that female was his lifeline, his beacon in the dark.

15

PETER

Marina squeezed Peter's hand as the car's windows turned opaque and the vehicle slipped into autonomous mode. "I'm so excited. I'm finally here."

"Almost." He leaned over and kissed her temple.

He'd warned her about the windows so she wouldn't freak out, and he also told her about the underground tunnel leading into the mountain that the village sat on top of.

When the car wound its way into the tunnel's hidden entrance, Marina's eyes widened, and her hold on his hand tightened.

Peter had seen this journey countless times before, and the James-Bond-style high-tech marvels that guarded their secret sanctuary no longer registered, but seeing them through Marina's eyes, he once again noted the miracle of ingenuity that was involved.

Most of the credit belonged to William, but the guy didn't work alone. He had a team of bright minds working under him, coming up with innovative solutions and technologies.

The air grew cold and damp as they descended deeper into the earth, and even though the windows were still opaque, they admitted light, which was absent in the tunnel. Peter wondered why no artificial lighting had been installed, or maybe it had been, and it just wasn't on when there was no need for it. The car drove itself, and it was perfectly able to navigate in the dark.

As Marina shivered, pressing herself closer to his side, he wrapped an arm around her shoulders. "Are you cold?" he asked.

"A little. But mostly, I'm spooked. I don't like dark places, and I don't like being underground. I hated that my cabin on the ship didn't have a window."

"Don't worry." He lifted their conjoined hands and kissed the back of hers. "We are not going to stay underground for long. After we park, we will take the elevator to the surface, and you'll see how full of sunlight the village is." He glanced at his watch. "The sun will set soon, but we still have enough time to see most of the village. It's not that big."

"When are the windows going to clear?" she asked.

"When the car enters the elevator, which will happen in one, two, and…three." The car stopped, and a moment later, they lurched up.

"Amazing," Marina whispered. "It's like a science fiction movie."

"It is." He smiled. "I've gotten used to it, so I don't see it anymore, but watching the marvels through your eyes makes me excited about it again."

When the elevator doors opened with a soft ding and a pneumatic hiss, revealing the cavernous underground parking garage, Marina's jaw dropped, her eyes darting from one sleek row of vehicles to the next.

"So many cars," she whispered.

It dawned on him then that Marina had never been to a mall or supermarket. She'd never seen a sprawling parking lot full of cars of every make, shape, and color.

"I need to take you to see the city."

Her cheeks pinked. "I sounded provincial, didn't I?"

He laughed. "Where have you ever heard that word?"

"I don't remember. Maybe I heard it in one of the movies or shows I've watched lately or dreamt it." Marina chuckled. "I don't know when it happened, but lately, I've started to think and dream in English."

"That's good." He opened the door. "It indicates mastery of the language, which you have." He stepped out of the vehicle.

One of the other Guardians beat him to Marina's door and opened it for her. "Welcome to the village, Marina."

"Thank you." She stepped out and looked around. "I'm already impressed, and I've only seen the parking garage. We have one bus and two cars in Safe Haven, and we didn't have much more than that in the compound in Karelia. I've never seen so many cars in real life."

There were still so many things he could show her that would make the parking garage seem like nothing, and Peter was excited at the prospect of being her guide.

As they gathered their luggage and made their way toward the elevators that would take them to the surface, Peter felt a flutter of excitement in anticipation of the moment Marina would lay eyes on the village for the first time.

He had told her about it, of course, painting vivid pictures of the lush greenery, winding paths, and cozy homes, but he wasn't great with words and could only convey so much without showing her actual photos, which he didn't have.

When the elevator doors slid open, revealing the sun-drenched pavilion with its soaring glass walls and displays of ancient artifacts, the look of slack-jawed amazement that crossed Marina's face made Peter grin.

She darted out of the elevator, her eyes wide and her steps faltering as she took in the display that lined the walls. Ancient pottery and intricately carved statues, gleaming blades, and clay tablets carved with ancient symbols were a treasure trove of history.

"What is all this?" Marina walked from one item to the next, her voice hushed with reverence as she ran her fingers along the glass.

"Kalugal is an amateur archeologist, and this is his collection," Peter explained. "Calling him an amateur is doing him a disservice. He might not do it for profit or fame, but he's very serious about it. When he moved to the village, he brought his entire hoard with him, and this is just a small sample of what he's got squirreled away in storage on the lower levels. From time to time, he rotates the exhibits, so we always have a fresh display." He walked over to stand by her side. "He also adds descriptions and explanations about each item."

Peter pressed a button, and a recording started, with Kalugal lecturing about that particular artifact. He let it play for a minute and then stopped it. "When you are bored and have nothing better to do, you can come here and listen to his lectures."

"I certainly will. This is fascinating."

He put his arm around her. "Maybe you'll discover that archeology is your passion."

"Maybe." She raised her glowing face to him, lifted on her toes, and kissed him on the lips. "Thank you for bringing me here."

"You're welcome, but you've seen nothing yet."

16

MARINA

Marina gasped as they stepped out into the sunlight, her free hand flying up to shade her eyes against the brightness. Peter had been right about the place being drenched in sunlight. It was almost as sunny as it was during the cruise.

The lush greenery was perfectly manicured, with narrow paths intersecting green lawns and patches of bushes and trees. There was a large pond and a playground, where several Kra-ell children were playing, most of them hybrid.

Out of everything that Marina had expected to see, this sight was the most shocking. The children were playing, laughing, yelling, and running around like human kids. She'd never seen them doing that in Igor's compound.

They had been highly disciplined, and their days had been spent learning and training.

Evidently, not only the humans of the compound had been freed, but also the Kra-ell, whom she used to think of as her masters.

"Welcome to the village, Marina," Peter murmured as he pulled her into his arms and spun her around in a giddy circle.

Clinging to him, she laughed, the sound bright and carefree to her ears.

Behind them, Alfie trundled along with their luggage and a long-suffering expression. "Are we walking or calling for the cart?" he asked.

Marina's eyes widened, her head whipping around to face Alfie. "There are carts?"

"There are," Peter confirmed. "But I thought we could walk so I can show you everything on the way and give you time to drink it all in."

Marina nodded. "I'd like that." She laced her fingers through Peter's once more.

They set off, with Peter pointing out the café, where people were sitting and having coffee and pastries. Recognizing her from the cruise, probably because of her blue hair, some smiled and waved, and she smiled and waved back.

As he showed her the office building and the clinic, Marina fought the impulse to look at the playground again and this time observe the parents. Or, more to the point, assess their response to seeing her.

But there was plenty of time to make assessments, and right now she needed to show Peter how happy she was to be in the village and respond with joy and enthusiasm to everything he was showing her.

He seemed even happier than she was about her being with him, and she didn't want to spoil the fun for him by introducing a potential problem he hadn't given any thought to.

"Do you want to see the playground?" Peter asked. "You keep looking at it."

"The children just look so happy. I never saw the Kra-ell kids smile like that back in the compound or heard them laughing out loud. It was always so grim, so oppressive there. I can't believe how quickly they have changed." She shifted her gaze to Peter. "It seems like the liberation of Igor's compound happened so long ago, but in reality, it didn't."

Peter nodded, his smile softening as he looked at the children. "It's easy to get used to good things. Jade is doing an incredible job with her people, but it wasn't smooth sailing by any means."

Marina chuckled. "I bet. They are such a combative people. I think they need a strong leader just to keep them from killing each other." She winced. "Sorry. I forgot that you dated one of them."

"I don't think Kagra is like that. She wants to be like Jade when she grows up, and she is emulating her leader. She's also more levelheaded than most of the other purebloded females."

Marina didn't like that he thought so well of Kagra, but she was smart enough to keep her mouth shut and not say anything snippy about the female. It would only make her look petty and jealous.

As Peter led her to the newest section of the village, he explained that it was home to the Guardians and council members, and he seemed excited about showing her his house.

They crossed a small pedestrian bridge, walked up the street for a few minutes, and then Peter stopped in front of one of the houses. "This is it. That's where we live." He turned to her. "Your new home."

"It's beautiful." She lifted her head and kissed him on the lips. "Are you going to carry me over the threshold?"

"Of course."

He swung her into his arms.

Behind them, Alfie snickered.

Peter turned to him. "Don't just stand there. Open the door for us."

"Yes, sir." Alfie reached over and pushed the door open.

"Welcome home, Marina," Peter said as he carried her inside.

Holding on to his neck, she looked around the beautiful living room. "Did you decorate it?"

Peter chuckled. "It wouldn't be so pretty if I had done it. Ingrid chose all the colors and finishes, and she also ordered the furniture and all the accessories." He kept going. "Alfie and I just brought over our clothes and shoes." He entered the bedroom and put her down on the bed. "Do you like?"

"It's all beautiful," Marina breathed. "And there is so much space. I could live in this bedroom."

Peter grinned, pulling her into his arms and kissing her forehead. "That can be arranged," he murmured, his voice low and filled with promise.

Desire stirred inside of her, but she pushed it aside. There would be plenty of time for that. Right now, she wanted to explore the wonders of her new house.

"Can I see the kitchen?"

"Sure." Peter offered her a hand up.

When they entered the living room, Alfie cleared his throat. "Should I start packing my bags?"

"Don't be ridiculous," Peter said. "This is your home. Nothing has changed."

Not looking convinced, Alfie turned to Marina. "Are you sure? I can find another Guardian to room with."

"Don't you dare." She smiled. "I would hate it if you left because of me. Besides, you'll regret it if you leave."

Alfie tilted his head. "Why is that?"

"You have yet to taste my cooking. Once you do, you will never consider leaving again."

"You are that good, eh?" He sounded skeptical.

"I am. And I will prove it to you."

17

JASMINE

Jasmine stepped out of the bathroom, her hair still damp from the shower, and changed into a comfortable pair of leggings and an oversized blouse that was still nice enough for an informal celebration. The pair of low-heeled mules would make the outfit a little more festive, but that was as far as she was willing to go in preparation for the party.

She was exhausted from the trip, her anxiety over the prince, and the drama of breaking up with Edgar.

Nevertheless, she was sufficiently energized to make a run to the clinic and check on the prince's progress. Bridget hadn't called, so there was no change, and he was still unconscious. However, Jasmine wanted to see if they had successfully taken him out of the stasis chamber and transferred him to the hospital bed.

Hopefully, the doctors hadn't broken anything or caused him additional damage in the process.

She couldn't shake the image of his emaciated body, the way his skin stretched taut over his bones—looking gray, dry, and brittle. She couldn't even imagine what he looked like when he wasn't starved and on the verge of death.

"I'm going to check on the prince," she told Gabi, the only one in the living room.

"Don't be long," Gabi said. "We have a party to prepare."

"I won't. He's still unconscious, so it's not like I'm going to stay around and chat." Jasmine forced a smile and opened the door.

As she exited the elevator on the clinic level, the clicking of her mules echoed in the empty hallway, making her regret her choice of footwear. She didn't want to announce her presence.

When she entered the clinic, the doors to the prince's room and Bridget's office were closed, and only the door to the princess's room was open. Jasmine peeked inside and wasn't surprised to see that the doctors hadn't removed her from the stasis chamber yet.

Morbid curiosity propelled her to look into the open chamber, and as she'd expected, the princess looked as skeletal as her brother. Still, it was easy to see that she was a female, even in her emaciated state. The bone structure was more delicate, and she was smaller.

As the door in the next room opened, Jasmine rushed out to catch whoever was there before they closed it.

"Doctor Bridget," she called out when she saw the red ponytail on the woman leaning over the hospital bed.

Evidently, they had moved the prince.

Bridget turned around. "Oh, hi, Jasmine. What can I do for you?"

"I just came to see how he was doing."

Bridget straightened and let out a breath. "As you can see, we moved him and hooked him up to the equipment."

An intravenous feeding tube was attached to the back of his hand, and various monitoring equipment was showing stats that Jasmine didn't know how to interpret. She could tell that things were working, though, and that they were steady.

"Is he going to make it?"

Bridget shrugged. "His body will, but I can't guarantee that his mind will as well. He's still unconscious, but he's stable."

Jasmine nodded, her gaze drifting to the prince's face. Even in his weakened state, his features had a regal quality.

He was so still, his chest barely rising and falling with each shallow breath.

"Are you going to stay here overnight?" she asked the doctor.

Bridget nodded. "Julian and I will stay in the keep for as long as the twins need us." She smiled. "My mate is used to sleeping with me on a hospital bed."

Jasmine swallowed. "You can take over my room. I can sleep on the couch in the living room."

Bridget smiled. 'Thanks for the offer, but I want to be near my patients."

"If you change your mind, just come up to the penthouse."

"It's okay." Bridget walked over to her and clapped her on the back. "This is the life of a physician, and I love what I do." She walked Jasmine to the door. "Go. Celebrate with your team." She opened the door and gently shoved her out.

"I'll come back tomorrow morning."

"Of course. Good night, Jasmine." Bridget closed the door.

With a heavy heart, Jasmine made her way back to the penthouse. As she entered, she found Margo, Frankie, Gabi, and Ella already hard at work, setting out platters of food and arranging bottles of various liquors on the kitchen counter.

They looked so full of energy and excitement, their immortal bodies needing much less rest than her human one.

Jasmine felt a pang of envy at their energy and high spirits. She was exhausted, both physically and emotionally, and all she wanted to do was crawl into bed and sleep for a week or at least one full day.

Ella turned to her. "Hi. How is the prince?"

"They moved him to the bed, and they are feeding him intravenously." Jasmine pushed a strand of hair behind her ear. "I guess it doesn't matter what his diet is for that, and they are only feeding him liquids."

Ella nodded. "Some things are universal."

"Is Edgar back?" she asked.

"Nope," Margo said. "Haven't seen him."

Jasmine wondered where he had gone. His things were still in the bedroom they had shared before the mission, so she knew he was coming back to collect them, and he had also promised her that he would be back for the party.

The prospect of not seeing him again triggered a pang of regret. Letting him go had been the right thing to do, but that didn't make the separation any easier. She still craved his company.

The prince was an unknown, and things might not take off between them, while with Edgar, she knew where she stood. If she were smart or a little less principled, she would have stayed with Edgar until she knew whether the prince was an option. As the saying went, it was better to have one bird in the hand than two up on the branch or something like that.

She smiled as her mind conjured an image of Edgar and the recovered prince sitting in a tree with their feet dangling below. Maybe they could be friends, but she doubted that.

The doorbell ringing startled Jasmine out of her reverie, and as she turned to see who was at the door, she expected it to be Edgar, but Margo's squeal of happiness indicated otherwise. Margo liked Edgar, but not that much.

Curiosity getting the better of her, Jasmine put down the glasses she was carrying to the table and walked over to the entryway to see what all the fuss was about.

Her jaw nearly hit the floor when she saw Mia, standing on her own two feet with Toven beside her. He was holding a large bag in one hand and extending the other towards his mate, ready to catch her if she stumbled.

"Your legs," she murmured like an idiot. "You are standing."

Mia's small feet were encased in a soft pair of slippers, and she walked inside with a hesitant but determined gait.

The regeneration process of her legs had been long and arduous, taking many months, but it was finally complete, and Mia was walking on her own two feet.

It was a miracle. Possible only because she had turned immortal.

Frankie started crying, and Margo quickly followed suit. Then, the three friends clutched each other in a fierce embrace, all of them shedding happy tears.

Jasmine felt her eyes well up as she watched them sharing this incredibly happy moment with Mia, celebrating her victory. The trio were more than just friends; they were more like sisters, and Jasmine envied their closeness.

All she had were two hostile stepbrothers, her manager, and her friendship with Margo. The rest of her so-called friends were fellow actors she'd met during the various productions she had participated in over the years. Those relationships could not compare with that of the three childhood friends.

Gabi came up beside her, wrapping an arm around her waist. "I love happy endings, don't you?"

Jasmine nodded, a lump forming in her throat. "Who doesn't?"

18

EDGAR

Edgar clutched a shopping bag full of books as he stepped out of the elevator on the penthouse level. It was his parting gift to Jasmine, and he hoped she would appreciate the gesture and the effort he'd put into thinking about it and acquiring it.

There should be a guide for clueless guys about what gift fit which occasion. Females seemed to know stuff like that intuitively, but most guys needed help.

At first, Edgar had thought of getting her some perfume, which most women liked, but it was too generic and meaningless. The same was true for chocolate or wine. Then it dawned on him. Jasmine had complained about having only two paperbacks with her, and somehow, they had never found the time to stop by a bookstore before heading out to Tibet. It had been mostly his fault for always finding other things to do that had been more important than that, and in retrospect, he realized that he had been too selfish, and

Jasmine had been too accommodating. She should have insisted.

He'd spent hours at the bookstore, going numb while leafing through the most popular romance novels of the day.

Ultimately, he'd chosen the ones that had more going on than just he-loves-me, he-loves-me-not. Jasmine was an intelligent woman, and he was certain that she needed more than such simplistic plots to fulfill her. But then, women were a mystery, and he might be totally off.

She'd said that she read to relax and forget about all the crap that was going on in the world, so maybe those simplistic storylines were precisely what she needed.

Well, she wasn't getting that. He'd taken a gamble and bought her one book with dragon riders that was pretty cool and appealed to the pilot in him, a couple about vampires, and a whole series based on fairy tale retelling. The saleslady assured him that it was trending and that he couldn't go wrong.

He tried to muster a smile as he walked in, but it felt forced. "Hello, everyone." He waved.

Jasmine looked up as he approached and cast him a smile that melted some of the ice around his heart. "You are just in time. Mia and Toven got here a few minutes before you, and we haven't started yet."

He glanced at Mia, noting that something was missing.

Her wheelchair wasn't there. She was sitting on the couch with Toven on one side and Margo on the other, and as Edgar's gaze drifted down, he saw that she wasn't wearing one of her long skirts or covering her legs with a blanket. She had on form-fitting pants, and her small feet were on full display, clad in shoes resembling slippers.

"Congratulations, Mia. I'm so happy to see your regeneration is complete."

"Thank you." She beamed at him and lifted her feet, twisting them this way and that. "I wish it was warmer outside so I could wear sandals or flip-flops and show off my new toes."

Smiling indulgently, Toven patted her knee. "Remember what Bridget said, love. You need to start with comfortable footwear and slowly transition to other styles."

Mia pouted. "She wanted me to wear orthopedic shoes, but I drew the line at that. I didn't suffer through all these months to go back to wearing granny shoes."

As the discussion moved to all the styles Mia wanted to try out as soon as possible, Edgar sat on the floor next to Jasmine and put the paper bag in front of her.

"I got you some books," he murmured.

Her eyes widened, and she pulled the bag closer to peer inside. "Thank you." She lifted her gaze to him. "Is that where you went? To a bookstore to look for books for me?"

He nodded. "You complained about having to reread the same two old paperbacks. I thought I'd replenish your supply before I left."

"That's so sweet of you." She leaned over and kissed his cheek.

"Take them out and see if they are to your liking. It was a challenging task finding something that you might like." He reached for one of the Snake Venom beer bottles lined up on the coffee table.

"I bet." Jasmine chuckled and reached into the bag, pulled out one of the fairy tale retellings, and cooed over it like it was treasure trove.

Edgar took a long swig of the beer, letting the cold liquid coat his throat. It would take much more than one bottle to numb the ache in his chest, but the night was still young, and the table was loaded with bottles.

"They are perfect." Jasmine returned the books to the paper bag. "Now I will have plenty to read to pass the time while I wait…" She didn't finish the sentence and cast him an apologetic look instead.

She didn't have to.

Edgar knew what Jasmine would be doing over the next several days. He'd stopped by the clinic and asked Bridget about her progress with the twins, and she'd given him an update. The prince was still unconscious, but he was being fed intravenously and monitored, and Edgar could see Jasmine sitting in the chair next to him like he was her mate or a family member, and not an alien she'd never met and knew nothing about.

As time passed and the drinks kept flowing freely, the tight sensation in Edgar's chest started to ease. However, his brain was still fully onboard, and the anger and disappointment that had been his constant companions for the past couple of days were just as vocal when drunk as they had been when sober.

"Are you okay?" Jasmine asked.

Edgar barked out a laugh. "No, I'm not okay." He took another swig of his beer. "I would have stayed, you know. To be with you. But I'm needed in the village. I'm the clan's only helicopter pilot." He snorted. "Well, Kian and Kalugal have learned how to fly helicopters on the simulator, so they can do that now, and maybe I'm no longer needed."

"That's nonsense, and you know it," Jasmine said. 'That's your job, and you are very good at it. No one is going to take it away from you."

He finished what was left in the bottle, put it down, and reached for a new one. "Yeah. They are both too important to fly themselves, let alone others." He took a swig from the new bottle. "Come with me, Jasmine," he slurred his words. "You'll be happy in the village." He waved a hand in a big arc. "You have nothing here. I can give you everything that he can't."

"I'm sorry, but I can't," Jasmine said with sadness in her eyes. "I wish I could."

The finality in her words was like a knife to his heart, and suddenly, he couldn't stand another moment with her. Pushing to his feet he staggered back, nearly tripping, and the room spun around him, the faces of the others blurring together.

He had to get out of there.

"I need to go."

"You shouldn't drive when you are in a state like this," Toven said. "Mia and I can take you back to the village."

Edgar waved a dismissive hand. "That's what autonomous driving is for. Good night, everyone." He stumbled toward the door.

Jasmine called after him, but he ignored her and closed the door behind him.

The elevator was right there, and as he got inside, the doors slid closed.

Alone at last, he leaned his forehead against the cool mirror glass and squeezed his eyes shut so he wouldn't have to look at himself.

19

JASMINE

Jasmine stood before the bathroom mirror and dabbed concealer on the dark circles under her eyes.

Despite the exhaustion and the discomforts of the trip to Tibet and the comfortable, fresh-smelling bed in a fancy bedroom inside the multimillion-dollar penthouse, she hadn't slept as well as she should have.

The opulent bedroom had felt empty and cold without Edgar beside her in bed, and when Jasmine couldn't fall asleep, she'd opened one of the books he'd gotten for her, reading until her vision blurred and her eyes refused to stay open.

That should have been enough to have her sleeping like a log, but she'd been plagued by strange dreams, or rather, nightmares. Upon waking, she realized that she'd dreamt scenes from the sci-fi movie *Stargate*, but she'd substituted the prince for the evil, life-sucking creature in the film.

It wasn't hard to guess why she'd had such nasty dreams about the prince. It had started with Edgar's comments, then she'd discovered that the Kra-ell needed blood for sustenance, and the kicker had been seeing the prince's emaciated form inside the stasis chamber.

When dressed and ready for the day, Jasmine stepped into the living room expecting to see her roommates, but no one was there. The only evidence of her companions' presence in the living room that morning was the half-full coffee carafe on the kitchen counter.

The coffee was cold, but Jasmine had no patience to brew a fresh pot. She poured a cup, sweetened it with sugar, and added milk so it didn't taste as stale.

She needed to find out what was going on with the prince.

Bridget hadn't called, which could mean that he was still unconscious or that the doctor no longer considered Jasmine as someone who needed to be informed.

She had served her purpose, and now she was not needed anymore. Should she go back to her apartment and her old job? She'd given in her resignation, but they would take her if she wanted to go back. There was always a need for experienced customer service reps at the call center.

Kian had promised to find her something better, but that seemed like ages ago, and now she was in limbo. She still had the credit card he had given her, but she didn't feel right using it for anything other than buying stuff related to the mission, and that was over.

With a sigh, Jasmine opened the penthouse door, stepped into the vestibule, and called for the elevator. Lifting her face to the camera above the door, she smiled and waved, knowing that the place was monitored twenty-four-seven.

Thankfully, her thumbprint had been inputted into the database as soon as they had returned, so she could use the private elevator to take her directly to the underground level.

She hadn't been granted access to that level before the mission, so it may mean she was now considered part of the team even though her part was done. Then again, she hadn't needed access to that level before.

She first peeked into the prince's room when she got to the clinic. He already looked much better than the day before, and the monitoring equipment readouts indicated steady outputs, a sign that he was doing well.

Or so she hoped.

Her medical knowledge was limited to what she'd seen on TV and in the movies, so it wasn't much. Come to think of it, however much it was, given the sources, it was all questionable at best.

"Good morning, Jasmine." Bridget startled her.

She spun around. "Good morning, doctor. How is the prince doing?"

Bridget glanced at the monitors. "He's doing well. Now it's a matter of waiting for him to wake up."

"So, he's not in an induced coma?"

The doctor shook her head. "There is no need. Physically, he's recovering as expected, given his condition. It's just his mind that I'm worried about." She gave Jasmine a sad smile. "You can sit next to him, if you like, and talk to him or read him a book."

Jasmine frowned. "He won't understand a word I'm saying."

"True, but he might be drawn to the sound of your voice. It's better than just letting the television provide the stimuli."

Jasmine nodded. "I'll do that."

"Do you want me to lend you a book?" Bridget asked.

Jasmine chuckled. "I'm an actress." She tapped her temple. "I have scores of scripts memorized. I can entertain him for hours with just what's stored in my head."

20

MARINA

The morning sun was climbing across the sky when Marina and Peter stepped out of the house, her hand tucked in his. The village was stirring to life, but the people she saw on the paths were not on their way to work. Given their sporty attire, they were on their way to some exercise facility, some fast walking, others jogging or cycling.

"Does everyone here start their workday late?" she asked.

"Most clan members work from home." Peter led her down the winding path. "So, they can set their own hours." He smiled. "And some don't work at all and engage in creative activity that is not commercial in nature. Every clan member gets a share of the profits the clan enterprises generate, and if they are okay with a modest lifestyle, they don't need to work." He leaned closer to whisper in her ear. "Guardians are very well paid, and I've been promoted twice already, and my pay increased accordingly. You don't have to work if you don't want to. You can be my pampered sex slave."

Marina chuckled. "As tempting as that sounds, I want to work and have my own source of income. I also want to meet people and not be chained to your bed twenty-four-seven." She smirked. "Although, I wouldn't mind that occasionally…"

Teasing aside, Peter might not always be around. He might tire of her or find his immortal or dormant truelove mate, and she needed to save for a rainy day.

It was a conclusion that Marina didn't like giving too much thought to, but she was painfully aware that she'd also once harbored the belief that her ex would be her forever one. Love blinded people to reality, and she wouldn't make the same mistake twice.

Peter kept introducing her to the people they were passing by, but there was no way Marina was going to remember all the names and faces. There were so many, and they all blurred together in a whirlwind of beautiful smiles and greetings.

The good thing was that no one had sneered at her or looked down their noses at her.

Finally, they arrived at the village café, a tiny building the size of a small train car with many adjacent outdoor seats. There were umbrellas over the tables, which probably served more to provide shade than to shield people from rain.

As the smell of freshly brewed coffee and baked goods wafted to greet them, Marina's stomach growled in anticipation.

"I wish I could stay and have breakfast with you." Peter squeezed her hand. "But all I can do is introduce you to Wonder, and then I have to run. My meeting starts in less than fifteen minutes." He pulled a card out of his pocket and pressed it into her hand. "Use this to pay for stuff in the café."

"I have money." She patted her pocket.

Peter shook his head. "You can't pay with money here. Only with the card."

Marina nodded. "Should I wait for you here until after your meeting?"

"Yes, but don't wait for me to have breakfast. I want you to eat, and when I come back, you can have coffee with me." He leaned down and kissed her cheek. "I hope to return bearing gifts."

He was getting her a clan phone, one of those fancy ones with internet access so she could read and watch movies.

"Yay!" Excitement thrumming in her chest, she lifted on her toes, wound her arms around his neck, and kissed him hard.

With a groan, he kissed her back, held her tightly for a few seconds, and then pushed her away. "I can't be late. Onegus will have my head." He turned toward the little booth where two gorgeous brunettes were serving customers. She knew Wonder, who had married the big redhead, but she wasn't sure she had seen the other one on the cruise. "Talk to Wonder. She's the one in charge."

"Okay."

He cast her an apologetic look. "I'll come find you as soon as I'm done." And then he was gone, striding down the path with his long legs.

Marina took a deep breath and walked over, but there was a long line of people waiting to be served, and she felt awkward about approaching Wonder and distracting her from her work, so she stood in line and waited until it was her turn.

"Marina," Wonder greeted her with a friendly smile. "Welcome to the village."

Marina was surprised that the female knew who she was. "Thank you. I was hoping I could talk to you about a job here."

Wonder grimaced. "I'm a little busy right now, but if you take a seat, I'll come to you when it gets a little less crazy here."

"Okay." Marina started to turn.

"Wait." Wonder stopped her. "Did you have breakfast yet?"

Marina shook her head.

"What can I get you? Do you want coffee, a Danish, a sandwich?"

It felt so awkward to be served by the immortal. "Coffee would be nice. And a Danish too, and a sandwich." She smiled sheepishly. "Peter has nothing in his house, and I'm famished. We just got here yesterday and didn't have time to go grocery shopping."

Wonder gave her a sympathetic smile. "Don't worry. I'll take care of you."

"Thank you." Marina pulled out the card Peter gave her and put it on the counter.

Wonder pushed it back to her. "It's on the house. Employees eat for free, and you are a future employee."

"You haven't even interviewed me yet."

Behind Wonder, the other female snorted. "If you want the job, you're hired." She handed a cup of coffee to the guy waiting for it and then offered Marina her hand. "I'm Aliya."

With a twinge of apprehension, Marina took the female's hand. "Nice to meet you."

The hybrid Kra-ell was surprisingly gentle as she shook her hand, and her smile was genuine. "Same here. I think I saw you on the cruise. You were serving food in the dining hall."

"That's right. I don't know how I missed you." Marina felt bad about not noticing Aliya.

"I didn't sit in the section you served."

Marina wanted to say that she had also attended some of the weddings as a guest, and she still hadn't seen her. Perhaps the female didn't like weddings and had stayed away.

After collecting her coffee, sandwich, and pastry, Marina took the tray to the only available table and sat down. She was lucky that most of the customers took their purchases to go, or she wouldn't have found a place to sit.

She was long done with her breakfast when the traffic in the café dwindled to a trickle and Wonder left Aliya to take care of things.

"Sorry it took so long." She pulled out a chair and plopped down. "It's crazy from six to nine in the morning, and then we have three hours of relative calm until the lunch rush starts. We close at six in the evening, though. So at least there is an end in sight."

"It's still a long day."

Wonder smiled. "It's not as difficult as it sounds. But that's because I'm immortal, and Aliya is half Kra-ell. Wendy used to work with us full time, which made things easier and allowed us to take days off from time to time, but after she enrolled full time in college, she switched to only working here on the weekends."

Marina tried to remember who Wendy was. The name

sounded familiar, so maybe she had been one of the brides, but which one?

"For a human, it's tough," Wonder continued. "I don't expect you to work as hard as we do. If you can work during the rush time, that would greatly help us. Six to nine, and then twelve to three. Six hours total with three hours to rest between shifts shouldn't be too hard."

"I can work six to three."

Wonder grinned. "That's even better."

"How come the café is so busy?"

"This is the only place in the village open during the day, so everyone stops by to get their caffeine fix and something to eat."

"What happens after six?" Marina asked.

"We have vending machines in the back for those who want some coffee and a snack after hours, and Callie's restaurant is open four nights a week. Atzil's bar is open only on Friday and Saturday nights, but he's looking for more help to expand his hours. The bottom line is that you can pick your jobs around here." Wonder leaned closer to Marina. "But I hope you pick the café. Aliya and I need a third set of hands."

Marina worried her lower lip. "I don't know how to operate that coffee machine you have there. I can make great sandwiches, though."

"The pastries and the sandwiches are supplied by Jackson's bakery and kitchen. We just serve them. We only make coffee, tea, and hot cocoa."

"Well, that makes things easy. When can I start?"

Wonder grinned. "You can start today if you want. Now that it's not that busy, it is the perfect time to show you how to work the cappuccino machine."

21

JASMINE

Jasmine sat by the prince's bedside, acting out scripts she'd memorized over the years. Some of them were musicals, so she sang the parts, the female and the male ones, just modified for her range.

She knew he couldn't understand her and that the words were just a jumble of meaningless sounds to his ears, but he might enjoy her singing, and since her acting imbued the words with emotion, he might understand that as well.

After all, people were the same whether they were humans, immortals, or Kra-ell.

She tried to keep it down, and she didn't want to distract or disturb Bridget and Julian while they were working on the princess in the next room.

Later, when Bridget walked in to check on the prince, Jasmine asked, "Am I bothering you and Julian?"

Bridget smiled. "Not at all. You are very talented and entertaining. It's like listening to a Broadway show from the dressing room."

Jasmine dipped her head. "Thank you. I wish the casting directors at all my auditions shared your opinion."

Bridget canted her head. "Looks and talent are two legs of the stool. The third is luck, and the Fates had different plans for you, so they didn't make you lucky."

Jasmine chuckled. "I'd like to think that. It's so much better than thinking I wasn't good enough."

Bridget turned to look at the prince. "Everyone is smart in retrospect, and the Fates don't like to show their hand. Perhaps your future is something you haven't even imagined yet." She stepped out of the room, leaving the door slightly ajar and Jasmine to ponder what she'd said.

What if the prince was just one more steppingstone toward a different future?

Jasmine closed her eyes and tried to think outside the box. What else could her future be? She was talented in many things but not exceptional in any of them. Her voice was strong, and she had perfect pitch, but it wasn't unique. She also wasn't a songwriter, and it seemed like these days, every successful singer had to come up with original pieces of their own.

A knock on the door pulled her out of her reveries, and as Jasmine turned and saw who it was, she tensed.

"Good morning," Kian said as he walked in with William.

"Good morning. My earpieces are in." Jasmine moved her hair aside to show William that she was wearing them.

William smiled. "Good. I'm glad that you are being cautious." He pulled out a small box from the bag he was carrying. "I have a new toy for you." He handed her the box.

"What is it?" She opened the top and looked inside.

William hadn't been joking. The thing looked like a toy. A small microphone and loudspeaker were housed in a teardrop-shaped pendant, which hung from a delicate chain.

"It works on the same principle as the earpieces, just without the compulsion filtering component. It will translate your words into the Kra-ell language so the prince can understand what you're saying. You can hang the chain around your neck."

She pulled the pendant out of the box. "How do I activate it?"

"It responds to voice commands." William smiled sheepishly. "The command to activate is 'Kra-on.'"

Jasmine chuckled. "That's easy to remember." She put the teardrop-shaped device in the palm of her hand. "It's so much more convenient than putting earpieces in the prince's recovering ears. Thank you for coming up with such a clever idea."

"It wasn't mine," William admitted. "My team has been working on improving the earpieces, and they've developed more great features. The device allows you to program it with your own voice, so it will sound like you when it translates your words into Kra-ell."

Jasmine frowned. "Will there be a delay, or will it translate simultaneously as I talk?"

"Simultaneously," William said. "And before you ask, the prince will only hear the Kra-ell translation, or mostly that. The device will cancel your voice waves by producing counter waves. It's not perfect yet, so he might hear some of it, but it won't be enough to confuse him."

"That's marvelous." Jasmine found three tiny buttons on the device, probably the manual controls. "Your technology is amazing." She turned the teardrop over. "What about singing, though? Will it also sing for him in Kra-ell?"

Kian regarded her with a puzzled look. "I don't think so. Is that an issue?"

She shrugged. "I sing to the prince. I don't know if he can hear me, but maybe he likes it. I would like to keep singing to him."

"Jasmine is very good," Bridget said from the waiting room. "Beautiful voice."

William and Kian exchanged glances, and William shook his head. "If you want to sing to him, deactivate the device."

"That's what I thought." She sighed. "It's a shame, though. I mostly sing songs from musicals, so the words are important. Still, this is a miraculous little device. You could make a fortune with it."

William ducked his head, looking embarrassed by her praise. "The next generation of earpieces will automatically learn the speech patterns and voices of the people around them, so they'll sound completely natural to the listener."

Kian chuckled. "The first generation was awful. The voice was male, and hearing my wife talking to me in a male voice was disturbing."

"I can imagine." She smiled up at him. "How complicated is it to teach it to use my voice?"

"I'll show you." William took the device from her.

"While you do that, I'll check on the princess." Kian turned around and left the room.

William spent the next few minutes showing her how to program the device and then left to give the new devices to the medical staff.

As Jasmine continued training the teardrop the way William had shown her, she thought about communicating with the prince the same way she would be talking to a human man in his situation.

The nuances of speech and the emotions behind them might be completely lost on him, and the same was true for her, even if William's team updated the earpieces before the prince woke up.

The prince was an alien from a completely different world with different values and beliefs. Would she understand him even if she could hear his voice?

Could she read him like she could read the people of her world?

Probably not. She would have a hard time communicating with someone from Tibet or Japan in a meaningful way, even if there was no language barrier. Their cultural expectations were too different.

Things would be so much easier with Edgar. He was an immortal, also alien in some ways, but he had been born on Earth, and he had grown up immersed in the same Western culture and values that had shaped her.

With him, there would be no language barriers, no cultural misunderstandings. Still, as the thoughts flitted through her mind, she pushed them aside because there was no escaping the fact that Edgar was not the one meant for her, and she should stop thinking about him as an option.

22

MARINA

Marina cringed at the number of cappuccinos she'd made that had gone down the drain. "I just can't get the hang of it. It looks so simple when you do it."

Wonder put a hand on her shoulder. "You need to develop the touch, which only comes with practice."

Leaning against the counter, Aliya nodded. "It took me days to master this beast and weeks until I could make all those fancy hearts and other designs with the frothed milk."

"Thanks for the pep talk, but I still feel like a failure."

Marina was getting used to the hybrid, who was very different from the other hybrids she knew from Igor's compound. The girl seemed more refined and better educated, but when Marina remarked on that, Aliya burst out laughing.

"I had the bare minimum of education when the clan found me. What you see now is the result of my mate's hard work. Vrog is a teacher and took it upon himself to educate his ignorant mate."

"Are you exclusive with him?" Marina asked hesitantly.

"I am." Aliya sighed. "When I came of age, I entertained following the Kra-ell ways and had several males in my unit, but it just didn't feel right. Vrog didn't want to share, and I didn't want to either. I'm very happy having only one mate." She crossed her arms over her chest. "Frankly, I don't know how the Kra-ell females manage several partners. It must be exhausting."

It had been quite a shock when the humans at Safe Haven had heard about Jade choosing one of the immortals as her exclusive mate, but evidently, she wasn't the only Kra-ell who had gone that way. Aliya and Vrog were also a monogamous couple. Emmett was another hybrid Kra-ell who was in an exclusive relationship with an immortal, but then Emmett was unlike anyone else on this planet.

"Hello, ladies." A tall, striking woman with long, silver-blonde hair approached the counter. "Can I bother you for a cappuccino and a pastry?"

Wonder cast her a warm smile. "Of course, Kaia." She turned to Marina. "Our newest hire will make your cappuccino."

Marina felt her cheeks get warm, and she wasn't quick to blush. "I'm not good enough yet."

"Welcome to the village, Marina." Kaia smiled. "I'll gladly be your first customer."

Marina winced. "Are you sure? Every cup I've made so far has gone down the drain."

Kaia shrugged. "I'm a scientist. I'm used to trying things a thousand different ways until something succeeds." She extended her hand. "I'm honored to try your cappuccino."

That was such a nice thing to say. "I'll do my best."

When the cup was ready, she put it in front of Kaia on the counter. Marina held her breath as the female lifted the cup to her lips and took a sip.

"Excellent." Kaia smacked her lips.

Marina very much doubted it, but she appreciated the white lie.

"Come back in a few days, and I promise it will truly be excellent."

"It already is." Kaia took another sip.

"What kind of scientist are you?" Marina asked.

"I'm a bioinformatician."

Marina had no idea what that meant and was too embarrassed to ask and admit her ignorance.

Kaia must have read her expression because she smiled. "Not many people know what bioinformaticians do. I work with biological data, trying to unravel the secrets of life." She tilted her head. "Who knows? We might discover how to turn ordinary mortals into immortals, no godly genes required."

Marina's heart rate accelerated, and her eyes widened. "Are you serious? Or are you just teasing me? Because if you are teasing, that's just cruel."

Kaia's piercing blue eyes seemed to hold the universe's secrets as she trained them on Marina. "The gods weren't always immortal. They found a way to modify their genes and make their bodies self-repair at such an accelerated rate that they turned immortal. What if we find a way to do the same?"

Marina's mind was reeling as she tried to process the implications of what Kaia was saying. If it were true, if there was a way for humans to become immortal, it would change everything. She could have forever with Peter after all. They could build a life together.

"How close are you to discovering the secret to immortality?" Wonder asked.

Kaia sighed. "Regrettably, I am not as close as I would like to be, but I believe I will be able to crack the code." She finished the last of the cappuccino, wrapped up what was left of her pastry, and put it in the paper bag Wonder handed her.

"Do you want to take another one for William?" Wonder asked.

"He's not here. He's at the keep today."

Wonder nodded. "Right. Anandur is there as well, guarding Kian."

Marina had a feeling that something important was going on in that place they called the keep, but she didn't dare ask what it was.

She was here because of Kian's good will, and if she didn't want to be kicked out, she should keep her nose out of where it didn't belong.

23

KIAN

TGIF, Kian thought as he rolled over and turned to look at Syssi, who was still asleep beside him. Or was it TTMFIF? 'Thank the merciful Fates it's Friday' didn't roll off the tongue as easily, though.

He leaned over and gently kissed Syssi's forehead before slipping out of bed and heading for the shower. He had a busy day ahead of him, with five phone meetings and a thousand and one details to attend to.

Nearly a month had passed since the cruise had ended, and he was still catching up.

As he stood under the hot spray, letting it sluice over his shoulders and down his back, he thought about the twins and the slow progress of their recovery. There had been some small improvements in their condition, but the road ahead of them was still long, and no one knew whether their minds would function properly once their bodies recovered.

Jasmine was keeping vigil at the prince's bedside, which was romantic given that all she had seen so far was a withered body. There was that one moment when the prince had opened his eyes and looked straight at her, but he hadn't done that since.

The poor woman was pining for what could be and not what was.

When Kian returned to the bedroom, Syssi wasn't in bed, and when he went looking for her, he found her as he had expected in Allegra's room.

"Good morning, my loves." He kissed Syssi's cheek and then his daughter's.

"Daddy!" She stretched her arms toward him.

"She is such a daddy's girl," Syssi murmured as she handed Allegra to him.

"Daddy." Allegra cupped his cheeks with her little hands and planted a kiss on the tip of his nose the way he liked to do to her.

"I love you, munchkin." He hugged her to him and turned to Syssi. "Do you want to get dressed while I get her ready?"

"Yes, please." She stretched on her toes and kissed him on the lips. "I'll be quick."

He knew she would be. Syssi's morning routine was no-fuss and efficient, with most of the time dedicated to breakfast rather than clothes, makeup, and hair. She had her priorities straight.

Their daughter, though, was a different story.

He went through eight different outfits until she settled on a frilly dress that was not practical for daycare in the university, where she would play in a sandbox that Amanda had recently added to the facility.

"You look very pretty," he said as he laced her pink sneakers.

Shoes were another quirk of hers. She abhorred Velcro. Allegra wore either laced sneakers or shiny Mary Janes.

He carried her to the kitchen and put her in her highchair.

Okidu placed a platter of his famous waffles on the table with all the toppings, and Kian handed Allegra a plain one. She didn't like anything mushy or gooey on her waffles.

Syssi smiled at him over her cappuccino machine. "What took you so long?"

"I think our daughter inherited her aunt's obsession with fashion. She's a very picky dresser."

"Tell me about it." Syssi rolled her eyes. "I think I'll start having her pick her outfits the night before to save time in the morning. And just so you know, I totally blame Amanda. She makes such a fuss over what Allegra is wearing that it is no wonder the child is striving to keep impressing her favorite auntie."

Kian pretended shock. "Just don't say Amanda is her favorite in front of Alena or Sari. They will be offended."

"Oh, they know." Syssi poured milk into their two cappuccinos. "She spends much more time with Amanda than with them, so it's natural."

Alena was due to deliver any day now, and although she was completely serene and unconcerned, Orion was going nuts. Not that it was a big surprise. This was his first child, while it was Alena's fourteenth.

The number was incomprehensible, especially for an immortal. "Have Alena and Orion chosen a name for their baby yet?"

Shaking her head, Syssi put the cappuccino cups on the table. "They are both superstitious and don't want to name the baby until it is born."

"Iti," Allegra said. It was her nickname for Bhathian and Eva's son.

Syssi smiled. "We already have an Ethan in the village, sweetie."

"Iti," Allegra insisted.

"Maybe there are other boy names that sound like Iti."

Syssi chuckled. "Yeah. E.T., the extraterrestrial who wants to go home. Does she think that her cousin is going to be an alien?"

"Or maybe she's talking about Nana's brother and sister." Kian grimaced. "I wonder if they will want to go home when they wake up."

He was just about to take a sip of his cappuccino when his phone buzzed, and when he lifted it to check whether he should answer it or ignore it, the name on the screen had him answering right away.

"Good morning, Mother," he said. "Were your ears burning? I was just talking about you."

She laughed, the sound raising goosebumps on his arms like it always did. "What were you saying about me?"

"Allegra insisted that Alena's baby should be named Iti, and Syssi said that it sounded like E.T. I responded that maybe Allegra had meant to name her Nana's siblings."

His mother didn't laugh. "That child of yours is definitely psychic. I called to tell you I want to see my brother and sister. Can you take me to the keep today?"

"There's nothing to see yet. They look a little better than they did when we brought them in, but they're still unconscious. They're barely more than dried-out corpses at this point, and I doubt you want to see that."

"Nevertheless, I feel like I need to see them." She was quiet for a moment. "I spoke with the queen last night through Aru and Aria, and the conversation made me worry."

Kian frowned. "What did she say?"

"I prefer not to discuss this on the phone. If you are not in a rush to get to the office, I would like to come over."

As if it was an option to refuse her. "I'm never in a rush when you need me."

"Excellent. I will be there in a few minutes." She ended the call.

"I'll start on the cappuccino," Syssi said, rising from her seat and moving towards the kitchen. "Okidu," she said, "can you make a few more waffles? The Clan Mother is on her way."

Allegra clapped her little hands, her face alight with excitement. "Waffles!" she cried, bouncing in her seat. "Nana!"

"Isn't it wonderful." Syssi turned to Kian with a smile, "to have your mother living just a short walk away?"

"You're probably the only daughter-in-law on the planet who feels that way about her husband's mother," he said, his voice teasing.

Syssi shrugged. "I love your mother," she said simply. "And your sisters, too."

Kian felt a rush of love and gratitude for his mate, for how she had embraced his family as her own. "I know, and it makes me the luckiest guy."

24

THE PRINCE

He drifted in a sea of darkness, his mind a jumbled mess of fragmented memories and half-formed thoughts. He couldn't tell where one ended and the other began, couldn't separate the dreams from the reality that once must have been his life.

Still, through the haze of confusion and uncertainty, one thing remained constant—the sound of her voice. It was a lifeline, a tether to hold onto in the endless expanse of nothingness that surrounded him.

He needed to find out who the female was and what language she spoke. He couldn't understand a single word. But her voice was a soothing melody that seemed to wrap around him like a warm embrace.

Sometimes, she sang, her voice rising and falling in a haunting cadence that stirred something deep within him. The songs differed each time, some joyful and uplifting, others sad and mournful. Some were passionate, filled with a yearning that he could feel deep in his soul, while others were light and playful, tunes that made him want to dance, laugh, and spin in circles even though he couldn't remember ever dancing.

He couldn't make out the words or decipher the meaning behind the melodies. But it didn't matter. Her voice was enough, a tether that kept him grounded in the void.

In the rare moments when the darkness receded and his mind cleared, he found himself grasping at the fragments of his past, trying to piece together the shattered remnants of his identity.

He saw flashes of a woman's face, who he knew was his mother. She was strong and brave, he knew that as well, and she did everything in her power to protect him and his sister, but she feared that even her formidable power would not be enough. She never said that, but he could see the fear in the shadows in her eyes.

"Your destiny awaits across the stars," she'd said. "The seer foretold your future. You will live, and you will thrive, and you will be safe."

He remembered the pain in his mother's eyes, the knowledge that she was sending them away and would never see them again.

The thought was too painful to cling to, so he drifted away, anchoring himself to that enchanting voice again. The female seemed to assume different roles as she spoke, sounding different with each switch.

It was so odd. Perhaps she was retelling tales of valor from days past, acting the parts of the heroes.

Time had lost all meaning.

He was trapped in the liminal space between life and death.

Gradually, though, ever so slowly, he began to feel a change. It started as a warmth in his chest, a tiny spark of life that grew and spread until it filled his entire being. It was like the first rays of dawn after an endless night, the promise of a new day and a new beginning. It was the feeling of blood flowing in his veins, of vitality returning, not in a torrent, but in a trickle.

The female was speaking to him again, her words a soothing murmur that washed over him like a gentle rain. He strained to listen, to make out the meaning behind the sounds. But it was like grasping at smoke, the syllables slipping through his fingers like sand.

And then, suddenly, something changed. The woman's voice shifted, the cadence of her words taking on a new pattern. It was as if a veil had been lifted, the sounds coalescing into something recognizable that he could almost understand.

It was a language he had never heard, the syllables strange and alien to his ears, soft, liquid, not guttural like his mother tongue. But somehow, he could make out the meaning behind the words, or perhaps he could feel the intent and the emotion conveyed through them.

He wanted to open his eyes and behold her, to reach out with his fingers and touch her, but the darkness was too strong and his weakness too profound. He slipped back into the void, back into the endless expanse of his mind. But even there, in the depths of his unconsciousness, he could still hear her voice, and he knew with a certainty that defied all logic and reason that she would be there when he finally managed to break to the surface of the murky waters under which he was submerged.

25

ANNANI

As Annani turned into Kian's walkway, she saw him waiting at the door with Allegra in his arms.

"She is excited to see her Nana," Kian said.

"Nana." Allegra stretched her arms toward Annani.

That was the best good morning possible, and Annani's heart felt immediately lighter. "Come to Nana, sweetness." She took the child and kissed her on both cheeks.

Allegra leaned away, looked into her eyes with that too-old gaze, and then leaned back in and kissed the tip of her nose.

"You are so precious, my sweet little granddaughter." Annani hugged her to her chest and followed Kian inside.

The smell of Okidu's famous waffles mingled with the

smell of Syssi's cappuccino and the sweet smell of the child in her arms was the best mix of aromas.

It smelled like home.

"I have your cappuccino." Syssi leaned to kiss her cheek. "Made with real milk the way you like it."

"Thank you." Annani sat down with Allegra in her arms. "I do not know how you can drink that vile oat milk." She held the child with one arm, lifted the cup with the other, and took a sip. "Perfect."

Syssi beamed at the compliment. "Thank you."

Annani tilted her head. "Am I keeping you from going to work?"

Smiling, Syssi sat down next to her at the kitchen table. "I called Amanda and asked her if leaving a little later today was okay. She has no classes on Fridays, so her schedule is more flexible. The postdocs can handle the research in our absence."

"I am glad I get to enjoy your company for a little longer." Annani reached for one of the waffles and handed it to Allegra, who snatched it with her usual glee at something tasty to munch on.

"So, what's got you so worried?" Kian asked as he sat on her other side.

Annani sighed. "The queen is insisting that we at least come up with a solid plan to fake the twins' deaths, and between the lines, she implies that if we cannot do that, we will have to resort to a less savory solution. We cannot afford even an iota of doubt to form in the Eternal King's mind regarding the twins' survival. He must be led to believe that they are dead and that their threat to him has been eliminated along with them. Our ruse needs to be perfect." Annani rose to her feet and put her granddaughter in her highchair. "I recommend doing so sooner rather than later because my grandmother is not a patient lady."

Kian chuckled. "I beg to differ. Someone plotting against her husband for thousands of years must be very patient."

"She deems my siblings a threat." Annani took a sip from her cappuccino. "Mostly, it is because the Eternal King will stop at nothing to ensure their elimination, even if it means obliterating Earth to achieve that goal, but also because of who they are and the powers they supposedly have, which might pose a direct threat to me. I tried to convince her that we need all the help we can get, and since we share a common enemy, the twins would naturally ally with me."

"That's an excellent argument," Syssi said. "How did she respond to that?"

Annani put the cup down. "She agreed with me but then pointed out that the twins might have their own agenda and that we must be careful."

"Nothing new there," Kian said. "We are taking every precaution with them. The plan is to induce momentary death, record it, and then revive them, but we can't do that until they are restored to full health. First, because they need to look as perfectly preserved as the Kra-ell who perished, so no one will suspect they entered unaided stasis, and second, so they survive the poison."

"Can I tell her that during our next chat?"

Kian hesitated. "Bridget needs to experiment with different doses of the poison to make sure it will work as intended and that she will be able to revive them. We might have to find another way if she says the poison is out. That's why I didn't want to tell the queen anything yet."

"We have to give her something," Annani said. "I think she is allowing us to nurse them back to health only because she knows it is important to me. If not for that, I do not doubt that she would have ordered Aru to get rid of them while still in Tibet. She might still do that once they no longer look emaciated." Annani glanced at her granddaughter, who was happily munching on the waffle.

"They are also her grandchildren," Syssi said. "How can she be so cold?"

Annani sighed. "Ani has been a queen for a very long time. She no longer thinks as a mother and a grandmother, if she ever did. I am precious to her not because I am her only son's daughter but because I am the heir, and she has no qualms about eliminating her other descendants if she deems them a threat to her plans."

Setting his drink down, Kian was considering the input. "Let me see how they are doing today and if Bridget has more insight about how to proceed. Hopefully, I will have more for you to share with the queen in your conversation with her tonight. But until the twins are awake, there is little point in you going to the keep."

26

JASMINE

Jasmine sat beside the prince's bed, her eyes fixed on his face.

Had anything changed?

His color was better, his face looked a little less hollow, and she could see his chest rising and falling as he breathed. It was progress, and she shouldn't expect more after only two days.

It seemed so much longer, though. It felt like the small patient room and the chair she was sitting on had become her entire universe. She'd gone up to the penthouse last night after Bridget had kicked her out, but she couldn't fall asleep, and after a few hours of tossing and turning, she'd come back down.

Thankfully, Bridget had been nowhere to be seen, and the nurse was much more sympathetic and let Jasmine stay.

Rising to her feet, she glanced at the slightly open door to make sure no one was watching her and started a stretching routine to get her blood flowing and relieve the stiffness in her muscles. After a few leg swings and arm circles, she moved into gentle yoga poses and concluded with a spinal twist to further unwind her body.

She should go to the penthouse and have something to drink and eat. Her friends had given up on calling her to join them for meals, but they had been kind enough to leave her leftovers in the refrigerator so she wouldn't starve.

Another option was the enormous commercial kitchen where she'd had coffee on the first day. Perhaps she could find something in its long row of refrigerators. What the heck did the clan need such a big kitchen for in its underground facility? Did they host parties down here? There could be a banquet hall somewhere for weddings and other celebrations.

She should take the opportunity to explore a little and see what else was there. The catacombs should be fascinating, but they were too creepy to visit alone, and she doubted she would find anyone to take her there.

Margo and Frankie had gone with Toven and Mia to the Perfect Match main office in the city for a tour, and Ella had returned to the village. Gabi had taken over the office in the penthouse to conduct Zoom calls with clients, so disturbing her was out of the question. She'd even posted a note on the door warning everyone not to knock or enter.

The gods were somewhere in the lower levels, working on the equipment they had salvaged from the pod, probably with William or others from his tech team.

Jasmine sighed.

She felt like a ghost, floating in limbo, not knowing what the future had in store for her. She didn't even know how long she could stay in the penthouse. She needed to talk to Kian and find out his plans for her.

Casting one more look at her prince, she slipped out of the room and was heading toward the clinic's main entrance when the door opened, and Edgar walked in.

In one hand he held a cardboard tray with two paper coffee cups, packets of sugar, and wooden sticks for stirring, and in his other was a large brown paper bag with something that smelled delicious.

Chocolate croissant. Jasmine was willing to bet that was what she was smelling.

"Hi," she said, looking at what he'd brought and hoping it was for her but not daring to assume. He had left in a huff after the celebration of the mission completion, and he hadn't been back since. "Who are you here for?"

He smiled. "You, of course. Who else? I came to see how you were doing and thought you could use some pick-me-ups."

"Oh, Goddess, I can." She reached for the coffee first. "Thank you. You are a lifesaver." She motioned for him to join her in the seating area of the waiting room.

He sat down, put his loot on the low coffee table, and handed her two brown sugar packets with two wooden sticks.

Jasmine felt a surge of gratitude and affection wash through her. "You still remember how I like my coffee."

He chuckled. "Of course, I do. We've not been apart long enough for me to forget." He pinned her with his blue eyes. "Not that I will ever forget. I will always remember you, Jasmine."

Why the heck did he have to be so sweet?

Not knowing what to say, she removed the lid from her latte, emptied the two sugar packets inside, and stirred.

Edgar reached into the paper bag and pulled out two croissants and two sandwiches. One of the croissants had gooey chocolate spilling onto its wrapper. He also produced a stack of paper napkins and put them next to the croissants.

"My mother always told me to eat my sandwich first and the dessert later, but the croissants are warmed up, so I suggest you start with them. One has chocolate filling and the other almond."

Jasmine grinned. "That's what I intended to do. This chocolate croissant has my name on it." She tore a large piece off and took a bite.

Her eyes rolled back in her head. "It's so fresh and delicious."

Edgar watched her mouth as if he wanted to lick the chocolate off her lips. "They are made fresh every night and delivered in the early morning hours. One of our clan members runs a large bakery and kitchen. The sandwiches come from the same place."

"Give him my compliments."

Edgar was quiet for a moment, regarding her with an intense look. "Come to the village with me, and you can compliment Jackson yourself. I'll also introduce you to him and everyone else." He smiled tightly. "We don't have to be together, but you are welcome to stay at my place until your situation clears. Not that I would be averse to us being together again, but that's obviously up to you."

It was so damn tempting to accept Edgar's invitation and leave all the uncertainty behind.

Well, nothing in life was certain, but having a roof over her head, food in her fridge, and a handsome man in her bed was a good start.

"I wish I could, believe me, I do. But I can't." She reached for his hand and gave it a light squeeze. "We had a good time together, and we probably could enjoy being together for a little longer, but in the end, it would have fizzled out because the Fates have different plans for us."

Edgar nodded, his face a mask of resignation. "I know, but it's so hard to let go. Especially when I see you sitting here all alone and looking dejected. I miss seeing the vibrant and upbeat Jasmine who stole my heart."

Jasmine rolled her eyes. "Perhaps she borrowed your heart for a bit, but she certainly didn't steal it. Your heart still belongs to you, waiting for the female you will gift it to. And as for me, I hope things will get better." She sighed. "I don't like the limbo I'm in. I want to know what's in store for me tomorrow and the day after that, but Kian rushed out yesterday before I could ask him his plans for me."

"Kian is here in the keep," Edgar said, his voice a little strained. "I think he went to see what Aru and his team are doing with the equipment from the pod. I'm sure he will stop by the clinic later."

"That's good to know." She lifted her cup and took several long sips. "I hope you will come to visit me again." She cast him a sidelong glance. "I was serious about staying friends."

He chuckled. "You just want me for the cappuccino and the croissants."

She was glad he was joking again. Seeing him suffering was paining her.

"I just want you in my life." She reached out, pulling him into a fierce hug. "Thank you." She leaned back and smiled teasingly. "For the coffee and the croissants and everything else."

27

KIAN

Kian strode through the keep halls, his footsteps echoing off the stone walls as he made his way toward the underground chambers he'd dedicated to storing the equipment from the pod. Beside him William kept pace, his face alight with excitement at the prospect of getting his hands on the advanced technology the gods had salvaged.

"Don't look so excited." Kian cast him a sidelong glance. "I talked with Aru earlier, and he said they hadn't been able to crack anything open."

The sparkle in William's eyes didn't diminish. "Even if we can't get anything open, we can probably connect it to a power source and see how it works. I would be happier if I could take every bit of equipment apart and reverse engineer it, but if I can't do that, I'll make do with figuring out what it can do."

"Fair enough," Kian said. "My main impetus is finding clues to the whereabouts of the other missing pods, but since I don't expect to find any more survivors, it's more out of curiosity and the need to prevent humans from finding them than the urgency to save people. All the Kra-ell are likely dead."

William arched a brow. "I'm not so sure about that. We didn't solve the mystery of Mey and Jin's parents, and we know for sure that their father must have been a hybrid Kra-ell, and we also know that he didn't come from Jade's tribe."

Kian used his phone to open the door to the suite of chambers the gods were using to work on the equipment. "Their father could have come from one of the other tribes that Igor found and subjugated. I don't know if the leaders of the other tribes kept their males on such a short leash as Jade. One might have fathered a hybrid boy outside his tribe, and that boy later became Mey and Jin's father."

William nodded. "That's possible."

As Kian opened one of the interior doors, they were greeted by Aru and his team hunched over a table littered with scraps of components.

"Any progress?" Kian asked.

Aru shook his head. "We've managed to power up some of the devices, but everything is solid state."

"That's great progress." William leaned over the table. "Can you show me what works and how?"

"I'll leave you to it." Kian clapped William on his back. "I'm going to check on our royal guests, and I'll let you know when I'm ready to head back to the village."

Waving Kian away, William didn't even lift his head.

"Evidently I'm no longer needed," Kian murmured as he stepped out of the room.

When he reached the clinic, he found Bridget in her office. He knocked on the open door and walked in. "How are you doing?" he asked.

"That's novel." Bridget leaned back in her chair, a small smile playing at the corners of her mouth. "Someone asking me how I am feeling."

"You look tired."

She sighed. "Sleeping on a gurney is not as fun as I remembered, but Victor is a good sport and doesn't complain. I think he enjoys it."

"Why don't you go home in the evenings? Julian and Gertrude can monitor the twins at night."

"I prefer to let Julian go home to his mate." Bridget smiled. "Besides, he's not experienced enough to deal with the twins on his own."

Kian tilted his head. "Are you sure? Maybe you are coddling him a little? Your son impressed me as a very capable physician."

Bridget grinned. "That's nice of you to say, and it's true, but he's not confident enough in his skills to deal with these two. Not only are they a unique medical challenge, but they are also the Clan Mother's siblings. Julian is terrified of them expiring on his watch."

"Is there a chance of that?"

She shrugged. "I think they are doing well. Their vitals are improving daily, and their brain activity is picking up. It's only a matter of time before they start regaining consciousness. Still, I've never encountered anyone who was in stasis for seven thousand years in a sealed stasis chamber that stopped working at some indeterminable point during those thousands of years."

"Still, it sounds like their prospects are good, right?"

"Unless something unexpected happens, yes. Jasmine's presence is helping. She keeps talking to him, and by talking, I mean that she is acting out entire plays and singing. It would have been much more boring here without that constant entertainment." She leaned forward. "I leave the doors to both rooms open so the princess can benefit from the stimulation as well."

"Good." Kian rose to his feet. "If you say that talking to a comatose patient is helping, then who am I to say otherwise?"

Bridget crossed her arms over her chest. "I know it does. Are you in a rush to return to the village?"

"I need to wait for William to be done, why?"

"Do you want to see our guests?"

"Of course. I would be remiss if I didn't, but first, I need to talk to you about something." He turned and closed the door before returning to his seat. "My mother visited me this morning. She's concerned that we are waiting too long to stage the death of the twins. I told her our plan, and she asked me to verify whether you still think it will work. Did you get any more insight into their physiology?"

Bridget nodded. "They are built like us, and their metabolism works like ours, not the Kra-ell's. I believe that the poison will work."

"Good." He let out a breath. "This will assuage the Clan Mother's fears."

Now, she could tell her grandmother to take a breather and wait patiently until the twins looked like their pod companions so their deaths could be faked convincingly.

Bridget pushed to her feet and rounded her desk. "They look better with every passing day. Come see for yourself."

The doctor walked out of her office and into the princess's room just across the waiting room.

"She looks much better." Kian leaned over the hospital bed. "Her eyes are shaped like ours, not the Kra-ell's."

Bridget nodded. "She is also not as tall. I measured her, and she's only five-nine. So, she is tall for a human but short for a Kra-ell female. She must have worn high-heeled shoes under her robes to pass for a Kra-ell."

"I wonder how old she and her brother were when they entered stasis. I should ask Jade if she knows."

"She should know, but I assume it was at least a few decades. It must have been a nightmare for them and their mother to hide their identities for so long. I'm sure other acolytes didn't take as long to become full-fledged priests."

"Indeed." Kian took another look at the princess. "We will know more when they wake up and tell us their story, provided they remember it."

28

JASMINE

Jasmine heard Kian talking about the princess over in the next room, and she wondered when he would come to see the prince.

She needed to talk to him, but he would probably walk in with Bridget, and she didn't want to have that talk with him in front of the doctor. Not that she had anything to be embarrassed about, but still. Some pleading would most likely be needed, and she'd rather do that with no audience.

Casting a glance at the prince, she decided she didn't want to talk in front of him either.

She stepped out of the room and waited by the door for Kian and Bridget to come out.

"Hi." She greeted him with a smile. "I was wondering if I could have a few words with you after you check on the prince."

"Of course." He returned her smile. "Bridget tells me that you are providing entertainment for the entire clinic and helping our patients find their way to us."

"I hope." She let out a breath. "I've been talking and singing for hours."

"Give me just a moment to look at him, and then we can talk in my office." He tilted his head. "That is if you are comfortable leaving your prince for a few minutes."

"That's fine." She waved a dismissive hand. "I come and go all of the time."

That was an exaggeration. She kept her absences to a minimum but didn't want to seem obsessed.

Kian took little time in the prince's room, and when he came out, he seemed encouraged.

"He is starting to look more like a prince than a frog," Kian attempted a joke. "Soon, he will be pretty enough to kiss."

Jasmine grimaced. "He's an alien to me, and I'm an alien to him. I don't expect any kissing anytime soon, if ever." She cast him a sidelong glance. "He's also a priest, and I was told that the Kra-ell priests are celibate."

"True." Kian continued walking down the corridor.

When they got to his office, he pulled a chair for her next to the oblong conference table, waited until she was seated, and sat beside her.

If he weren't a hundred percent loyal to his wife, Jasmine would have been worried about the intimate setting.

Mated immortals were not supposed to be capable of sexual attraction to anyone other than their mates, and Kian was an honorable guy. Still, she'd been in enough situations like this for the proximity to trigger apprehension.

"So, what did you want to talk to me about?" Kian asked.

"I was wondering if I was still in danger from the cartel. Can I go back to my apartment or my job? How long can I stay in the penthouse before I need to vacate it, and did you consider my employment prospects with Perfect Match?"

Smiling, Kian lifted his hands. "Whoa. That's a lot of questions. I'll answer them one at a time."

"Sorry." Jasmine winced. "I've been thinking about it for two days straight, so it was like releasing the relief valve on a pressure cooker."

Kian leaned back in his chair. "No one has come looking for you or put a tracker on your car. I had it checked. They snooped a little around the agency Margo worked at, but they didn't bother with her parents or her brother. They are back in their homes, and Margo's brother is supposed to get married next month. They ended up postponing the wedding after Margo told them she would have to stay in witness protection for a while longer. Her brother refused to have a wedding without her."

"Good for him," Jasmine said. "So, basically, I'm free to go if I want to?"

Kian leaned forward, his elbows resting on his knees as he fixed her with an intense gaze. "Do you want to go back?" he asked. "Because if you do, we'll make it happen. But I thought you wanted something different for yourself."

"I do," she answered with no hesitation. "I mean, I want something different. I want to be part of your world and see where this thing with the prince goes. It might go nowhere, and then I will need to reevaluate, but for now, I need to know that I can stay in the penthouse and that you are not going to kick me out. I mean, I don't have to stay in the penthouse. I can sleep on a cot in the clinic. I just need to know that I can stay here. With him."

Kian smiled indulgently. "You can stay in the penthouse for as long as you want. I told the gods the same thing. They are all welcome to use the penthouses as their base even when they have to travel."

"Thank you," she whispered as relief washed over her. "Right now, I can't work yet, but as soon as he is stable, I can start filling any position needed. I'm not choosey."

"No rush." Kian pushed to his feet. "For now, your job is to keep talking and singing to the prince and princess."

"I can do that."

"I'll arrange an allowance for you, and if you need help getting things from your apartment, terminating the lease, bringing your car over here, or any other arrangements, let me know, and I'll have someone assist you."

That was so much more than Jasmine had expected, and for a moment, she was stunned by the generosity.

"Thank you," she finally managed to say. "I really appreciate that, and I will take you up on your offer."

"You are welcome. It would be best if you also kept using the credit card I gave you. Just to be cautious, don't use your own cards yet. I don't want the Modanas tracing you here."

29

KIAN

Kian scowled at his cappuccino, absently stirring the oat milk and watching the swirls form. A new problem had been brought to his attention, and even though it seemed like a poorly conceived prank, it still disturbed him because things like that had never happened in the village before.

Across the breakfast table, Syssi watched him with a knowing look in her eye, her breakfast untouched. Allegra sat between them, happily munching on a piece of toast with cream cheese.

"What's that frown about?" Syssi asked. "You've been staring at your coffee as if it has done something to offend you."

"It's not the coffee." Kian sighed, running a hand through his hair in frustration. "Things have been happening around the village that leave a bad taste in my mouth. People are complaining about items missing from their yards and packages that were marked as delivered disappearing from the mail room. Stuff like that has never happened before, and naturally, everyone thinks it's either the humans or the Kra-ell, and they are not shy about giving both the stink eye. It's difficult enough to run an integrated community without someone perpetrating stupid pranks and petty thefts."

"It sounds like something bored teenagers would do, but we only have three in the clan, and they are all wonderful kids who would never do anything like that. From the new arrivals, there is just one human teenage girl who is so timid that the thought of stealing things would have never even occurred to her, which leaves the Kra-ell. There is a larger group of teenage and young adult Kra-ell, purebloods, and hybrids, and those who need to survive on blood are getting antsy because they don't get to hunt often enough. Jade only took two small groups so far, and it was mostly pureblooded females and some of the younger children. She needs to step up the outings."

Kian was surprised that Syssi knew so much about the Kra-ell. Working nearly full-time at the university and taking care of a young child didn't leave her with a lot of spare time.

"How do you know all that?"

She shrugged. "When Amanda and I return from the university, we usually stop at the café and hear all the gossip from Wonder and Aliya. Those two know everything that's going on in the village, and now that they've added Marina, she will soon become a good source of information as well."

"Amazing." Kian shook his head. "Maybe you can ask them if they've heard anything about the missing items?"

"They don't know who is doing it, but the hypothesis about the teenagers is floating around." She sighed. "I hope it's the teenagers and not adults who want to stir things up."

"Yeah. That's what I'm worried about. So far, the missing items are not very valuable, and it's more of an annoyance than a significant loss, but I'm afraid that whoever is doing it is just testing the waters."

She chuckled. "If I'm right and the Kra-ell are responsible for the thefts, they are definitely not testing the waters. Pushing their boundaries is more apt."

Given the Kra-ell's aversion to deep water, Syssi was right, but Kian wasn't concerned with semantics. "It's not just the missing items. The nighttime shutters have been malfunctioning in some of the houses, letting light spill into the darkness, and that's a security risk. If someone were to fly over the village at night, they'd see the lights and know that something was up here that shouldn't be."

William's ingenious devices kept the village hidden from electronic detection. During the daytime, the clever reflective roof tiles made the entire top of the mountain look like there were only trees. But something as simple as light in the window at night could destroy the illusion.

"Which houses had their shutters malfunction?" Syssi asked.

"They are all in phase two. Either the crews that built those homes did a shoddy job and cut corners, or the shutters we ordered were of crappy quality."

The second part was less likely because he had personally reviewed all the large purchases, and he would never have approved anything that wasn't considered top-notch.

She frowned. "I didn't know about the shutters, and that sounds like deliberate sabotage."

"I agree. But why would anyone do that? The safety of everyone residing in the village depends on us staying hidden and keeping the village a secret from the rest of the world, especially the Doomers. William's devices ensure that we're invisible to electronic detection. If that's sabotage, then whoever is doing it has a death wish." He leaned back in his chair and crossed his arms over his chest. "Besides, they are all under compulsion to not harm anyone living here."

Syssi shook her head. "There are always loopholes. They could convince themselves they are doing it for the greater good or some other nonsense that allows them to circumvent the compulsion. You need to put surveillance cameras in the mailroom and around the houses in phase two."

Kian nodded. "As much as I hate spying on my people, it has to be done."

Syssi shrugged. "We already have cameras in strategic places, like the bridge to phase two and at the perimeter of Kalugal's enclave. We also have cameras all over the mountain. A few more will not make a difference."

"It's a slippery slope, Syssi. Where does it end?"

"We don't put cameras in people's bedrooms and bathrooms." She chuckled. "It's funny that I find myself on the side of adding security features while you push back on that."

"I am not pushing back. I agree a hundred percent. I'm just playing devil's advocate." He sighed. "What if we suspect something nefarious is happening in private spaces?"

"Like what?"

He arched a brow. "Do I need to spell it out for you? We have humans living in the village. It's very easy to take advantage of them."

"Right." She scrunched her nose. "Maybe that's something we should leave to Edna. Did she ever approve a search or something along those lines?"

Kian snorted. "Clan law predates all the fluffy laws of today. If I suspect someone is taking advantage of a human or a minor, I don't need a search warrant to break down the door."

Syssi's eyes became hooded. "Why does that make you so sexy to me?"

He cast a glance at Allegra. "Is there a chance you can put her in front of the television to watch the Wiggles?"

Syssi laughed. "I could, but I told Amanda I would meet her at the playground."

He leaned closer to her. "Call her and postpone your playdate. It's Saturday. Tell her that you overslept."

30

JASMINE

"Good morning, Bridget." Jasmine handed the doctor a large cappuccino and a bag with a warmed-up chocolate croissant. "Enjoy."

The doctor smiled. "Thank you, I will." She took both to her office while Jasmine headed to the prince's room.

"Good morning, my prince." She leaned over and gently kissed his cheek.

He was still unconscious, and he didn't react to the kiss, but something told her that he could feel it. It was probably her imagination, but it seemed like his lips curved up a little.

Yeah, she was hallucinating.

Sitting on her chair, she put the coffee on the floor and bit into the croissant. After Kian had told her that she was part of the team and that her job was to talk to the prince and princess and stimulate them with her acting and singing, he'd also reminded her that the credit card he'd given her was still at her disposal and she could buy whatever she wanted with it. He had still advised against using her cards, to be on the safe side.

It was nice to stop at the café in the lobby and get coffee and something to eat. She would have ordered delivery from a supermarket and cooked proper meals, but not if she was the only one to cook for.

Margo and Frankie had started training in the Perfect Match center, Ella had returned to the village, and Gabi was busy working or visiting her family there. The gods spent most of their days in the bowels of the keep, working on the salvaged equipment, and she had no idea where they were getting their food from. Maybe they ordered deliveries, collected them at the guard station, and ate them where they worked.

Talk about dedication.

Pulling the teardrop from her pocket, Jasmine regarded it with suspicion.

She was not tech-savvy, and it took her time to adapt to new gadgets. She already had the earpieces, which she had to wear all day long, and now she needed to program the teardrop so it would sound like her.

It was important that she did that before the prince woke up.

He was used to the sound of her voice, or so she hoped, and when she used the teardrop to translate for her, it would confuse him if it didn't sound like her.

In fact, perhaps she should start talking to him through the device while he slept. If he could hear her, it would be good if he could also understand her.

Activating the device, she spoke a few lines from a play, but even though it got the tonality right so that it didn't sound flat, it still sounded strange and distorted. Then again, she'd recorded herself speaking enough times to know that she sounded different to herself than she did to others and that the way her voice resonated in her head was not the same as how the outside world perceived it.

Which gave her an idea.

She pulled out her phone and recorded herself speaking to have a baseline.

Next, she recorded the teardrop's output and compared the two. It was the start of a long, painstaking process of training the device to reproduce her voice accurately. She recorded herself repeatedly, listening to the playback and making tiny adjustments until the words that came out sounded more like her own.

It was a tedious task that required patience, persistence, and a willingness to listen to her voice until it began to sound like a stranger's. But Jasmine was determined and refused to give up until she had achieved the perfect balance of tone and inflection and the near-perfect replication of her own cadence.

Even then, however, the device had its limitations. When Jasmine tried to sing, the teardrop spoke the lyrics, translating them into the harsh, guttural sounds of the Kra-ell language without any of the melody or rhythm that made music powerful. She remembered then that William had told her to deactivate the device when she wanted to sing.

Jasmine considered transcribing the lyrics herself, trying to capture the essence of the songs in the alien tongue. But as she listened to the Kra-ell words that the device produced, she realized it would be impossible. The language was too different, too foreign to her ears and her understanding.

What about Shakespeare, though? Would the teardrop be able to tackle that?

She began to recite lines from *A Midsummer Night's Dream*, the words flowing from her lips in a steady stream of iambic pentameter. But even as she spoke, she could hear the way the teardrop struggled to keep up, and she did not doubt that the meaning of the words was lost in the translation.

She activated her earpieces in a stroke of inspiration, letting them translate the Kra-ell translation back to English. She'd been right. It was a mess.

Switching to a more contemporary play, Jasmine watched the prince's face for any sign of awareness, not expecting to see anything, but then she saw something that hadn't happened before.

The prince's eyes were moving beneath his closed lids.

Her heart racing with excitement, Jasmine rushed out of the room and ran into Bridget's office.

"You have to see this." She waved the doctor on and rushed back into the prince's room.

Bridget came running, her forehead creased with concern as she hurried to his bedside.

"Look at his eyelids," Jasmine said. "They are twitching."

"I can see that. He's dreaming. His brain activity is increasing, and his eyes are moving, suggesting he's experiencing REM sleep. It's a good sign, Jasmine. A very good sign." Bridget spent a few more moments checking the readouts on the equipment before leaving the room.

Jasmine felt a wave of emotion washing over her as she looked down at the prince's face. He looked so peaceful, so vulnerable in his sleep.

"I'm here for you," she said.

Then, realizing that she hadn't activated the translating device, she turned it on and repeated the same sentence. "You are not alone. Your sister is in the next room, and the doctor is taking good care of you both. You are safe, and you are going to be okay. I promise."

She leaned down and brushed her lips over the back of his hand.

31

PETER

"I've never seen so many cars," Marina breathed as Peter pulled into the mall's parking lot. "Not even in the village. There is a sea of them."

He smiled. "You ain't seen nothing yet." He found a spot, which was a stroke of luck on the weekend, slid his car into the narrow space, and cut the engine. "Wait until you see the inside."

He planned a whole day of wonders for her, and the mall was just the first stop. It might be too much for her first outing in a major city, but his Marina was a trooper, and she would do just fine.

She released her seatbelt. "I'm still amazed that I was allowed to leave the village."

He leaned over and kissed her pouty lips. "I told you that no one would object to that as long as you were with me. If you wanted to venture out on your own, the answer would have most likely been no."

She smiled. "My protector, my keeper, my Guardian."

Her tone was clear of sarcasm or ridicule. Marina enjoyed being under his protective wing, and he enjoyed the fact that she was okay with him hovering over her like an overprotective, over-possessive, overly romantic boyfriend.

Hell, he loved it.

Peter also loved that she waited for him to go around the car and open the door for her. All it had taken was him asking her just once to allow him to be a gentleman. He hadn't asked her permission, though, to show her all the wonders and delights the world had to offer and make up for all the years she had spent locked away in Igor's compound and then isolated in Safe Haven.

He was going to surprise her with that.

As she took his offered hand, he pulled her to him for a quick kiss. "Let's go shopping like there is no tomorrow. I want you to get a whole new wardrobe, with clothes for every occasion, shoes to match, sexy lingerie, makeup, jewelry, hair color, whatever you need to feel like a princess."

But not a Cinderella.

When he'd seen the duffle bag containing all her earthly possessions, he'd found it difficult to hide his wince. The bag hadn't even been full. He took more things with him on a weekend vacation than everything Marina owned.

She chuckled. "I've only been working in the café for two days, and I don't even know how much they will pay me. I can't afford all this."

Shaking his head, he wrapped his arm around her. "When you are with me, you pay for nothing. It's my treat."

She cast him an amused sidelong glance. "Since I'm not allowed to go shopping without you, I will always be with you when I buy things."

"Precisely." He leaned and kissed the top of her head. "As I told you, Guardians are paid very well, and until now, I've had nothing to spend my money on. Now that I have you, there's nothing I would rather spend it on than making you happy. Everything I own is yours."

She stopped walking, turned to him, and opened her mouth, probably to argue, closed it, and then opened it again. "We are not married, Peter. And even if we were, it wouldn't be fair for me to come into your life and share the fruits of your labor that you've accumulated over hundreds of years."

"I'm not that old," he grumbled. "And you buying a whole new wardrobe won't even make a dent in what I have in my bank accounts." He wracked his brain for something he could say that she wouldn't be able to rebut. "We are together, Marina, which is as good as being married. We don't need any official document to legitimize our union."

Huffing out a breath, she resumed walking. "We are just starting out, Peter. We are in love, and everything is great, but things might change."

"They won't. Not for me."

As impossible as it was for him to bond with a human, Peter felt bonded to Marina. She was his mate, but he knew she wouldn't just take his word for it. She didn't know what it meant to be fated to a partner, and if he tried to explain, she wouldn't believe him.

As Kagra's taunting resurged in his mind, he wondered if perhaps she'd been right and he was in love with the notion of love.

Marina leaned into him, resting her head on his bicep. "I love you."

"I love you too." He tightened his fingers on her shoulder. "Do it for me. It will please me to no end to have you buy as many things as we can both carry."

"Okay," she murmured.

"Yes!" Peter pumped his fist in the air.

Hand in hand, they entered the mall, a blast of cold air greeting them as they stepped through the automatic doors. Marina's eyes widened in wonder as she took in the vast expanse of the atrium, the gleaming storefronts, and the throngs of shoppers milling about.

"It's so beautiful." She squeezed his hand. "Look at the height of the ceiling and the skylights, oh my, so marvelous. It's like a wonderland."

"Come on, beautiful. Let's shop till we drop."

Peter led Marina into the fray, guiding her from store to store and helping her pick out outfits, accessories, and everything else he'd planned.

As they made their way through the racks of designer gowns and cocktail dresses, Peter felt excited at the thought of what lay ahead. He had never been one for grand gestures or elaborate schemes, but with Marina, everything was different. It was charged with a sense of possibility and promise that made his blood sing.

At first, she'd needed some coaxing, especially when hit with price tag shock, but once he'd gotten her over that hurdle and she gained confidence, Marina turned out to be a natural-born shopper with an eye for fashion and a love of all things beautiful.

They lost themselves in the simple pleasures of the moment, laughing and chatting and trying on things just for fun, like the cowboy hat that Marina insisted he had to get.

"I will need matching boots," he said with a fake Southern accent.

"Then let's get them." She tugged on his hand, leading him to the men's shoe section in the department store.

It was uncanny how quickly she'd got her bearing and knew where everything was.

"We don't have time for that." He laughed, grabbing the first pair he saw and motioning for the clerk to get him a pair in his size.

His other hand was going numb from the number of bags he was carrying, and Marina had a whole bunch of them, too.

The hunting had been fruitful, and Marina had everything she needed for tonight and the rest of next week. He planned on taking her to the mall again.

"Why don't we have time?" She plopped tiredly on the chair next to him. "When is the mall closing?"

He turned to her with a smile. "There is plenty of time until closing, but I've made dinner reservations at a fancy restaurant tonight at eight, and we still need to go home and get showered and changed."

She turned to him and smiled with her head resting on the back of the chair. "You've planned a full day of fun for us."

"I did," he said with no small amount of pride. "It wasn't easy to get reservations for *By Invitation Only*. I had to beg Kian to give me the spot tonight. There is a long waiting list for spending a small fortune at the best kept secret in town."

Marina frowned. "If the restaurant is so good, why is it a secret?"

"It's a super exclusive place owned by a clan member. People pay hundreds of thousands for a membership just so they have the privilege of making a reservation. It's the kind of place where the rich and famous enjoy themselves away from the public eye."

Marina's eyes nearly popped out of her head. "And you want to take me there? I don't belong in a place like that."

"Don't worry about it." He took her hand. "Neither do I. But it's dark and intimate, and no one will pay us any attention."

He didn't add that it was a place where illicit affairs were conducted in shadowy corners, and the air was thick with the scent of forbidden desires.

She eyed him with suspicion. "Are you sure?"

"I'm sure." He lifted her hand and kissed the back of it. "Remember the wrap dress I told you was perfect for dinner in a fancy restaurant?"

She smiled. "How could I forget? It was the most expensive item you bought me. That and the shoes that went with it." Her eyes sparkled. "They are so sexy. I can't wait to wear them."

Just then, the clerk returned with a tower of shoe boxes and put them on the floor next to Peter. "I took the liberty of bringing several styles for you to try, sir."

Peter stifled a chuckle. Seeing the number of bags he and Marina were hauling between them, the clerk must have assumed that he was dealing with serious shoppers who were worth his time and effort.

32

MARINA

When Marina collapsed into the passenger seat of Peter's car, her body was exhausted, but her spirit was exhilarated. The trunk was filled to bursting with shopping bags, a testament to the whirlwind day of indulgence they had spent.

Growing up in Igor's compound, shopping had been as foreign to her as the idea of freedom. Her life had been simple, defined by her duties and designated place in the hierarchy. The funny thing was that, at the time, she hadn't considered her life terrible. She had known her place and what had been expected of her, and as long as she'd toed the line, she was safe. Others in the compound hadn't had it any better, not the humans anyway, and even the Kra-ell had lived modestly, including Igor himself. He had been a glutton for power but not for luxury.

It was so easy to get used to all the good things Peter introduced her to. The lovely big house was professionally decorated, with a comfortable bed that felt like sleeping on a cloud. And now the shopping extravaganza had been so over the top that Marina was having difficulty internalizing the amount of money Peter had wasted on her. A village could buy food for a month with that kind of money.

Still, it was his money, and he didn't owe it to anyone. He had earned and saved it, and if it made him happy to spend it on her, she would oblige him.

As Peter glanced at his watch, his brow furrowed. "We will have to rush things a bit to make it in time to *By Invitation Only*." He looked at her with a smirk. "And we do want to make it on time. They are very strict about that. If you are not in their parking lot at the scheduled time, they will not wait for more than fifteen minutes."

Marina wanted to ask why they were meeting someone in a parking lot to go to a restaurant, but she didn't want to appear too provincial.

Besides, she didn't have the energy. She was tired, and the prospect of dressing up and going out to a fancy restaurant seemed daunting. Not that she was going to say a thing. Peter had gone to a lot of trouble planning this day for her, but he had forgotten that she was human with human limitations and reserves of energy. Nevertheless, she had no intention of disappointing him and putting a damper on the magic.

Summoning a smile, she pushed down the fatigue and focused on the thrill of anticipation. "I can't wait."

Peter wasn't fooled, though. He was too attuned to her to fall for the brave face she put on. Reaching over, he took her hand. "Shopping is hard work." He sighed dramatically. "I suggest that you recline the seat and nap on the way home to recharge your batteries for tonight."

That was a good idea, but it wasn't as easy as just closing her eyes. "Can you thrall me to feel sleepy?"

Peter hesitated. "I'd rather not. I don't take thralling lightly, and I don't do it casually. I can sing you a lullaby, though."

Marina didn't want him to do anything he wasn't comfortable with, so she reclined her seat, curled on her side, and closed her eyes. "I'd like to hear you sing."

Not surprisingly, Peter had a beautiful singing voice. It was deep and velvety, and his pitch was perfect. In no time, she felt sleepy.

"Wake me up when we get home," she murmured.

As they merged onto the highway, Marina was carried away by the gentle rocking motion of the vehicle and the soft, steady thrum of the engine, and she let her mind drift,

Hovering on the edge of sleep, the word *home* echoed through her mind.

She'd lived in the village less than a handful of days, yet it felt more like home than any other place she'd lived in because she was with Peter, and Peter was her home.

33

PETER

Peter selected a dark red silk tie from his collection, the color complementing his charcoal-colored suit. Standing in front of the mirror, he draped the tie around his neck and, with practiced movements, crossed the wide end over the thin one, looped it underneath, and brought it up through the neck opening.

The truth was that he didn't wear ties often, but when a man was almost two centuries old, he'd had enough practice to do it blindfolded.

He tucked the wide end down through the loop he had created, tightening and adjusting the knot to sit neatly against his collar. After ensuring that the tie was centered and the length was right, he smoothed down his suit jacket and inspected his reflection with a satisfied nod.

He looked handsome and debonair if he said so himself.

The gold cufflinks had been a present from his mother upon his acceptance to the Guardian training program, and they added to the look he was going after tonight, which was refined sophistication.

Peter chuckled to himself. Was he a good enough actor to fool anyone?

Not likely. A tailored suit and a pair of fancy cufflinks could not replace years of formal education in snobbery.

As Marina stepped out of the bathroom with a towel wrapped around her chest and another around her hair, Peter lifted his hand and smoothed it over his goatee.

"Don't worry." She patted the one on her head. "I'm the queen of quick blowouts."

He snorted. "Yes, you are. But it's called blow jobs, not blowouts."

Marina rolled her eyes. "Nice try." She dropped the towel covering her body, which was a pure act of revenge because she knew he could do nothing about it.

They needed to arrive on time.

"You are wicked," he said, his eyes glued to her sashaying naked ass.

She looked at him over her shoulder, her eyes hooded, and a naughty smirk lifted her lips. "I know."

Oh, she was going to pay for that.

"Wear the wrap dress," he called after her.

"I am. You told me you wanted me to wear it tonight when you bought it for me."

He had, but he hadn't told her the rest of his plan. He would tell her later.

"Can you find it for me? It will save us time. Also, the black shoes."

"Sure thing, sweetheart."

When she emerged from the bathroom fifteen minutes later, with her hair and makeup done and sporting a new, sexy lingerie set, he held the dress up but didn't hand it to her.

She reached for the hanger, but he held it up.

"Peter." She tried to jump for it. "We are going to be late."

He shook his head. "Take off your bra and panties."

Noting the mischievous glint he no doubt had in his eye, she shook her head. "We don't have time for games." Her voice sounded breathless.

He'd known that it would excite her. "We are not going to play now. Take them off, and I'll give you the dress."

Her eyes widened. "You can't be serious."

"I'm dead serious. Do as I say."

The scent of her arousal hitting his nostrils was all the confirmation he needed that she was very much on board for the game he had in mind.

"Yes, sir."

She reached behind her and unclasped her bra, sliding the shoulder straps down her arms, letting it fall off, and tossing it on the bed. Next, she hooked her thumbs in her thong panties and shimmied out of them.

As Peter's erection threatened to escape the confines of his boxer shorts and he began to sweat, he realized that his plan was going to be sweet torture that would last long hours unless he got some creative ideas, like sneaking Marina into the bathroom or the supply closet in his cousin's restaurant and fucking her into oblivion, or having her prove her claim that she was the queen of blow jobs.

Striking a pose, Marina extended her hand. "Are you going to hand me the dress or not?"

He offered it to her without a word, knelt at her feet, and helped her into the impossibly high heels.

Marina was a beautiful woman, but she was a vision standing naked in four-inch stilettos, with her hair and makeup done to perfection.

Still kneeling, he watched her put the dress on, wrap it around her body, and secure it with a belt, which she tied tightly around her narrow waist.

"I hope I'm not going to flash anyone but you."

He pushed to his feet and wrapped his arm around her middle. "Don't worry. I'll make sure no one gets to see what's mine."

34

JASMINE

As Jasmine walked into the penthouse, holding a stack of laundry under her arm, her back was aching from the long hours spent sitting by the prince's bedside, and her shoulders felt tight even though she'd tried to remember to stretch from time to time.

They should invest in better chairs for the patients' loved ones sitting at their bedside.

Not that she was the prince's loved one, but he didn't have anyone else to watch over him, and Jasmine had nominated herself. Well, nominating implied a voluntary decision when it was more like a compulsion. She didn't have a choice in the matter. There was no other way to explain why she slept on the floor near his hospital bed, only a sleeping bag cushioning the hard surface, and why she showered in the small, utilitarian en suite bathroom. She had barely left his side in the days since his arrival, her heart aching with the need to be near him like they were connected by some invisible thread that had tied them together across time and space.

Somehow, everything she had ever strived for and worked so hard to achieve seemed less important than nursing this stranger, this alien from a different planet, back to health.

Thankfully, the medical staff didn't notice the sleeping bag she'd hidden under the hospital bed and that she didn't spend every moment sitting in the damn chair but stretched out on the floor for a quick nap here and there. Or maybe they had noticed and were pretending that they didn't because no one had the heart to kick her out.

"Hello, stranger." Margo's voice startled her.

Jasmine gasped, her hand flying to her chest, and when she scanned the room to find where the voice was coming from, she found Margo sprawled out on the living room couch with her phone clutched in her hand.

"You startled me. I thought you were still training in the Perfect Match center."

"It's Sunday." Margo sat up. "Frankie went to visit her family, the guys are working in the basement, and Gabi and Ella are in the village. I'm all alone up here."

Calling the sprawling underground labyrinth under the high-rise a basement was the epitome of an understatement, but Jasmine didn't correct Margo. "I'll just drop this in the washing machine and come sit with you for a bit."

She wanted to return to the prince as soon as possible, but Margo looked like she could use a friend.

"Do you want coffee?" Margo pushed to her feet.

"Sure. I planned to drop my dirty stuff in the machine and carry a fresh stack back to the clinic, but I'm a little hungry. Are there any leftovers in the fridge?"

The truth was that she was famished, and she would have raided the fridge on her way out anyway. The café in the lobby was closed on Sundays, so she'd gotten coffee in the kitchen and instant oatmeal she'd found in one of the cabinets. The medical staff must have assumed that she ate at the penthouse, which she did when she could find leftovers.

"I'll put together a plate for you," Margo said.

"Thank you."

After loading the washing machine, Jasmine went to the bedroom and collected a fresh change of clothes and a few towels.

When she returned to the kitchen, two fresh cups of coffee were on the counter and a large plate of assorted fruits and cheeses.

Not the meal she'd had in mind, but it would do.

"That looks awesome." She snatched a strawberry and popped it into her mouth.

"I'm glad you like it. That's all I could find." Margo lifted her coffee cup and took a sip. "How are the twins doing?"

Jasmine shrugged, the familiar words rolling off her tongue with practiced ease. "Still unconscious, but they look better with every passing day. It's amazing how quickly you people recover. It would have taken a human several weeks or even months to make the progress these two have made in three days."

"They are half gods." Margo smiled tightly. "I'm just an immortal, but I get what you are saying."

Sensing that something was weighing on her friend's mind, Jasmine frowned. "What's going on, Margo? Trouble with the family? Or are you feeling lonely because Negal is spending his days in the basement?"

Margo chuckled. "Both. But it's mainly about my brother's wedding." She lifted her phone and showed Margo the screen. "Lynda changed her mind about the bridesmaids' dresses and sent me a link to choose a new one. She always makes life as difficult as possible for everyone around her."

"I don't get it." Jasmine put a piece of cheese on a cracker. "I thought that the wedding was postponed because your family was whisked away to safety to hide them from the cartel, but then no one came looking for them, and they were allowed to go home. Everything was already arranged, including the bridesmaids' dresses."

Margo sighed. "It's never as simple as that with Lynda. Besides, it was postponed again."

"Why?"

"Because of me. I told them that I was still in the witness protection program because of the trip to Tibet, and Rob refused to get married without me."

"Good for him," Jasmine said. "Do you need help choosing your new bridesmaid dress?"

Margo shook her head. "I don't care about the damn dress. I care about Rob's future." She turned a pair of pleading eyes on Jasmine. "Can I ask you for a favor?"

"Of course. Anything."

"What I need is for you to do your card magic to tell me if Rob is going to be happy with Lynda."

Jasmine stifled a wince. "Are you sure you want me to do this? I know the cards have proved themselves regarding the prince, but they might not always be right."

It was also possible to misinterpret their meaning, and Jasmine was far from the best at reading them.

"I know." Margo clutched her cup of coffee as if it was a lifeline. "But I'm desperate. I have to know."

"I'll get the cards." Jasmine pushed to her feet.

Margo put a hand on her arm. "Finish your coffee and your meal first. The tarot can wait a few more minutes."

35

PETER

The night was unusually dark when Peter drove through the city streets. Clouds obscured the moon and stars, and the air smelled like rain.

Beside him, Marina stared out the window at the passing scenery. "This city is huge, and each neighborhood looks different." She turned to him. "I still think the village is much nicer than anything out here."

"I agree." He put his hand on her knee.

Knowing that she was naked under the dress and that he could fondle her any time he wished, it had been a struggle not to part the skirt and explore how turned on she was. But part of the fun was the anticipation, and he wanted to save the game for when they were seated in a dark corner booth.

As he turned down a narrow, nondescript alley, Peter guided the car into the parking lot and eased into the spot marked with a large number twenty-three on the pavement.

Cutting the engine, he glanced at Marina. "Ready to be wowed?"

"By what?"

"You'll see." He opened the door, stepped out of the car, and walked to the passenger side.

The restaurant's nondescript limousine pulled up behind them just as he opened Marina's door and offered her a hand.

"Good evening." The limo driver opened the back door for them.

They slid in and, a moment later, were again on their way.

"It's like some spy movie," Marina whispered.

"It's all part of the mystique, a cultivated air of exclusivity that makes *By Invitation Only* the exclusive club it is." He chuckled. "And you don't have to whisper. The driver can't hear us." He pointed at the glass separating the back from the front.

She frowned. "How can you be sure of that? He might have a microphone back here."

"That's an excellent observation, but he doesn't. The owner ensures that his staff obeys the rules."

Understanding glinting in her eyes, Marina nodded.

As the limo stopped in front of a gate, there was nothing there that would indicate the presence of a world-class restaurant on the other side. There were no signs or markers that would betray its existence beyond the ordinary-looking gate. To the untrained eye, it looked like just another residence of some wealthy family that wanted to protect its privacy.

Peter squeezed Marina's hand as the gate slid open and the limo crawled up the long and winding driveway. "This is a new location. It's my first time here."

Her eyes widened with surprise. "Really? I thought you'd been here before."

"Only once, and it was in the previous location. The demand became so high that Gerard had to buy a larger place. Not that it was a problem, given the fortune he makes. When he first came up with the idea, I thought he was nuts because no one would pay that much for a membership that only gave them access to make reservations and still pay for the meal, but he was right. I underestimated how the rich really live and how much they are willing to spend on exclusivity and privacy and belonging to a club that only accepts the elite of the elite."

"I'm surprised your cousin demanded Kian buy a membership."

Peter grinned. "Kian co-owns the place with Gerard, so I don't think he had to pay full price, but I don't know that for sure. Gerard is a gifted chef, but he also has an ego to match, and he's not easy to work with. Kian is probably a very silent partner who only collects profits in proportion to his investment."

As the limo stopped in front of the grand entry, Marina swallowed, and her eyes flooded with trepidation. "I can't go in there, Peter. I don't know how to act around people like that."

He intertwined his fingers with hers. "Neither do I," he said in a playful tone. "I just try to remember that this is a classy joint, so no getting drunk and singing Scottish lurid love ballads. If you can do that, you'll do just fine."

Marina laughed nervously. "I'll do my best, but I make no promises."

As the driver opened the door, Peter stepped out and offered his hand to help Marina out while blocking her from the view of the guy in case her skirt parted.

The driver went ahead of them and opened the door with a flourish almost rivaling Okidu's. "Welcome to *By Invitation Only*."

A hostess greeted them with a warm smile as they stepped through the door and into the dimly lit foyer. "Good evening."

She didn't ask for their names and didn't utter the name Peter had made the reservation under. Anonymity was the name of the game or, rather the pretense of it.

The rich and famous wanted to be seen and acknowledged by their peers but left alone to their illicit affairs and clandestine meetings. As long as no names were spoken, there was no definite proof of who they were. There were plenty of lookalikes, and Peter wouldn't have been surprised to discover that the elite used doubles to mislead the paparazzi and perhaps even one another.

"Please, follow me." The hostess led them through the cavernous room, which was divided into intimate seating arrangements.

"I've requested the booth," Peter said.

The woman nodded. "A booth was reserved for you, sir."

A jazz band was playing soft, sultry tunes that seemed to dance on the air like wisps of smoke, but no one was dancing yet.

It was too early for that.

Peter cast a sidelong glance at Marina, watching her reaction to the grandeur and the beauty of the room, the celebrities they were passing by, and the way the candlelight flickered across the faces of the diners and made their jewels sparkle.

Squeezing her hand, he leaned to whisper in her ear, "Welcome to the magical and wondrous world of *By Invitation Only*."

36

JASMINE

Jasmine retrieved her well-used tarot deck from the bedroom and returned to the living room.

"I made fresh coffee," Margo said with a nervous smile.

"Good." Jasmine sat next to her on the couch. "Do you know anything about tarot?"

"A little. My roommate in college introduced me to them, but I never took her readings seriously. It was just a fun thing to do to pass the time and have a good laugh." She smiled apologetically. "No offense."

"None taken." Jasmine shrugged. "As long as you don't think that they are the devil's toys, I have no problem with you doubting the readings."

Margo laughed. "The devil's toys? Are you serious? Has anyone ever told you that?"

Jasmine grimaced. "My father, but I don't want to discuss it." She took the cards out of the pouch.

With a deep breath and a silent prayer to the Mother of All Life, she shuffled them a few times and then put the deck on the coffee table in front of Margo.

"Put your hand on the deck and think about your question. Hold the image of your brother and his fiancée in your mind while you ask."

Margo did as she was told, her hand resting on the deck for a long moment, and her eyes closed.

"Okay." She removed her hand. "What now?"

"Now it's my turn." Jasmine closed her eyes, letting her mind drift as she also put her hand on top of the deck, feeling the universe's energy flowing through her.

When the tingling sensation stopped, she opened her eyes and began to lay out the cards in a familiar spread. The Lovers reversed. The Tower upright. The Three of Swords piercing a heart with its sharp, gleaming blades.

Jasmine felt her heart sink as she looked at the cards and their message. Betrayal, heartbreak, the shattering of illusions, and the crumbling of foundations.

She didn't want to say it out loud and give voice to the painful prediction of Rob's future, but as she looked at Margo, she saw that her friend had formed her own interpretation of the cards and the message they conveyed.

"I knew it." Margo sighed. "The way Lynda acted in Cabo made it obvious that fidelity was not something she concerned herself with."

Jasmine hesitated, not wanting to confirm her friend's fears. "I can make another spread. Perhaps your suspicions influenced the results. It is also possible that the infidelity will happen in the distant future, not in the past. It can also mean that it happened in the past but will not happen in the future. It can possibly mean that Rob is the cheater."

Margo shook her head. "I asked if Rob was going to be happy with Lynda, and the answer was obvious. There's betrayal and a lot of pain and heartbreak on the horizon. This time, I will be more precise with my question." She looked at Jasmine. "I will ask if Lynda is cheating on Rob or will cheat on him in the future."

"Let's do this." Jasmine collected the cards, reshuffled them several times, and put the deck in front of Margo. "Go ahead. Put your hand on it."

Regrettably, the second spread turned out identical to the first one, which was eerie.

"I'm sorry." Jasmine collected the cards.

Margo let out a breath. "I don't know how to tell Rob. He's not going to believe me. It's not like I can tell him I'm basing my accusations on a tarot reading."

Jasmine chewed on her lower lip. "You need real proof.

Did you ask the cards if she was cheating on him currently?"

Margo nodded.

"Then you can catch her in the act and bring him proof. You don't have much time before the wedding."

Margo snorted. "I doubt she is sleeping with someone while at the same time running around town and driving everyone crazy with her wedding plan changes. If she is, she must make very effective use of her time." Margo closed her eyes. "There isn't enough time to do anything, and even if there was, I don't have the money to pay a private detective, and I don't want to ask Negal for the money either."

Margo's comment gave Jasmine an idea. "You could ask Negal to spy on Lynda. He can shroud himself and be invisible."

"He's too busy with the equipment salvaged from the pod," Margo said. "I can't ask him to do that."

"Yes, you can, and he will do it for you." Jasmine reached for Margo's hand. "Rob is a Dormant, just like you. Marrying Lynda the cheater might cost him a chance at immortality."

Margo stared at her for a long moment. "You are right. I didn't think of that. Rob is a couple of years older than me, so it's not like he has endless time to attempt transition. Not doing anything about him throwing his life away on Lynda is not an option. I have to make it my number one priority."

Jasmine nodded. "I'm here for you. If you need me to do anything, say the word." She winced. "Just don't ask me to put a hex on Lynda. I only do positive stuff."

Margo chuckled. "I wouldn't dream of it. I don't wish Lynda ill. I want what is best for my brother, and Lynda is not it."

37

MARINA

Marina had a death grip on Peter's hand, not because her shoes were dangerously high and the heel was so thin that she was afraid it would snap if she made a wrong move. And it wasn't even the opulence of the plush, velvet-covered curved chairs in the circular booths. The people truly took her breath away, the faces she recognized from television and movies, from the glossy pages of magazines and gossip columns. They were the elite, the kind of people she'd never dreamt of meeting, nor had she wanted to.

And yet here she was, the lowly human girl who had grown up as a serf in a Kra-ell compound rubbing elbows with the crème de la crème.

The hostess led them to their table, a secluded corner booth cast in shadows, intimate, that would hide her from the crowd to which she didn't belong.

Peter guided her into the booth and slid in beside her, his body a solid, comforting presence that anchored her to the moment and shielded her from her anxiety and feeling of inadequacy.

"Your server will be with you momentarily," the hostess said. "Can I offer you something to drink while you review the menu?"

"Yes, please," Peter said. "The bottle of wine I reserved."

The hostess's eyes glistened with excitement, but Marina felt that it wasn't because she found Peter hot, or maybe it was, but it wasn't the only reason. "Of course. I'll be right back with your bottle."

Marina leaned against his arm. "She seemed very happy about the bottle you reserved. Does she get a cut?"

"Probably." He leaned in close, his lips brushing the sensitive skin of her neck in a way that made her shiver with anticipation. "I'm glad you don't feel intimidated by all this."

"Oh, I do. I'm very happy to be hiding in this booth with you." She turned to face him and brushed her lips over his. "Doing all kinds of naughty things that we are not supposed to do."

Peter's eyes started glowing. "Did I tell you already how much I love you?"

She smiled. "You did, but I don't mind hearing it again and again."

"You are perfect."

"Thank you." She batted her eyelashes. "Tell me more."

He fake-groaned. "I've created a monster." He kissed the pulse point on her neck, the spot he liked to bite.

"But you love me anyway." Smiling, she let herself sink into the plush, velvet-covered cushions of the booth.

The hostess returned with the wine and made a big production of uncorking it, pouring it into their glasses, and then waiting for them to approve.

Marina didn't know much about wines, but this one tasted exquisite, and she told the hostess that.

"Wonderful." The woman beamed.

"You'll have to order for me," Marina told Peter after the hostess left. "I don't understand most of the menu. What language is it written in?"

"Snobbish."

She laughed. "Seriously."

"French."

"Do you know French?"

He nodded. "But the easiest and best way to order in this place is to get the day's special. All the items are perfectly coordinated and complementary."

"That's convenient." She let out a relieved breath. "That's what I'll have."

The menu didn't have prices, and she wasn't going to ask how much it cost because Peter wouldn't tell her.

As the meal began, Marina got lost in the culinary sensations. Every item was a work of art and a symphony of flavors and textures that danced on her tongue and made her moan with pleasure.

The portions were small, almost laughably so, but each was a masterpiece. The chef and his helpers must all be obsessed perfectionists to produce things that looked and tasted like that, and she could understand why people were willing to spend a fortune on the experience.

Through it all, Peter's hand occasionally wandered to her thigh beneath the table, his fingers tracing idle patterns on her skin that made her pulse race.

She didn't know when he was going to up the game, but she was sure he would do so soon. His eyes had been glowing throughout the evening, but he somehow managed to keep his fangs from elongating.

When the first bottle of wine was gone, Peter ordered a new one and poured them both a glass.

He lifted his and waited for her to do the same. "To life, love, and joy."

Marina repeated the toast and clinked her glass against Peter's, the sound ringing out like a bell in the hushed, intimate space of the booth.

It was then that Peter's hand began to wander higher, and his fingers brushed against the soft, sensitive skin of her upper inner thigh, eliciting a strangled moan from her throat.

A flicker of fear mingled with excitement as he coaxed her legs to part wider, her cheeks flushing with embarrassment at the thought of being caught in such a compromising position. But then Peter's lips were at her ear, his voice low and husky with desire as he whispered to her in the darkness.

"No one can see," he murmured, his fingers doing naughty things, teasing and tormenting her in a way that made her squirm on the soft velvet seat. "Lean back and enjoy, love."

She let her head fall back against the cushions of the booth, and her eyes fluttered closed as Peter's fingers dipped into the soft, slick heat of her core.

As he teased and tormented her, she bit back a moan, her hips arching up to meet his touch, and as he brought her to the brink of ecstasy and then pulled back, leaving her gasping and trembling with need, she nearly lost her mind.

It was a delicious torture, a sweet, agonizing pleasure that left her breathless and dizzy with desire. In the dark, intimate cocoon of their booth, with Peter's touch setting her skin on fire and his lips whispering wicked, delicious promises in her ear, Marina found that she didn't care if anyone heard her moan or saw her expression of ecstasy.

She was lost as he held her on the edge for so long that she was ready to scream, and when he finally whispered in her ear the command to come, she bit so hard on her lip that she drew blood.

Long moments passed until her heartbeat stabilized, and she opened her eyes. "That was positively wicked." Marina reached with her hand and cupped him over his pants. "What about you?"

"Don't worry about me, love." He removed her hand and leaned to kiss her. "I have everything planned."

She snorted. "Do I even want to know?"

38

PETER

The drive back to the village was quiet, the silence broken only by the soft purr of the engine. The night had been magical, with the finest food and wine, dancing and laughter, as well as a naughty game that had Marina climaxing all over his hand.

Peter smiled, remembering how long it had taken her to catch her breath and calm her heartbeat. His Marina was a closet exhibitionist, and he intended to coax more of that from her in Brundar's club.

Not yet, though.

He would let a few days pass before he suggested it so she wouldn't feel overwhelmed. It was his responsibility to make sure that she expanded her boundaries at a comfortable pace and didn't force herself to do more than she was ready for just to please him.

He glanced over at her, taking in the way her eyes drooped with satisfied fatigue and her head lolled against the headrest as if it were too heavy to hold up on its own.

"Don't fight it, love." He reached over to clasp her hand. "Sleep. I'll carry you home."

Marina smiled, her fingers tightening around his. "I have an account to settle with you. I still owe you an orgasm."

Heat rushed through Peter at her words. He would've loved to collect on that debt tonight, but he could wait until tomorrow.

"I'll take an IOU, love. Tonight, it's going to be straight to bed for you."

She sighed. "Your resilience and boundless energy are what I envy the most about your immortality." She turned to him and smiled. "Well, that and not getting sick, and staying young forever."

Peter's gut clenched at the reminder that his time with Marina was limited.

"I hope that my frequent venom injections will keep you young and healthy for much longer than normal for humans."

"I hope so, too." She lifted their conjoined hands and kissed his knuckles. "And perhaps the solution to our predicament will come from an unexpected source."

She slanted him a smile. "I met Kaia on my first day in the café, and she said something about working on a way to turn ordinary humans immortal. I thought she was saying that just to make me feel good, but Wonder said she was a scientist, so maybe she's actually onto something?"

"Kaia is a brilliant bioinformatician, and I know that she is working on something, but I don't know what it is exactly. It's classified."

Marina frowned. "But you are a Guardian?"

"Even Guardians don't have access to everything."

Peter had heard rumors, of course. But they were mainly about building a more primitive version of the Odus, not finding the secret to immortality.

"That's a shame. I thought you knew something about her work."

"Well, I do." He scrambled for something optimistic to say. "Our ancestors became immortal through genetic manipulation, so it's possible, and if anyone can find the answer, it's Kaia."

Marina sighed. "Kaia has endless time to find the answers she's seeking and figure out how to make humans immortal, but I don't. If I'm lucky, I might have a decade before I start showing signs of aging. And if I'm not lucky, it could be even sooner than that."

Peter wanted to take Marina in his arms and promise her that everything would be alright and that science would find a way to keep her young and beautiful and vibrant forever, but she was right, and there was nothing he could say to make it better without resorting to lying.

"I believe that the Fates brought us together for a reason, Marina," he said instead. "I feel the bond forming between us, which shouldn't be possible between a human and an immortal, and yet, here we are."

"Oh, Peter." Marina smiled indulgently. "I'm not a Dormant. I think we've established that by now."

She was right, of course. No Dormant had ever taken this long to transition, especially given the steady supply of his venom.

Still, he couldn't shake the feeling that there was more to their connection than met the eye, that the Fates had woven their threads together for a purpose that he could not yet see.

"Every Dormant is different, and every transition is unique. You could be the rare case of a late bloomer."

She laughed. "That's not likely, Peter. For that to be true, my mother would have to be a Dormant too, right?"

Peter shrugged. "There are many Dormants in the human population; it's just that there are so many humans that it's like looking for the proverbial needle in a haystack. Even if your mother was born in the compound, she could still carry the godly genes."

Marina closed her eyes. "I wish you were right."

Damn, he hated the resignation in her voice.

"Assume the win," he murmured.

She opened her eyes, confusion flitting across her face. "What does winning have to do with anything? Winning what?"

Peter just grinned, his heart pounding with reckless excitement. "Let's get married."

"Peter..." she said as if she was admonishing him for making a stupid joke.

"I'm serious. Let's have a ceremony in the village square, in front of all our friends and family, and show the Fates that we have faith in them and that we believe in the power of our love to overcome any obstacle."

Marina shook her head. "You're such a romantic, Peter."

"I know, so? Do you want to marry me or not?"

She stared at him, her eyes wide with disbelief. "You can't be serious."

But he just smiled. "Yes or no?"

For a long moment, Marina was silent, her eyes searching his face as if looking for some sign of doubt or hesitation. But there was none to be found, only love and devotion and his fierce, unshakable determination and belief that he was right.

And then, with a smile that lit up the darkness like a beacon, she nodded. "Yes, but I expect a proper proposal with a ring and you down on one knee."

39

THE PRINCE

His mind drifted aimlessly among fragments of hazy memories of mostly sounds, clouded visuals, smells, and tactile senses.

Fabrics.

For some reason, he had the impression of how different fabrics felt against his skin. But those were memories.

He felt nothing now.

He knew he was male, so there was at least that, but he didn't know his name or what he looked like. Had he never seen his own reflection?

There was no sense of time, no concept of how long he had been floating in this confusing void or why.

Maybe this was death?

This could be what being dead felt like.

After all, he had no sensation of having a body or being inside a physical shell. As far as he knew, he could be just a floating consciousness.

But why was he conscious if he didn't have a purpose? Wasn't the soul supposed to end up somewhere special according to its merits?

And there was that sound again. A female voice that was somehow whole and clear among the haze of his fragmented thoughts and distorted memories of sensations. He could not understand what she was saying, so that was aligned with the rest of his confusion, but the sound was so clear, as if she was right there beside him, talking to him, singing to him.

Was the sound a lifeline or a beacon he was supposed to follow to find his place in the afterlife?

No, it couldn't be the afterlife because if he were dead, the sound wouldn't evoke such longing in him. He wanted to see the female's face, knowing that she would be beautiful, to feel the touch of her hand, knowing it would be soft and gentle.

Clinging to the sound, he followed it, his consciousness clinging to the tether...

If he could open his eyes...

If he only had eyes...

He should concentrate on remembering what it felt like to have them—having eyelids, closing them, opening them, moving his head from side to side.

A sense of apprehension assailed him every time he thought about anyone seeing his eyes. There was an instinctive need to cover them so no one would see them.

Why?

What was wrong with them?

And why was the sound gone?

He needed the female's voice so he could follow it. Where had she gone?

Had something happened to her?

The sudden flash of fear and anger was like a bolt of energy, like a lightning strike that animated the body that he was becoming aware of, not enough to move anything but perhaps enough to lift his eyelids and look at the world he was in without reaching for a veil.

Dangerous. It was so dangerous. But he was tired of living in fear.

Commanding the shutters on his eyes to lift was at first futile, but he was not ready to give up. With a monumental effort, he forced the movement and almost lost consciousness just from the exertion of that slight action.

Then it dawned on him. He was conscious.

The view that greeted him was alien and terrifying. He hated small, confined spaces, and this chamber was small and devoid of color. White walls, various equipment, and all kinds of tubes and wires were attached to him.

A scream lodged in his parched throat, but then he saw her.

A female was slumped in a chair beside his bed, her wavy dark hair spilling over her shoulders, her face softened by the gentle embrace of sleep.

For a moment, he simply stared at her.

Who was she?

Why did she sit in this alien room with him, guarding, talking, and singing to him? Was she a medic?

Did he know her and had forgotten who she was?

Perhaps this was home, but he had forgotten that as well.

He tried to speak, to force the words past the dryness of his throat and the heaviness of his tongue, but all that emerged was a rasping, guttural sound that seemed to echo in the room's stillness like a cry of despair.

The female didn't rouse, but suddenly the door flew open with a bang, and another female rushed in, red hair the color of fire flying behind her like a torch in the wind.

The dark-haired female jerked awake, her eyes wide open as she sat up straight in her chair.

They spoke to each other in urgent tones, their words a jumble of unfamiliar, incomprehensible sounds. But then, with a movement almost too quick to follow, the dark-haired female lifted a pendant that hung around her neck and spoke a command, "Kra-on."

The redheaded female followed her example, and suddenly, miraculously, their words became clear, the meaning of their conversation snapping into focus like a puzzle piece falling into place.

With a start, he realized that the devices hanging from their necks translated their foreign language into one he could understand.

"My sister," he managed to croak, his voice a hoarse, broken whisper that seemed to scrape against the inside of his throat.

The dark-haired female rushed over to his bed and leaned over him, her smile soft and reassuring and her strange golden eyes glowing with warmth and affection as she brushed cool fingers over his forehead. "Your sister is fine," she said through the device. "She's in the next room, still unconscious like you were, but getting better with every passing day."

Tears gathered in his eyes, a wave of relief and gratitude washing over him like a cool, cleansing rain. "Thank the Mother," he whispered, his voice choked with emotion.

The female's smile widened, her eyes crinkling at the corners with a warmth that seemed to radiate from her every pore. "Welcome back to the world of the living, my prince."

"Prince?" Why had she called him a prince? "I'm no one's prince."

But the redheaded one stepped forward before the dark-haired female could answer him. "I need to examine the prince," she said briskly, her voice crisp and businesslike as she gestured for the other female to move aside. "Please, give me some space."

The dark-haired female nodded, stepping back from the bed with a lingering glance that seemed to promise she would never be far away.

And then the red-haired female was leaning over him, her hands moving over his body with the practiced efficiency of a medic.

A medic. That was what she was. And this was a medical facility.

Was the dark-haired female another medical provider?

"I'm senior medic Bri–" the translation device seemed to have a problem with the sounds.

The dark-haired one stepped forward and said, "Bri-jet," without the device's help.

When he repeated the sound, the senior medic nodded. "You have got it right. Good job. I am going to touch you now to do a more thorough check of how you are doing. If this is agreeable to you, say yes or nod, and if you cannot do either, blink once; if it is not agreeable and you prefer a male to check you, blink twice."

Did he prefer a male?

He was not sure, so he blinked once.

The medic pulled out a metallic device, rubbed it for some reason, and put it on his chest.

It suddenly occurred to him that he might be naked, and he did not want the female to see him, but she was a medic, and it was too late to say that he preferred a male to conduct the examination.

"Can you feel this?" she asked after doing something he couldn't feel.

"No," he rasped.

She paused what she was doing, stepped away from him for a moment, and then returned with a cup.

"I will start by wetting your lips." She poured some water on a white square of fabric and rubbed it over his lips. "Better?"

He licked his lips, the water tasting fresh on his tongue.

"Yes. Can I have more?"

The medic smiled. "Do you usually drink water?"

"Yes," he replied, wondering about the odd question.

The doctor nodded, her eyes narrowing as she studied him with a gaze that seemed to see straight through him. "I am going to raise the back of the bed to bring you to a semi-reclining position. There will be a whizzing sound when I activate the mechanism. Ready?"

Too tired to say the word, he blinked once.

"Here it goes." She pressed something, and then, with a soft whirring sound, the back of his bed began to lift, the angle shifting until he was propped up in a semi-reclined position.

The medic put in the cup a strange, tubular device bent at one end and held it out to him with an expectant look on her face. "Suck gently," she instructed. "I only want you to wet your mouth. You can swallow a little, but not a lot. Your stomach can't handle anything more than that right now."

He did as he was told, drawing the cool, clear water into his mouth and letting it sit on his tongue for a moment before swallowing it. It felt strange, almost foreign, as if his body had forgotten how to perform even the most basic functions.

When the medic took the cup away, the prince looked up at her, his eyes searching her face for some hint of familiarity, some clue that might help him piece together the shattered fragments of his memory.

"How can you understand me?" he asked.

The device that translated their strange language into

the one he understood did not work in reverse. It did not translate what he had been saying to them.

The female pushed her flaming hair behind her ear, revealing a small device lodged inside her ear. "This translates for me," she explained, tapping it with one slender finger. "The same way the teardrop translates for you." She tapped the pendant that hung around her neck.

So, they had two kinds of translation devices—one for hearing and one for talking.

Interesting.

But even as he marveled at the ingenuity of the gadgets and wondered how they worked, the thought that bothered him was that he still didn't know who he was.

They called him prince, but a prince of what?

What had happened to him that made him unable to remember his own name?

40

JASMINE

The prince was awake, and his eyes were the brilliant blue she remembered from the moment he'd opened them.

Jasmine's heart was pounding so loudly that she had no doubt Bridget and the prince could hear it, but she didn't care.

This was the moment she'd been waiting for.

She wasn't a medical professional, but it seemed to her that he was out of the coma for good. He was keeping his eyes open and talking in whole sentences.

It would have been nice to hear his real voice and how he sounded in his own language, but she didn't dare defy Kian and take the earpieces out. They were staying no matter what, but not because she feared the prince's compulsion. She just didn't want to give anyone an excuse to kick her out of the room.

Her prince was still painfully thin, but he was breathtaking, with his chiseled features and regal bearing, his skin smooth and unblemished despite the ravages of time and stasis. Julian had cut short the tufts of long hair that had stayed attached to his head through thousands of years of stasis, and the bald spots were starting to sprout new hair.

Brown. It was a beautiful shade of chestnut brown, not black like Jade's.

Regrettably, by the time Bridget was done with her checkup, the poor male had fallen asleep again, but the doctor reassured Jasmine that he was resting, not unconscious.

"I'm going to dim the lights," Bridget said. "Now that he's conscious, he will be more comfortable sleeping without direct light shining into his eyes."

Jasmine nodded.

"He is very weak," Bridget said. "I expect he will be drifting in and out of sleep for the next day or two. Right now, it seems he only has the energy to stay awake for a few minutes."

The doctor sounded apologetic, as if it was her fault that Jasmine hadn't had a chance to talk with her prince yet.

"That's okay. I'll wait until he wakes up again."

Bridget chuckled softly. "It will most likely take a while, so I would have suggested that you take a break and go for a walk to stretch your legs, but I have a feeling that wild horses won't be able to drag you away from this chair."

"Your feeling is spot on," Jasmine admitted. "Now that he's finally awake, I'm not going anywhere."

She had a bottle of water and a couple of energy bars in her purse, so she was all good.

"Very well," Bridget said. "I will call Kian and tell him the good news."

Jasmine nodded, excitement and trepidation mounting inside her, making her gut clench with worry about what was still in store for her fragile prince. Kian would be thrilled to hear the news, but he would also have questions and exhaust her poor guy, robbing her of the few precious wakeful minutes during which she and the prince could get to know each other.

When the doctor left, Jasmine rose to her feet and stood over her prince, admiring the incredible progress he'd made in a few short days.

"Were you the one I heard in my dreams?" He startled her when he spoke.

His eyes opened, glowing blue in the dark room.

"Yes," she answered before remembering that the teardrop wasn't on.

"Sorry," she murmured. "Kra-on. Yes."

"Your voice kept me tethered to life," he said. "I followed it out of the void."

His admission filled her with warmth. "The doctor, Bridget, said it was good to talk to people in a coma. I didn't have the teardrop or the translation device, so I just sang and recited plays and poems in my own language, hoping that my voice would soothe you and make you feel less lonely. But then William brought me this." She lifted the device. "And it translated what I said to your own tongue. It didn't work with singing, so each time I wanted to sing to you, I had to turn it off."

The prince smiled, a soft, gentle curve of his lips that made Jasmine's heart skip a beat. "I loved the singing and the talking even when I couldn't understand it. You have such a lovely voice."

"Thank you."

As a wave of emotion washed over her, Jasmine felt tears prick at the backs of her eyes. She had never felt so needed as she did in that moment, with the prince's eyes fixed on her face.

"I am the one who should be thanking you," he said in a near whisper. "You brought me back." The prince's eyes began to drift closed, his lids heavy with exhaustion and his breathing slowing to a steady, even rhythm.

Jasmine's heart sank, a flicker of disappointment washing over her. But then she remembered what Bridget had said about the prince drifting in and out of sleep for the next couple of days, and she sat back down.

Hopefully, he would wake up again before Kian arrived so they could talk some more.

41

KIAN

"What's your impression of him?" Kian asked when Bridget was done telling him about the prince.

There was a long moment of silence. "He opened his eyes and spoke. He recognized Jasmine as the one whose voice he had been hearing, and he responded to my questions with clarity and coherence. On the other hand, he had no idea that he was a prince and asked a prince of what? He remembered having a sister; that was the first thing he asked about. When Jasmine told him that his sister was alive, there were tears in his eyes. I might be wrong, but he doesn't seem like the scary, powerful creature that the Eternal King is afraid of. He didn't try to use compulsion on me or Jasmine, and if he even has the ability, he doesn't remember having it."

"How do you know that he didn't try?"

Bridget chuckled. "Come on, Kian. Do you think that I wouldn't have known? He didn't even ask me to do anything. Aside from asking about his sister, he was just reacting to me and my questions."

"He's recovering. I'm sure he will be less agreeable when fully healed."

"I don't think so," Bridget said. "He seems like a gentle soul to me."

Beside him, Syssi nodded sagely. "The prince was raised as a servant of the goddess. I don't know what that implies, but if it's anything like human monks and priests, it requires a certain level of humility and compassion."

Kian lifted a brow. "Not all monks and clerics are blessed with those two qualities, and that's putting it as mildly as I can. Some of those who call themselves men of god are servants of evil."

"I know, my love." Syssi patted his thigh as if she was gentling a wild horse. "But there are many good ones as well, and there is no reason to get all upset over nothing."

"Daddy?" Allegra looked at him with worried eyes from her spot on the floor.

"Everything is okay, sweetie." He forced a smile. "Daddy is not angry."

When she nodded regally and returned to her toys, the gesture was so like his mother that it made him smile.

He turned back to his phone and the doctor, who was still on the line. "I'll let my mother know. I'm sure that she would want to see her brother immediately, so get ready for a visit."

He'd managed to keep his mother away from the twins by convincing her to wait for them to wake up, and now that one of them had, she wouldn't want to wait another minute.

"You should bring Jade along," Bridget said. "Maybe seeing his people will jog his memory. I was very surprised he didn't react to how Jasmine and I looked. I thought he would assume we were goddesses, and maybe he did, but it didn't prompt a negative reaction from him, which is strange for someone who grew up surrounded only by Kra-ell and fearing gods."

Syssi shook her head. "He and his sister grew up in isolation. We don't know what they were taught by the priestess they were apprenticed to."

"True," Bridget agreed. "Let me know when you are on your way."

"I will." Kian ended the call.

"Your mother will be so thrilled," Syssi said.

Kian nodded, his mind already racing ahead to the safety measures needed to protect her.

With a sigh, he dialed his mother's number.

"Good morning, Mother."

"Good morning, my son." Annani sounded cheerful. "Are you bringing Allegra over?"

"Not today. Bridget just called to tell me that the prince was awake. He's weak and confused, but he's alive and speaking. I'm sure that you want to visit him as soon as possible."

"Of course. When are we leaving?"

"As soon as you are ready, I want you to wear a disguise."

There was a long moment of silence. "Why?"

"Precaution. I don't want him to know who you are until we are sure of his intentions. I wish you still had the Nurse Rachel costume."

Annani laughed. "Oh, yes. That was such a lovely outfit, but I am afraid that I do not know what happened to it. I might have donated it along with other old clothing."

"You probably did. I think a pair of jeans and a T-shirt will do the trick. That and tamping down your glow and making yourself less beautiful. He is only half god, so he might not be immune to your shrouding."

His mother scoffed. "If I need to shroud myself anyway, what do I need a costume for?"

"It's less tiring when you don't have to shroud everything for a long period."

Syssi leaned in close to whisper in his ear. "I could get a

pair of jeans and a shirt from Lisa. She's much taller than your mother but just as slim."

Kian nodded. "Good idea." He turned back to his mother. "Did you hear that?"

"Yes, but it did not make me happy. You know how much I detest jeans."

"I do." He pulled out his trump card. "But I also know how much you want to see your brother."

"Very well," she said. "Are you coming over to collect me?"

"It's up to you. I can come over, and we can continue from your place, or you can come here. I still need to call Jade, and Syssi needs to get the clothing from Lisa, so let's make it an hour?"

"I will come to your place," his mother said. "Do I need to bring along my Odus?"

"That's an excellent idea, but one will suffice."

The Odus were the best protection for his mother, and they were immune to compulsion, but given the prince's weakened state, there was no need for more than one.

"I will be there in an hour." His mother ended the call.

Syssi pushed to her feet. "Can I come with you? I'm curious to see the twins."

"Of course, you can." He stood up and pulled her into his arms. "You don't need to ask. I'm always at your command."

"I know, my love." She stretched up on her toes and kissed him. "But I'm worried that your sisters will be upset for not being included while I was."

"Don't worry about them. Alena is not going anywhere because she can barely walk and is about to go into labor at any moment, and Amanda doesn't like to get involved in the early stages of anything."

Syssi laughed. "You know your sisters well. What are we going to do with Allegra? I don't want to take her with us, and I don't want to leave her with Okidu either."

"Take her to Andrew. Allegra loves playing with her older cousin."

"What if he asks why?"

Kian shrugged. "You can tell Andrew. It's not a big deal if he knows. By now, the entire village knows the twins are at the keep."

"That's good." She kissed him again. "The fewer secrets I need to keep, the better."

42

THE PRINCE

The senior medic had left the back of the bed elevated, and as he lay back against the pillows with his eyes closed, his mind reeled with what he had learned in the brief moments of his waking.

He felt overwhelmed, his thoughts still fragmented and scattered and refusing to coalesce into a logical tapestry that could help him orient himself in this strange world he had found himself in.

Was it strange, though?

How would he know what was strange and what was not when he had no reference, anchor, or name?

He wanted to fall asleep again and let the blessed oblivion of unconsciousness take him away from the confusion and fear, but the female sitting beside his bed, the one with the golden eyes and the gentle touch, seemed determined to keep him awake and anchor him to the waking world with the sound of her voice and the warmth of her hand in his.

What had she been saying to him?

He had lost the thread at some point. "I am sorry, but my mind wandered off. Can you repeat what you have just said?"

She smiled. "Of course. I am sorry for talking nonstop and keeping you awake. Do you want me to let you sleep?"

He did not wish to offend her and lose the only person who seemed to care about him in this world. "No, please continue." He managed to turn his head so he could look into her bright, golden eyes. "I do not know your name."

When she said something that the translating device couldn't interpret, she tried again, and when it still refused to cooperate, she shook her head. "I'm going to turn it off for a moment." She pressed on the device.

"Jaaz-min." She patted her chest. "Jaaz-min."

When he slowly repeated the two syllables, she smiled and activated the translation device. "It's the name of a white, sweet-smelling flower. Some say that it grows in the gardens of the gods. Do you have anything like that in your world?"

Something tickled his memory. "Dull-or. It's a white flower with a pleasant smell." He was so happy to remember anything at all.

"Wonderful," Jasmine said. "I will program the teardrop to translate Jasmine to Dull-or and the other way around. Can you remember any other flowers from your world?"

"Shorga. It is a purple flower." He felt stupidly happy for remembering such an unimportant detail.

They spent the next few minutes trying to jog his memory about other things, but he became tired, and his mind became sluggish.

"I am sorry," he said in a near whisper because he did not have the energy to speak up. "I am tired."

"You are also thirsty. Your lips are dry." She reached for the cup of water beside the bed and brought the tubular thing to his lips. "I don't know how much you should drink, so take only a little."

He still remembered the medic's instructions, sucking in a little bit of liquid to wet his mouth.

When Jasmine took the tube away, he sighed. "I wish I could remember my name so I could give it to you."

She retook his hand, her touch warm and reassuring as she leaned in close. "It will take time, but you will remember. Small steps. And for now, I'll call you prince."

"Prince of what? No one's answered that question for me yet."

"Prince means that you are the son of a queen or a king. I was told just a little bit about why you were sent here, and I'm not even clear on all the details, so I don't want to give you the wrong information. Besides, I think that it's better if you remember it yourself." She gave him a small smile. "That way, you will know it is true, right? I could tell you all kinds of pretty lies and you won't know because you don't remember anything. I could also tell you the truth, but you won't believe me."

She was confusing him, but since he was enjoying just looking at her smiling face and hearing her voice, he didn't say anything and let her talk.

"You can also decide what being a prince means to you and adopt it. You don't have to be limited by what others expect from you. In stories, a prince is the leader of his people, a brave warrior of great honor and courage."

Was that who he was?

Somehow, the description did not fit. He was not a warrior; or was he?

A memory flashed through his mind of training with a sword; his partner was his sister, clad from head to toe in fabrics that concealed even her face. She was fast on her feet, and he'd had trouble keeping up, but there had been joy in their dance.

He tried to cling to the memory, but it disintegrated into smoky fragments, dissipating completely.

"Tell me what you know about me," he commanded.

"I don't want to give you the wrong information. Those who know more about you and can give you better answers have been notified that you are awake, and they will arrive within an hour or two."

He tensed. "Who are they?"

"Don't worry." She squeezed his hand. "No one means you or your sister harm. You are in good hands."

"Can you at least give me their names and titles, so I know how to address them?"

"Kian is the leader of this community. He doesn't have a title or a last name, so you just need to call him Kian. He's a little grumpy, but he is a very good guy. I owe him my life."

He frowned. "How so?"

Jasmine shrugged. "It's a long story that you will not understand without context that you don't have, but I'll try to make it simple. I got involved with some bad people who had nefarious intentions for me. One of Kian's people got pulled into my mess by mistake, so he sent a rescue team. They got us both out."

The prince put his other hand over his heart. "Then I owe Kian a life debt for saving you."

Her eyes widened. "No, you don't, but thank you for offering. I have repaid the debt by myself."

He narrowed his eyes at her. "How?"

Jasmine laughed. "Not the way you think. Kian is happily mated."

He had no idea why that was relevant and what she imagined he had thought.

"I do not understand what Kian's mate has to do with your life debt to him. Did you save her life?"

Jasmine opened her mouth, closed it, and then opened it again. "Talk about cultural differences. We have a lot to learn about each other."

"I still do not understand." He was too exhausted to guess what she could have meant by her odd comment. His eyelids felt heavy. "I'm sorry," he mumbled, his words slurring together as he fought to keep his eyes open. "I'm too tired to think."

Jasmine's smile was soft and understanding. "It's okay. Your body and mind need time and rest to heal."

He nodded, his eyes fluttering closed as he drifted off into the welcoming embrace of sleep.

43

ANNANI

Annani did not know which feeling was stronger, the excitement at the prospect of meeting her half-brother for the first time or the annoyance at having to wear jeans.

Why did Kian think plain human clothing would make a difference to her appearance?

Her brother did not know how the people of this world dressed. He did not know that a gown was a formal dress or that jeans were casual. It would not influence what he thought of her.

Sometimes, appeasing her son's paranoia was tiring.

As she reached Kian's front door, Okidu opened it and bowed.

"Good morning, Clan Mother."

"Good morning." She swept past him and headed straight toward Kian's office.

His door was open, and she did not wait for an invitation.

"Hold on, William." Kian put the phone down and pushed to his feet. "Good morning, Mother." He rounded the desk, leaned down, and kissed her cheek. "I'm almost done talking to William. Please take a seat."

Nodding, she accepted the invitation and listened as he continued the conversation with William.

"I only need two devices. One for Syssi and one for my mother."

"I can do that," William answered. "Give me half an hour."

"No problem. Can you send someone to my house with them?"

William chuckled. "I'll come myself. It's Sunday, and there is no one in the lab. It's just me."

"Right." Kian raked his fingers through his longish hair. "I forgot what day it was today. Thank you for doing this for me on a weekend."

"No problem, boss. I live for this stuff."

As Kian ended the call, Annani arched a brow. "What devices is William bringing for Syssi and me?"

"It's a translator device that works similarly to the earpieces, only it translates from English to Kra-ell and broadcasts the speech through a small speaker. We assume that the twins speak only Kra-ell."

"You probably assume correctly." She let out a breath. "I am so excited. Do you think he looks like me?"

Kian smiled indulgently. "No one looks like you, Mother, and the last time I saw him, he looked only a little better than a corpse."

She grimaced. "Can you please stop saying that word regarding my siblings? It is upsetting to me."

"I'm back!" Syssi walked into the office with a bundle of clothing clutched in her arms and a smile on her face. "Good morning, Clan Mother. I've got the teenage clothes to help make you look more ordinary, although I doubt it would move the needle."

"I doubt it as well." Annani took the bundle from Syssi's hands, her brow furrowing as she unfolded the garments and held them up.

Jeans and a pink T-shirt with a picture of a white cat on the front. "This is ridiculous." She gave the bundle back to Syssi. "I despise pants in general and jeans in particular. Perhaps you have a dress that I can borrow?"

Syssi smiled, her eyes twinkling with mischief. "I had a feeling that you would say that. I'll be back with something you might be more comfortable wearing." She rushed out of the office.

Kian sighed. "It's just for a couple of hours, and you've worn jeans before. I don't know what the big deal is."

Annani gave him a haughty look down her nose and did not bother to answer.

When Syssi returned, she brought a sundress made from red fabric with white and black flowers printed on it. The pattern was pretty, and it probably looked adorable on Syssi, but it was not something Annani would have ever gotten for herself.

"It's a little small on me," Syssi said. "But it will still be too big on you. Luckily, it comes with a belt to cinch the waist."

Annani took the dress from Syssi and regarded it with a frown before holding it against her body. It was too long. Her usual style was floor-length gowns, so the length in itself was fine, but for that particular style and cut, the hem should be at the knee, not mid-calf. She would look like a girl in her mother's dress.

"Very well. I will try it on."

She took off her breezy silk gown in the bathroom and slipped the sundress over her head. The fabric felt pleasant on her skin, so there was a small comfort in that, but that was the only positive thing she could say about it.

With a sigh, she braided her long hair, pulled out the sunglasses from the pocket of her gown, and put them on.

The reflection in the mirror depicted someone who wasn't her. The female looking back at her was not the queen that she had always been, the leader of her clan, the Clan Mother.

She was not meeting her brother for the first time looking like a beggar in an ill-fitting dress. When he first saw her, he would see a queen.

Annani was out of the sundress and into her gown in seconds, but it took her a little longer to unbraid her hair.

"Mother," Kian said reproachfully when she walked back into the office with Syssi's dress draped over her arm.

She shook her head, her jaw set with resolve. "My brother's first impression of me will not be based on falsehood. I will meet him as me," she said firmly, her voice filled with authority that brooked no argument. "The only concession to security that I am willing to make is to not mention my father or that the prince and I are related, but if I feel that he poses no threat to me, I will reveal this as well."

Kian looked like his mouth was full of broken glass, but he knew better than to argue with her. "As you wish, Mother."

Syssi took her dress back. "I'm sorry you didn't like it." She sighed dramatically. "Now I will have no choice but to lose weight to fit into this."

Kian growled. "Give it to charity. You are not losing anything."

She sent him an air kiss before turning to Annani. "How about a cappuccino while we wait for William?"

"That is a wonderful idea." Annani threaded her arm through Syssi's. "Is there any chocolate cake left?"

Syssi smiled brightly. "Of course."

44

JASMINE

Jasmine let out a breath when the prince's eyes fluttered closed, and his breathing slowed to a steady, even rhythm.

He was so lost, and when he finally remembered who he was and why he had been sent to Earth, he might be even more lost than he was now.

Her heart ached for him.

She hadn't lied about not knowing all the details, but she knew that he and his sister were considered abominations in their home world and that they had been sequestered in the temple and covered from head to toe to hide who they were.

If their secret came out, they would have been killed by their people, and their mother would have shared their fate for her transgression. That was why the queen had sent her children to Earth on the settler ship, knowing she would never see them again.

She had done it to save them.

Although now that Jasmine had seen what the Kra-ell looked like, she couldn't fathom how the queen had thought to pull it off. The prince looked like the gods, not the Kra-ell; the same was true for his sister. If everything had gone according to plan and the ship had arrived when it had been supposed to, the settlers would have woken up and discovered the two hybrids among them.

Perhaps the plan was for the twins to pretend to be gods who had joined the expedition.

That actually made sense.

There had not been all that many gods on Earth, and the settlers could have chosen to settle somewhere far away from them so they wouldn't have anyone to compare the twins to.

If only the prince could remember his mother's instructions, they could have had answers to so many questions.

Perhaps his sister would remember more, although Jasmine doubted that. She hadn't woken up yet, which implied a worse condition than her brother's, so her brain might be more severely damaged.

At least the prince was coherent, and she was thankful for that.

With a sigh, Jasmine let go of his hand, rose from her chair, and made her way to the kitchen.

The enormous place was deserted as usual, but she knew where the coffeemaker was and got busy brewing a fresh pot.

What did they use this kitchen for? It looked like something that belonged in a venue. She could easily imagine a large team of chefs and kitchen staff preparing food for a wedding or some other event.

Sitting at the counter with a mug of coffee, she thought about Margo and wondered if her friend had talked with her mate about shadowing Lynda.

She pulled out her phone and typed up a message to Margo.

Her phone rang a few moments later.

"Yes, I did," Margo said. "And Negal had a much better idea than following her around. We will attach a tiny bug drone to her, and it will record everything she does until it runs out of power. Hopefully, we will get something by then, and if not, I will collect the dead drone and replace it with a new one. Lynda is so self-absorbed that she won't even notice."

"How small is that drone?"

"Smaller than a mosquito. They brought a bunch of them from their home planet, and it's precious, so they can't afford to lose any of them, but I don't intend on letting it get lost. I'll get it back for them."

"Sounds good to me. By the way, the prince is awake."

"I know. Negal told me. He also told me that the guy doesn't remember his name."

"He doesn't, and he's very upset about it. Where are you now?"

"Negal and I are collecting my stupid bridesmaid dress."

Jasmine chewed on her lower lip for a moment. "Are you going to introduce him to your family?"

Margo sighed. "Eventually I'll have to, but not yet. I told them I met someone in the witness protection program, and I'm dating him, so I can keep telling them he's on missions until I'm ready to present him. What about you?"

Jasmine laughed. "Thankfully, I don't have such problems. Even if I had someone to introduce to my father, I wouldn't. The less he knows about my life, the better."

"You have someone," Margo said. "The prince. How did he respond to you?"

"He's very sweet and grateful for my presence, but he can't stay awake for more than a few minutes at a time, so it's not like we have fallen madly in love and are about to live happily ever after."

Jasmine had a feeling that the road ahead was full of obstacles, and not just because of the prince's damaged memory. Naturally, there were obvious cultural differences between them, and if she wanted to bridge them, she needed to find someone who knew about the Kra-ell culture.

Not that the prince had grown up like other Kra-ell boys. His only companion had been his sister, and the only other people he'd come in contact with were his mother and the priestess, who must have known who and what they were and had protected them.

"Well, according to the cards, you will have your happily ever after with him," Margo said.

"I was shown a prince in my future. The cards didn't promise me a good ending."

"Then do another spread," Margo suggested. "If they could tell you that Lynda was unfaithful to Rob, they can tell you whether you will live happily ever after with your prince. You just need to ask the right question."

Jasmine swallowed. "I'm not ready to ask them that question. In fact, I don't think I should."

"Why not?"

"Because not everything is predetermined, and some things need to unfold on their own."

45

KIAN

The mood in Kian's old office was a mixed bag of anticipation, excitement, worry, and even introspection.

The last one seemed to afflict his mother and Jade, but his mother was more excited than contemplative, while Jade was the other way around.

Kian knew what was going through his mother's head, but he wasn't sure about Jade. For her, the prince was a reminder of the life she'd left behind on Anumati. It had been a different world when she and the other settlers had been put in stasis chambers inside the escape pods that had comprised the bulk of the interstellar ship. Seven thousand years had passed, give or take a few decades, but that wasn't how Jade felt it. The thousands of years spent in stasis had passed without any awareness, so for Jade, time had resumed only after her stasis chamber had opened, which had happened not so long ago.

Next to him, Syssi thrummed with pure excitement, seemingly not worried at all that the prince might have nefarious intentions, and Aru was on the other side of the spectrum, mainly looking worried.

"How is your Kra-ell?" Kian asked him.

"It's good."

Jade snorted. "The Kra-ell the prince and I speak is an ancient dialect compared to yours."

"You can still understand me, and I can understand you," the god said. "That's all that matters."

Her shrug indicated that she had nothing further to say on the subject.

"We need to decide how much to tell the prince," Kian said. "We don't know the queen's plan and how much of it she'd shared with her children. They might have been sent to do damage, or they might have been sent to their father for protection. Those are two opposite ends of the spectrum. Right now, the prince does not even remember his name, so perhaps it's better to keep him in the dark and wait for his memory to start returning so we can evaluate the kind of person he is and his intentions."

His mother shook her head. "That will only create mistrust. He will remember eventually, so there is no point trying to keep him in the dark until he does. It is better that he regains those memories sooner rather than later, so we know what we are dealing with while he is still vulnerable."

Kian groaned. "The guy has just woken up after seven thousand years of stasis. We can't dump on him the entire history of Anumati, the conflict between the gods and the Kra-ell, the gods with the resistance, and what happened on Earth. There is only so much he can absorb. What I'm trying to figure out is what to tell him today."

Annani nodded. "You are right, my son. We should give him a few tidbits of knowledge and see how he reacts." She lifted the translating pendant. "I am glad to have this gadget and to be able to communicate with my brother. It would have been impossible without it."

Jade dipped her head at his mother. "With all due respect, Clan Mother, I think that I should be the one to talk to him. Even if he does not remember anything, he will instinctively feel more comfortable with a Kra-ell female that will remind him of his mother and the head priestess who de facto raised him and his sister."

Annani did not look convinced, but she gave Jade a nod. "We will play it by ear."

Jade tilted her head. "What does that mean?"

Syssi smiled. "It means that we will decide who will tell the prince what depending on the situation, and how receptive he seems to you or the Clan Mother. Who knows? Maybe he would prefer to hear it from Aru?"

"I doubt it," Aru said. "He will be more receptive to females, but I don't think he will have a preference for Jade. Given what Bridget and Julian reported, the prince doesn't know what species he belongs to. It's a miracle that he has even retained his language."

"That is interesting," Annani said. "Wonder, my dear childhood friend who spent five thousand years in stasis, woke up with similar amnesia. She knew she was an immortal female and remembered her language, but she did not know which people she belonged to and where she came from."

"How long did it take her to regain her memory?" Aru asked.

"Months," Kian said. "I hope it won't take the prince that long."

Syssi sighed. "The princess is probably going to be in an even worse state. I hope she didn't sustain brain damage."

"The prince's amnesia presents both an opportunity and a challenge." Kian drummed his fingers on the polished surface of the conference table. "On the one hand, it gives us a chance to shape his understanding of the world and his place in it. On the other hand, there is a chance that he's immensely powerful and not aware of it yet, and we will have an unpredictable wildcard on our hands that can turn into an ally or an enemy, depending on how we handle the situation. That's why we need to tread carefully and take it slow."

He turned to Jade. "You can start by introducing yourself as you would if you were still on Anumati. I'm curious to see his reaction to you. If he asks you questions, answer them, but try not to overwhelm him with too much information at once. Don't mention anything about who his father was and his relationship to Annani."

As Jade inclined her head in acknowledgment, his mother turned to him. "How long do you want me to hide from my brother that I am his sister?"

"Not long. I just don't want you to tell him right away. I want to see if he knows anything about Ahn, and that means waiting for him to remember and not feeding him information that might skew his responses. You should also tamp down your glow."

His mother grimaced. "Only until I reveal who I am."

Kian nodded.

"What about Jasmine?" Syssi asked. "She sits by his side day and night." She looked at Kian. "Are you okay with her meeting the Clan Mother?"

He winced. "Not yet. We will have to get her out of there."

"I'll do that," Jade offered.

Syssi arched a brow.

"What are you going to tell her?"

"I don't need to give her a reason. I'll instruct her to wait in the penthouse or the kitchen until I tell her it's okay to return." Jade smiled coldly. "People usually don't argue with me."

46

THE PRINCE

Time seemed to slip away as the minutes and hours blurred together in a haze. The prince drifted in and out of sleep, his mind still a jumbled mess of fragmented memories and half-formed thoughts, but things were not as chaotic as they had been when he had first become aware. He wondered why he felt calm instead of frantic.

It was the smell.

The female, Jasmine, the one who was named after a white, sweet-smelling flower. She didn't smell sweet, not entirely. There were spicy and musky undertones, too, and he wondered whether the scent was natural or artificial.

Feeling the first tendrils of wakefulness pulling at his eyelids, he opened his eyes, a smile lifting his lips when he saw her sitting by his bed and still holding on to his hand.

"Well, hello." She grinned at him. "I'm so happy that seeing me makes you smile. You must be feeling a little better."

"I do feel better, and seeing you makes me happy." He tried to squeeze her fingers, but his hand didn't obey his command.

He couldn't remember if he had ever held a female's hand other than his sister's. He must have held his mother's hand but didn't remember that either. How old was he?

"You are sad again. What were you just thinking about?"

"I do not know how old I am. Is there a way to tell?"

"I can tell you are an adult, but I do not know enough about your kind to even try to guess your age."

"What is my kind?"

"Don't you remember anything besides your sister?"

He had a feeling that she was avoiding answering on purpose. Maybe she didn't know what he was.

Maybe he was a survivor of a crash landing on a distant planet?

Something tickled his memory again.

A uniform.

It was a disguise. He had never worn one before. He had been used to comfortable, loose robes...

Princely robes?

"You are remembering something," Jasmine said. "I can tell by the faraway look in your eyes."

"It's just fragments. I remember wearing loose robes, I remember the feel of the fabric on my skin, and I remember vowing to my mother that I would protect my sister with my life." His eyes prickled with tears. "But I failed. She was hurt."

Jasmine intertwined her fingers with his. "You didn't fail. Your sister is alive, and she's getting stronger every day."

"Not thanks to anything I did."

"How do you know that? You don't remember anything. You might have done heroic acts to save your sister, and she might be alive thanks to you."

"I wish that was true." He knew it wasn't.

He wasn't injured. He hadn't fought for his sister. Something happened to both of them. But what could it have been to render them both unconscious while not injuring them?

But wait, what if he was injured and did not know it? He could barely feel his body. He was numb all over. Perhaps the medics gave him something to numb the pain of his injuries.

"Am I wounded?" he asked. "Is my sister?"

Jasmine frowned. "I thought you knew what happened to make you weak and forget everything. You and your sister were in stasis for a very long time. We found you, brought you here, and the medics resuscitated you. It takes time for your bodies to replenish themselves."

He was not sure he knew what stasis was, but he could guess. Had it been natural or induced?

He took a deep, shuddering breath, trying to steady and anchor himself in the present moment. "Where did you find me?"

"A place very far from here. Your escape pod landed on a mountain and made a big hole." She hesitated. "Only you and your sister survived. The others in your pod didn't. I'm so sorry."

Another tear escaped his eye for the lives lost of people he couldn't remember. "Tell me about this place."

"Where we found you?"

"Yes, and everything else in this world." He needed a distraction from the sadness. Something good to lift his spirits and make him feel like there was hope for him and his sister. Like there was a reason he was there.

Other than Jasmine, that is.

Perhaps he was meant to arrive on this world to find her?

She hesitated. "I don't know where to start. There is so much. There are so many different people, cultures, and ways of life. Some good and some not so much. It's a place of great beauty, but also great danger, a place where anything is possible, for better or for worse."

He nodded. "Tell me more about the people. In what ways are they different from one another?"

She took a deep breath. "This planet orbits a star that we call the sun. We have oceans and mountains, forests and deserts, great cities with millions of people living in them, and vast wildernesses and deserts where there are no people at all."

He listened, enraptured, as Jasmine painted vivid pictures with her words of towering structures that seemed to touch the clouds, all kinds of vehicles that moved on land, oceans, and the sky, and other technologies that, for some reason, failed to impress him. He found the many different races and cultures, each with their traditions and beliefs and their many different ways of seeing the world, fascinating.

"But for all its wonders, Earth is also a place of great strife and conflict," Jasmine said. "There are wars and famines, injustices and cruelties, but there is also great kindness and compassion, people who dedicate their lives to helping others and making the world a better place."

What she was describing resonated with him. "Good and evil, creation and destruction, life and death, honor and dishonor. It's all a duality." He closed his eyes. "I don't even know what it means, but I'm supposed to know."

Jasmine sighed. "You were raised to be a priest. You should know those things. They will come back to you."

He frowned. "So, you know things about me. Why didn't you tell me before?"

She lowered her eyes. "I didn't want to tell you that."

"Why not?"

"Because I wanted you to like me."

47

JASMINE

The prince looked so puzzled that his expression was almost comical, but the last thing Jasmine felt like was laughing.

Did she really say that?

I wanted you to like me.

"I don't understand," he said.

"No, of course, you don't." She grappled for words to explain what she'd said without sounding ridiculous, but before she could come up with something profound, Jade strode into the room without bothering to knock or announce her presence in any other way.

Evidently, there were significant cultural differences between what Jasmine considered polite and what the Kra-ell considered acceptable behavior.

"Greetings, holy brother." Jade lifted a fist to her chest.

"I am Je-Kara, first daughter of the tribe of Thar'ok, a former member of the queen's guard."

The prince's eyes widened, a flicker of recognition sparking in their depths as he struggled to push up against the back of the hospital bed.

"Greetings, Mistress Je-Kara. Do I know you?"

Jasmine wasn't surprised that Jade wasn't the female's real name, and Je-Kara was much more fitting, but why had the prince prefixed it with mistress?

The female made him nervous, which Jasmine could understand. Jade was intimidating as hell, but she couldn't be his superior if he was the prince, and she was just a guard, right?

"No, you do not," Jade said. "I have seen you and your sister from afar, but you've probably never noticed me."

Some of the tension in his shoulders released, and he offered Jade a tentative smile. "Even if I did notice you, Mistress Je-Kara, the first daughter of the tribe of Thar'ok, I am afraid that my memory is malfunctioning, and I cannot even remember my own name. If you know me, I would very much appreciate it if you could tell me what I am called."

Jade inclined her head. "In our culture, priestesses in training are called holy sister in training, and in your case, holy brother in training. You were the first Kra-ell male ever to enter the priesthood." She smiled. "And please, call me Je-Kara or Jade, as I prefer to be called here on Earth. Je-Kara was never a name fit for a warrior."

His eyes sparkled with amusement. "Perhaps I should also adopt an earthly name until I remember the one that was given to me at birth. What would you suggest?"

Jade glanced at Jasmine. "Any ideas?"

Jasmine chewed on her lower lip, thinking hard. The prince was gentle, sweet, and polite. What kind of name would fit him?

"Would you like the name Cedric? It means kind and loved." She turned off the teardrop and repeated the name so he could hear it as it sounded and not translated.

Jade grimaced. "That's a soft name. The prince needs a strong name. Something like Kor-rug or Or-gul." She slanted a look at Jasmine. "Kor-rug is a lion-like creature on Anumati, and Or-gul is a bird of prey."

"I like Cedric," the prince said.

Jade looked like she had just sucked on a lemon, but she inclined her head. "As you wish, my prince. I hope your memory will return soon, and you will remember the name your mother, the queen, gave you when you were born. I am sure it is a powerful name."

Jasmine exchanged an amused look with the prince and swallowed a chuckle.

Jade turned to her. "I must ask you to leave us for a time. The prince is about to receive several visitors, and we need to discuss some matters privately. You can wait in the penthouse or the kitchen for me to tell you when you can return."

Jasmine knew that Kian was on his way, so it made sense that he wanted to talk to the prince in private.

"Of course. I'll be in the kitchen if you need me. I could use another cup of coffee."

Jade nodded in approval.

Jasmine looked at her prince. "I'm not going far. I will be just down the hall."

She gave him a reassuring smile when he nodded and stepped out of the room.

As usual, the kitchen was deserted, the counters clean and gleaming under the strong fluorescent lights, and it reminded Jasmine how much she hated to be alone, especially in a room with no windows. This whole underground structure was depressing.

Perhaps she should go to the penthouse after all?

She could drink her coffee on the terrace and enjoy some fresh air. Even in downtown Los Angeles, the air was fresh so high up.

But she'd told Jade that she would wait in the kitchen, and if she went back to the clinic to tell her that she was going upstairs, it would seem as if she was snooping.

With a sigh, Jasmine set about making herself a fresh pot of coffee, her hands moving through the familiar motions with mechanical precision. She measured the grounds, filled the carafe with water, and watched as the dark liquid dripped and hissed into the waiting pot.

As she worked, her mind drifted back to the prince and the moments of connection and understanding.

He liked the name she had given him.

Cedric.

Did he look like a Cedric?

The name evoked an image of a British lord, someone who had graduated from a classy university and spoke with an upper-class diction and vocabulary.

Yeah. She'd read way too many historical romance novels.

Come to think of it, maybe that was where her obsession with royalty had begun.

Half of the heroes in those books were princes. Or maybe it was the other way around, and she'd always known she was destined to meet a prince, and that was why she'd been drawn to those kinds of stories.

As the coffee finished brewing with a final, sputtering hiss, jolting Jasmine from her reverie, she poured herself a mug and sat on one of the barstools next to the polished, stainless steel counter.

48

EDGAR

Edgar stopped in front of the clinic door and wondered whether he should leave the takeout bag outside. The smell of the dishes was delicious, but it could be overwhelming for the clinic and disturb the prince.

That was actually a good reason to bring it in, but he wasn't that much of an asshole. Besides, Bridget might have a problem with Chinese food being brought into her space, and he wasn't stupid enough to get on the doctor's wrong side.

Leaving the bag by the door, he pushed it open and walked in.

Anger rolled in like thunder when he saw the inner door to the prince's room closed. Had Jasmine closed it because she'd wanted to be alone with her prince?

She can do whatever she wants, he reminded himself. *You have no right to feel possessive.*

"Edgar," Bridget said as she walked out of her office. "What brings you here?"

"Takeout from the Golden Dragon. Are you hungry? I got it for Jasmine, but I have enough for everyone."

He'd gotten it for Jasmine as a gesture of friendship but also to remind her that he was still around, and if her prince turned out to be a frog, she was welcome to return to his arms.

Still, in case Jasmine thought it was creepy, he'd gotten enough to feed the entire clinic staff.

Bridget smiled. "I can't right now, but I'll gladly partake if there are any leftovers." She tilted her chin toward the closed door. "The prince is awake, and Kian is with him along with the Clan Mother, Jade, and Aru."

Edgar didn't know whether he should be relieved that Jasmine wasn't with the prince behind that closed door or more worried because the prince was awake.

Hopefully, the prince had disappointed Jasmine, and she was ready to embrace reality instead of the fantasy she'd created about the half Kra-ell.

"How long has he been awake?" he asked.

"Since early this morning, but he's still frail and sleeps on and off every so often."

"Where is Jasmine?"

Bridget smiled knowingly. "She's in the kitchen, and I'm sure she will be thrilled about the takeout."

"I hope so." He returned the doctor's smile. "I'll leave the leftovers in the fridge so you can feast when your guests are gone. The Golden Dragon is the best."

"I know, and I will."

After collecting the bag he'd left on the floor, Edgar continued down the corridor to the keep's kitchen and pushed open the door.

Jasmine looked up from her coffee mug as he entered. "Hi." She rose to her feet and walked over to him. "What brings you here?"

He held up the bag of food. "Brought you some lunch." He set the bag down on the counter. "Thought you might be hungry after all the excitement of the day. I've heard your prince is awake."

She didn't take the bait about the prince. "That's so sweet of you." She reached for the bag. "I didn't even realize how hungry I was until just now."

"I must have sensed it." He tapped his temple.

Edgar watched as she unpacked the food, satisfied by the small, appreciative noises she made as she inhaled the savory aromas of the dishes he had chosen.

He knew her tastes and had chosen accordingly, but there were other dishes there as well that were more aligned with his preference for spicy stuff.

"You got enough to feed an army." She put two plates

on the counter, one for him and one for herself. "Do we need more plates? Who else is joining us?"

"I thought that Bridget, Julian, and Gertrude would appreciate some fresh food, but they can't leave while the distinguished guests are visiting. Bridget asked that we store the leftovers in the fridge."

Jasmine probably didn't know about the Clan Mother being there, so he wouldn't mention her unless she did.

She nodded and lifted a pendant he hadn't noticed before. "Did you see William's latest gadget? This can translate what I'm saying into Kra-ell and still sound like me. Do you want to see how it works?"

"Sure."

Edgar's heart sank. If she could communicate with the prince, she would make him fall in love with her, and then she would fall in love with him. Or maybe she already had?

Well, it had to happen one way or the other.

"Kra-on!" she said and then added a few more words that came out sounding like the guttural Kra-ell language.

Edgar frowned. "How come I didn't hear what you said in English?"

She turned the device off. "William said something about it producing counter sound waves to absorb what I say so only the Kra-ell is heard. I might be confusing stuff because I don't understand anything about these kinds of things."

He didn't like Jasmine's tendency to put herself down and try to appear not as smart or capable as she was. Perhaps he should say something. They might not be a couple anymore, but they were friends.

He smiled at her to gentle the sting of his words. "Why do you do that?"

"Do what?"

"Pretend to be less smart than you are?"

She shrugged. "I don't want to be a show-off, and I really don't think I should speak with fake authority about things I understand little to nothing about."

"Now, that was a much better answer. You basically said the same thing but without disparaging yourself." He picked up the box closest to him and opened it. "Fates. Those smells were killing me on the way here. Let's eat before things get cold."

Jasmine laughed. "Let's."

Her laugh was a relief. It signaled that she hadn't been hurt or offended by what he had said.

They got busy shoveling food into their mouths for the next few minutes. Well, he shoveled. Jasmine ate with her usual restraint and ladylike manner.

She would fit the princess role well, but she needed to develop more hutzpah.

"So, tell me. What do you think of the prince so far?"

Lifting a napkin, Jasmine patted her lips to clean them. "He's very different from what I expected."

"In what way?"

"Everyone kept talking about how powerful and dangerous he was and that we needed earpieces to protect ourselves from his immense compulsion ability. But he doesn't seem powerful at all. He was visibly intimidated by Jade even though she was being perfectly polite."

Edgar chuckled. "I don't blame him. She intimidates me as well."

Jasmine nodded. "Yeah. She has a presence about her, which is kind of sexy."

Edgar lifted a brow. "Really? I didn't know that you swing that way."

"I don't. It's just an observation. I'm attracted to power, but I am purely into males."

Maybe that was what he had been missing?

"Anyway," she continued. "The prince is gentle, fully devoted to his twin sister, and gets teary-eyed when talking about her because he thinks he failed her." She pushed a strand of hair behind her ear. "I think he and his sister were so sheltered and isolated that they are still very naive and fragile."

He didn't know if Jasmine realized it, but she sounded like she was already in love with the prince, even though he was the direct opposite of what she'd imagined and found attractive.

If her description of him was accurate, then instead of a fearsome leader, the prince was a lost soul searching for a nurturing heart.

The surprising part was that Jasmine was uniquely suited for the task. She was quick to accept people the way they were and was open to new ideas. Perhaps the Fates had been right to send her to the prince. But if that was true, what did the Fates have in store for Edgar?

Why had they involved him in this mess?

Then it hit him. What if he was destined for the princess?

He wasn't as nurturing and open-minded as Jasmine, but he would make the effort for the right female.

"What about the sister? Is she showing signs of waking up?"

"She's still unconscious. What is clear, though, is that her brother cares a great deal about her, and since he's a good guy, she must be a good person as well."

Edgar leaned his elbow on the counter. "Perhaps I should sneak into her room and see if I can wake her up with a kiss."

Jasmine laughed. "It's worth a try. After all, a little kiss on the cheek is not going to do her harm."

He laughed along but was more serious about the idea than he was letting on. "Who knows? Maybe the Fates have brought me here for a reason. Perhaps she's my one and only."

"Perhaps." Jasmine reached for his hand and gave it a light squeeze. "I'll keep my fingers crossed for you."

49

THE PRINCE

The medics brought three more chairs into his room, arranging them around his bed, which didn't help calm his nerves.

Meeting Je-Kara had already shaken him; now, he was expected to receive more visitors, who were obviously even more important than the imposing female.

When the door opened again, Je-Kara walked in and nodded to him. "Are you ready?"

He wasn't, but he nodded.

The first to enter was an imposing male with piercing blue eyes. He had the same teardrop translation device as Jasmine and the medics hanging from his neck. Taking an assessing look around, he nodded his greeting and then walked out and returned with two females. One was pretty and golden-haired, and the other was a stunning, regal female with flaming red hair who had to be a goddess.

He didn't know why and how he knew that other than her perfection indicating that she could not be anything else.

Were more memories percolating up from under the thin barrier of his subconscious?

The female had a regal bearing, and the power emanating from her was a tangible presence. The male who had entered first acted with authority like he was the group's leader, but that was a ruse.

The goddess was in charge.

The male was not fully a god, nor was the golden-haired female.

Then another male entered, with dark hair and dark eyes, and the last one was Je-Kara.

"Good afternoon," the one with the blue piercing eyes said through the translating device, his voice coming out deep and growly. "My name is Kian; this is our Clan Mother, Annani, my mate Syssi, and my good friend Aru."

So, he had been right, and the redheaded goddess was in charge. There was something about her, something that tugged at the edges of his memory like a half-forgotten dream. She reminded him of someone, a face that hovered just beyond the reach of his fractured recollections.

Given his limited range of motion, he inclined his head the best he could. "I am honored by your presence," he said to all of them while looking into the goddess's eyes.

The Clan Mother smiled and inclined her head slightly.

"You've met Jade already," Kian said as Je-Kara entered.

It took the prince a moment to remember that Je-Kara preferred to be called Jade because Precious was not a name befitting a warrior. She was right, but was being named after a shade of green any better?

"Yes, I have." He forced a smile. "I wish I could give you a name, but I do not remember mine. Jasmine suggested that I use the name Cedric until I remember the name I was given by my mother."

"Do you remember your mother?" the goddess asked.

"I have one partial memory of vowing to her to protect my sister. I do not remember anything else about her."

"Do you remember your sister?" the golden-haired one asked.

"I remember I have a sister and am supposed to protect her. I do not remember her name or what she looks like either." He had planned to ask to see her, but since he could barely move his arms, that would be a problem.

He did not want to ask the medic to carry him to her room.

The goddess regarded him with affection in her wise eyes. "I am so happy that we have found you, and I agree with Jasmine that the name Cedric fits you. I can call you Prince, Cedric, or Prince Cedric. Which one do you prefer?"

He thought for a moment. "I do not feel like a prince, so I guess I will use Cedric until I remember my name."

The Clan Mother smiled. "Very well, Cedric. You can call me Annani, and I want you to know that you are safe, and that I am here for you and your sister. You both have my protection and my hospitality."

"Annani," he repeated the name with reverence. It reminded him of another name, but again, his faulty memory refused to cooperate. "Such a beautiful name. Thank you for sharing it with me."

"You are very welcome." The goddess sounded almost as emotional as he felt. "I am looking forward to the day I will also learn your real name."

He swallowed. He had been lost, adrift in a sea of confusion and uncertainty, and now he had someone to turn to, someone powerful and benevolent who had just vowed to protect him and his sister and take care of them.

50

ANNANI

Annani felt her heart swell with emotion as she sat beside her half-brother's bed. She wished to reach for his hand and clasp it, but the gesture would seem improper given that he did not know they were related, and she was not ready to tell him yet.

He looked so fragile, so unsure. He needed to be told things a little bit at a time.

She could see her father in the prince. The same strong, chiseled features and even the same eye color, but where her father's gaze had been determined and powerful, the prince's was soft and a little lost.

And to think that they had all feared that he and his sister were terrifying creatures who could wield unimaginable power. The earpieces were there to protect her from him in case he was more powerful than she was, but they also translated Kra-ell to

English, while the teardrop pendant translated English to Kra-ell, breaching the barrier of language.

The devices were Fates sent, or rather William sent, even though they could do nothing to bridge the cultural divide that Cedric was not even aware of yet, but he would be.

His eyes were misted with tears, and it was not an act because Cedric did not even know that he was supposed to act like a tough Kra-ell prince, with all the arrogance and dominance of the purebloods.

He was not one of them, but that was how he was raised.

Or maybe not. He and his sister had grown up in the temple, with the priestess being the strongest influence on their lives. Perhaps she had taught them compassion instead of a thirst for war.

Annani's eyes started to sting with sympathetic tears.

There was just something very touching about a grown male tearing up.

"Oh, my dear Cedric." She reached for his hand despite the impropriety. He did not know what was acceptable behavior and what was not, and since he did not pull his hand back, she assumed he was agreeable. "I am so incredibly happy and thankful that you and your sister are here. If only my Khiann and my Lilen were here as well, my life would be complete."

Next to her, Kian shifted on his chair, and on his other side, Syssi wiped tears from her eyes. Aru and Jade just observed, unmoved and untouched by the moment.

"Who were they?" Cedric asked.

"Khiann was my mate and the love of my life. He was taken from me mere months after we were married, murdered by a jealous and vengeful god who could not stand the thought that I chose Khiann over him."

The prince frowned. "I do not understand. Why did you have to choose one over the other? You could have had both."

Annani smiled. "I see that some of your memories are coming back. You grew up among the Kra-ell, where males outnumber females four to one, so Kra-ell females take several mates. I am a goddess, and gods are born in equal numbers. We choose only one mate."

He dipped his head in embarrassment. "I apologize for the improper comment. I meant no disrespect."

"I know." She patted his hand. "If you had all of your memories back, you would have known that gods mate only one person, even though gods and Kra-ell come from the same planet. We are all Anumatian."

He looked at her for a long moment. "What am I?"

"You are part god and part Kra-ell. Your mother was the queen of the Kra-ell."

His eyes started glowing in excitement. "And my father?"

"We are not sure who he was." Annani hated to lie to him, and she was not sure she should.

Until she had laid eyes on the prince, she had no proof that he was indeed her half-brother, so her statement might have been true, but seeing him and realizing how much he looked like their father, only a little darker and a lot softer, she could no longer harbor doubt.

The prince glanced at Kian and then back at her. "Who was Lilen?"

He could have asked her more about himself and where he had come from, but instead, he asked about Lilen. That spoke volumes about the kind of person he was.

"Lilen was my son. He fell in battle, defending our clan."

His fingers closed around hers with the gentlest of squeezes. "I am so sorry that you have lost so much."

She nodded. "Thank you."

"If I may…" The prince glanced at Kian and then back at Annani. "Can I ask if you know why my sister and I are here?"

Annani looked at Kian, who nodded.

Her son was observing the prince closely, checking for any signs of him remembering why he was sent to Earth.

"Some of what I am going to tell you will be upsetting, so before I start, I want you to look at my son and his mate. They are half god and half human. They are immortals like gods and have many of the other traits that the gods on Anumati have, but to a lesser degree, and they are perfect the way they are."

"Of course," the prince said. "Why would anyone claim otherwise?"

Annani smiled. "I am glad you asked. On Anumati, gods and Kra-ell do not mix. Even though they are genetically compatible, probably because they originated from the same common ancestors, mixed-race relationships are forbidden by both. The claim is that any children born of such unions will be abominations."

His eyes widened. "So, my sister and I are considered abominations?"

Annani nodded. "That is why your mother hid you behind veils from the day you were born and then sent you away from Anumati the first chance she had. She did that to save your lives."

51

THE PRINCE

So much of the fragmented memories suddenly made sense. The reason why he couldn't remember what his sister looked like even though he'd remembered them sparring with swords.

The tactile sensations of different fabrics against his skin. The absence of other people.

They had been covered from head to toe, veiled, and isolated.

"If relationships between gods and Kra-ell are forbidden, how did my sister and I come to be?"

The goddess smiled. "Love, I guess. Or maybe the rebellion of the young. Your mother was still just the princess when she became pregnant with you and was part of the resistance that tried to bring more equality to the Kra-ell. She worked closely with gods championing the Kra-ell cause, and she must have fallen in love with one of them. The birth of twins is extremely rare on Anumati and nearly unheard of among the Kra-ell, especially fraternal twins when one child is a female and the other a male. That alone cast suspicion on the newly crowned queen, but she was a clever female who spun a protective web around you. Taking advantage of the rarity of your twin births, she declared that you would both serve the Mother of All Life and consecrated you to the priesthood, effectively removing you from the public eye."

The goddess turned to look at Jade. "Am I doing your history justice so far?"

Jade inclined her head. "Yes, Clan Mother. But if you wish, I can take it from here."

The prince tensed. He did not want the cold Kra-ell female to tell him about their world. He wanted the gentle goddess to keep talking.

She must have sensed his wish and shook her head. "Thank you for the offer, Jade, but I will continue the story. If I get anything wrong, though, do not hesitate to correct me."

Jade's lips quirked up in an almost-there smile. "I would not dare, Clan Mother."

"Please do," the goddess said. "I do not want to provide our dear Cedric with the wrong information."

When Jade nodded, Annani turned back to him. "There are no male Kra-ell priests, but since the Kra-ell believe that twins share one soul, your mother proclaimed that by virtue of your sister, you would become a priest too. The advantages were clear. You were kept isolated in the temple, where the chief priestess of the Kra-ell ruled supreme and could protect you. You were never seen without your veils covering every inch of your body. Still, your mother could not do that forever, so she hatched a scheme to sneak you onto a settler ship bound for Earth."

"How could she have done that if we look like hybrids?" he asked. Annani looked at Jade. "You had a theory about that, right?"

Jade nodded. "I believe that you shrouded yourselves. Gods can make themselves look any way they want or even disappear from view. I believe that you shrouded yourselves to look like purebloded Kra-ell." She shifted slightly in her chair. "I was in the next pod over when you and your sister arrived, and something about you looked familiar. As I mentioned before, I was on the queen's guard and saw you walking the palace gardens between the palace and the temple. You were always veiled, but I recognized your particular gait and bearing. There were other hints as well. All the other pods had three or four females and seventeen or sixteen males, which is the natural Kra-ell gender distribution. Your pod had an equal number of males and females. I don't know what your mother's plan was, but I assume she wanted you to find your father when you got to Earth."

This was so much information that he was struggling to organize it all in his head. "What happened to the other people in our pod?"

"None made it, regrettably," Kian said. "The Kra-ell cannot enter stasis without a stasis chamber. Gods can. The stasis chambers stopped working when the pod malfunctioned, and the Kra-ell perished. You and your sister remained in natural stasis and survived like that for thousands of years."

He must have misunderstood, or maybe the translation device had made a mistake.

"Thousands of years? Is that how long it takes to travel from Anumati to Earth?"

Kian shook his head. "Aru tells me that it takes approximately five hundred years, but the ship carrying the Kra-ell settlers was old, so it might have taken longer. Still, not that much longer. It either malfunctioned or was sabotaged, and it arrived seven thousand years later. The ship exploded over Earth but managed to expel some or all of the stasis pods. Some made it safely and opened, like Jade's, but most were lost. We found yours thanks to Syssi and Jasmine."

His head was spinning. "I do not understand. How could they have known where to look for us?"

Syssi smiled shyly. "I'm a seer, and I foresaw that Jasmine would be instrumental to finding your pod, and I was right. She has very unique talents none of us even dreamt about."

His heart swelled with pride even though he could not take credit for Jasmine's talent. "Jasmine is special. I knew that from the first moment I saw her."

Kian chuckled. "Which was earlier today. But you are right. You and your sister owe the woman your lives. The physician who was part of the rescue team says that you were both running out of time. A few more days or at most weeks, and you would have perished, even in stasis, because your chambers were sealed."

He didn't know what that meant, and he did not really care. All he could think about was that Jasmine had saved his and his sister's lives, and he owed her a life debt, which he would gladly spend the rest of his life repaying.

He had known her for mere hours, but already he could feel a bond between them. How apt therefore, that it was Jasmine who had named him upon his rebirth.

52

KIAN

The prince was nothing like any of them had expected, but then the guy didn't remember anything, including possible instructions to eliminate Ahn or whatever other agenda he had been ordered to follow.

Kian didn't like how close his mother was sitting to the guy or that she was holding his hand like he was a child. He was weak, that much was obvious, but it wouldn't take much for him to snatch the earpiece out of Annani's ear and compel her to do his bidding.

He couldn't imagine the amount of damage his mother could do if someone else hijacked her power.

At least she hadn't told the prince that she was his half-sister, but Kian wasn't sure how long she would be able to hold that back. If he were a human, his mother's impulsiveness would have given him an ulcer.

Still, it was difficult to feel threatened by a male who teared up over everything.

This male didn't appear to be the powerful, dangerous creature they had been warned about, which on the one hand was a relief because he didn't seem like a threat, but on the other hand, he was not a powerful ally who could help their cause either.

It was too early to make a definitive judgment, though. Time would tell, and in the meantime, Kian would ensure that no one neglected safety precautions just because the guy had leaky eyes.

He had seen enough monsters who had done horrific things, crying like babies when the tables were turned on them.

Filthy cowards.

Kian shook his head, dispelling the thoughts that didn't belong in this room.

The prince seemed like a genuinely gentle soul, and Kian was starting to think that the warnings about the twins' powers had been deliberate misinformation.

Their mother might have spread the rumors of their power and their danger on purpose to protect her children from their grandfather and others who might have wished them harm.

If so, it was a clever plan, he had to admit. It made the twins seem too formidable, too terrifying to attack, but the queen had miscalculated.

The worst thing she could have done for her children was to draw the Eternal King's attention to them and make him think that they might pose a threat to his throne.

"He's like a child," Jade whispered almost inaudibly behind him. "No grown Kra-ell male would tear up over every other sentence. His mother did a poor job of raising him. She didn't teach him the way of the sword or prepare him for life."

Her words were harsh, but they echoed Kian's thoughts. The prince had grown up sheltered and coddled, which hadn't done him any favors.

It didn't make sense, though.

Kian's mother had pushed him to take on responsibilities and become the leader she'd needed him to be from a young age, and Annani was a sweetheart. The twins' mother had to be a tough female, or she wouldn't have been a queen of the Kra-ell.

Perhaps she had done precisely what she had intended, though, and had raised her son to be gentle and loving and to value compassion and empathy over strength and power.

It was a radical idea, a concept that went against everything the Kra-ell valued, but maybe the queen hoped that her children would create a different society in the colony on Earth. The odd configuration of the twins' pod fit this radical idea. It was the only one with an equal number of females and males. Another possibility was that the sister was the powerful one of the two.

In the Kra-ell society, males were subservient to females, so it wasn't such a far-fetched idea.

"Why did you ask Jasmine to leave?" the prince asked Jade. "Is anything we discuss a secret that should be kept from her?"

"I am the secret," Annani said. "I do not wish to burden you with too many details, so I am not going to explain why I like to keep my identity hidden from any who are not part of my clan or affiliated with it. At the moment, Jasmine's affiliation is still in question."

The prince looked troubled. "Why is it in question?"

Annani was about to answer when the door opened, and Bridget stepped inside. "I apologize, Clan Mother, but I'm afraid this will have to do for today. The prince is exhausted, and his vitals are all over the place. He needs to rest now."

"Of course." Annani rose to her feet and leaned over the prince. "I shall visit again." She kissed his cheek. "Hopefully, next time I come, you will be well enough to tolerate me for a little longer."

The guy looked at her with so much affection, admiration, and longing that even a cynic like Kian was touched.

"I enjoyed every moment of your visit, Clan Mother. Every word was a revelation and a comfort. I am looking forward to many more talks with you." He smiled. "Someone needs to tell me who I am and where I came from."

Annani cast a glance at Jade. "There may be no need because your memory will return. It would be better for you to remember who you are than for someone else to shape your self-perception."

"Then we will spend time together talking about you and your world."

"I would like that," Annani said. "Now, close your eyes and sleep, my sweet brother."

Kian froze, but the prince just smiled. "Thank you, my lovely sister. I will obey your command."

He must have thought that Annani had called him her brother as a term of endearment and that it meant something other than an actual blood relationship.

Nevertheless, it was a slip-up that shouldn't have happened.

53

JASMINE

Jasmine tensed as Jade walked into the kitchen with a grimace twisting her mouth.

"Is the prince okay?"

"He's fine." Jade's gaze swept over the array of open takeout boxes on the counter. "Your food stinks."

"I beg to differ," Edgar said. "It smells delicious."

"I believe it does to you, but the smell of cooked meat is repulsive to me." She shivered in disgust. "Anyway, I came to tell you that you can return to the clinic. He's asleep and will probably stay asleep for a while after all the excitement, so there is no rush." She gave them both a two-fingered mock salute, pivoted on the heel of her combat boots, and strode out.

"The nerve of her criticizing what we eat," Edgar murmured. "As if drinking blood from a live animal's vein is not repulsive."

Jasmine winced. "That's gross. I hope the prince does not like drinking blood. Bridget says his digestive system is like ours, but he also seemed disgusted when she mentioned meat. I guess it's a cultural thing."

Edgar shrugged. "So, what do we do with all the leftovers? Put them in the fridge, or call Bridget and the others to come and eat now that the guests are gone and her patient is sleeping?"

"Let's call her so she can eat it while it's still warm. Reheating Chinese food ruins the taste." Jasmine started closing the boxes and arranging them in a neat row.

"I don't have anything scheduled for today." Edgar finished closing the last of the boxes. "I can come and sit with you, keep you company while he sleeps." He gave her a lopsided smile. "So you won't be bored."

"I'm not bored," Jasmine said. "I've been singing to him, reading him stories. It helps pass the time."

Edgar frowned. "You can't do that anymore, remember? He is no longer unconscious, and you should let him rest."

"You're right." She canted her head. "It's strange how fast habits form and how difficult it is to change them. It's like I've spent my entire life, not just a few days, sitting in that chair in the clinic, talking and singing to an alien prince who I wasn't sure could even hear me." She smiled. "But he did. He told me that my voice soothed him."

Edgar nodded, but she wasn't sure whether it indicated that he understood or agreed or both.

"I'm curious to see what he looks like now," he said. "That's another motive for me to get Bridget out of there. She might not allow me to see him." He started toward the door.

"Why wouldn't she?" Jasmine followed him out of the kitchen. Edgar shrugged. "I have no reason to be there other than curiosity."

That was true of all the visitors, but Edgar was the only one who might not have the prince's best interests at heart.

Jasmine hated even to think that, but she should encourage at least one medical staff member to remain so Edgar wouldn't have free rein to do as he pleased. She could not physically protect the prince from the immortal and had no defenses against his mind manipulation. If he was planning to harm the prince, he could thrall her to do it for him.

Then again, Edgar didn't need to be in the clinic with her to do that. At any time, he could have thralled her to put a pillow over the prince's face and smother him or do something else to him that was less obvious.

He didn't, though, and she felt awful for even thinking that. Edgar might have a mile-long jealous streak, but he wasn't a bad guy.

The door to Bridget's office was open as they entered the clinic, and Edgar knocked on it before walking in. "We didn't put the food in the fridge. We left it on the kitchen counter. If you hurry, you might still eat it warm."

"Don't mind if I do." The doctor rose to her feet. "I'll ask Julian and Gertrude to join me."

Jasmine tensed despite her earlier rationalization that if Edgar meant the prince harm, he could have used her to do that already.

"Shouldn't at least one of you stay here in case of an emergency?"

Bridget smiled. "The kitchen is seconds away, and if anything out of the ordinary is registered on the monitoring equipment, our phones will sound the alarm."

"Oh, okay." Jasmine hid her embarrassment by turning to look at the slightly open door to the prince's room. "I didn't know that. I should check on him."

"I'll come with you." Edgar followed her.

When she walked up to the prince and gazed at him, Edgar walked around to the other side of the bed.

"He looks good." He lifted his eyes to her and smiled. "He's handsome. I was afraid he would look like the Kra-ell. Jade is pretty, but she's a bit too alien-looking for my taste, and the males look too feminine with their long hair and narrow waists. They are strong bastards and fierce warriors, so their looks are misleading, but still. If I were a female, I wouldn't have been interested. Then there are their strange mating rituals. No thank you."

"What strange mating rituals?" Ella hadn't said anything about that.

"They are violent, and they fight for dominance." He grimaced. "Did you

watch Star Trek: The Next Generation?"

"I did. I loved it."

"Remember the Klingon matings? It's something like that."

Jasmine shivered. "I'm glad that the twins were celibate and were not exposed to such barbaric practices."

"Yeah, me too." He smiled sheepishly. "Let's go see the princess."

Jasmine was also curious, but mostly, she wanted to get Edgar out of the prince's room. "Let's do it."

As they slipped inside the other room, Jasmine sucked in a breath. "Oh, wow, she looks much better as well."

The princess was beautiful; her features were delicate and finely wrought beneath the fragile skin, and her body was long, lean, and graceful. The few strands of hair still attached to her head were stringy and the same color as the prince's. A warm chestnut brown that would be gorgeous once it was restored to health.

"She's beautiful," Edgar murmured, his voice soft and filled with a quiet reverence as he studied the princess's face. "Regal, even. But it's a shame that her hair is in such bad shape. It would be better to shave it all off, let it grow back evenly." He looked up at Jasmine. "She'd look good bald. She has the bone structure for it."

Jasmine snorted. "Are you smitten, Edgar?"

He shrugged. "A princess is probably out of my league."

She laughed. "The prince is out of my league as well, but that's not stopping me. Why should it stop you?"

Edgar was silent for a long moment, and his brow furrowed as he considered her words. And then, slowly, a small, rueful smile began to tug at the corners of his mouth. "Would it be a little creepy for us, as former lovers, to be involved with the twins?"

She winced. "Yeah, it is a little creepy. But given that we are dealing with ancient aliens who are royals from another world, I think we're allowed a certain level of weirdness. As long as we don't mind and they don't, what's the harm?"

"Fair enough."

54

THE PRINCE

He stirred, his eyelids fluttering open as he emerged from the depths of sleep. For a moment, his mind struggled to reconcile the strange surroundings with the fragmented memories that danced at the edges of his consciousness.

Slowly he turned his head, his gaze falling on the female curled up in the chair beside his bed, and a smile blossomed on his face.

Jasmine looked soft and relaxed in sleep, her dark hair spilling over her shoulders in soft waves.

Extending his arm, he tried to reach the strands with his fingers, but the bed was too high, too far away. He tried to move sideways and stretch his arm closer, but his arm was already trembling from the effort, and his muscles were still weak.

With a groan, he tried harder to force his body to obey his commands, but he'd reached his limit and had to give up. It was unsettling to be trapped within his own flesh and unable to control his most basic functions.

Perhaps he could rest a little and try again.

Yeah, he should rest and try to recall what he had learned from his visitors.

How long ago had they sat in his room and told him things he had already mostly forgotten?

While he'd slept, someone had removed the extra chairs, and Jasmine had returned, but that still did not tell him how long he had been asleep.

They had told him about his mother, who had made him vow to protect his sister. As if he needed to make a vow to do that. It was his honor and duty to protect her. Even his memory loss could not erase his devotion to his twin. She was his entire world.

Had been his entire world.

Now, there was also Jasmine, but his sister had to come first. They told him that she was in the next room over and doing fine, but he had to see her with his own eyes to believe it, to reassure himself that she indeed lived, that he hadn't failed.

So close, and yet so far.

How could he reach her if he could not reach Jasmine's hair? Rest. He needed to rest.

Closing his eyes, he let his mind drift off until sleep overtook him, and when he woke up again, he felt a little stronger.

Jasmine was still asleep on the chair, and he felt a pang of guilt about her discomfort. She was there for him, and he now knew why. She felt responsible because she helped find him and his sister, saved them from the grip of death.

He owed her a life debt, and he couldn't wait for her to wake up so he could make the vow to her.

Right now, his vow would be worthless because he couldn't protect her any more than he could protect his sister, but when he was back to full strength, he would protect them both with his life.

He had to get stronger fast, and he wasn't going to achieve that by lying in bed. With a sudden burst of determination, he gathered his strength and pushed his legs down the side of the bed. Now, if he could only force his torso to lift off the mattress and move him to a sitting position...

The door burst open, and Bridget came rushing in. "What do you think you're doing?" She crossed the room in a few quick strides and gently but firmly pushed him back onto the bed. "You could have torn out your IV feed, and you're in no condition to be moving."

"What's going on?" Jasmine rubbed her eyes. "What did I miss?"

"Your guy tried to get up."

Jasmine turned to look at him with a shocked expression on her face. "What were you thinking?"

"I have to see my sister."

Bridget's expression softened. "You will, but not today. She's in the room next to you, and she's doing fine. That's all you need to know for now."

She tilted her head. "I can show her to you if you want."

"How?"

The medic pulled out a device from her pocket. "We have cameras installed in each patient room, so I can take a look even if I'm away from the clinic." She cast a glance at Jasmine, who blushed for some reason.

He shook his head. "I need to see her with my own eyes. I need to touch her hand and feel the warmth of life under her skin."

55

JASMINE

The prince's desperate plea to see his sister tugged on Jasmine's heartstrings. She turned to Bridget. "What if we wheel his bed into the other room?"

When the doctor started shaking her head, Jasmine looked up at her. "Before you say 'no,' I think that seeing his sister might jog his memory."

Bridget hesitated for a moment. "It's worth a try. The rooms are small, and these beds are bulky. Before I call Julian and the nurse to see if we can make it happen, I need to measure the space we have to verify that it is doable." She looked at the prince. "Don't worry, we will find a way for you to see your sister even if Julian has to carry you."

When he nodded, Bridget pulled a measuring tape from her coat pocket and stepped out of the room.

Jasmine stood next to the bed and took the prince's hand. "I keep trying to refer to you as Cedric in my mind, but it doesn't sound right. I want to know your real name."

"So do I." He squeezed her hand. "Thank you for suggesting rolling my bed to my sister's room."

"It was nothing." She chewed on her lower lip. "I saw her earlier. She's beautiful."

He smiled. "For some reason, you sound guilty."

"I do?" She closed her eyes. "I snuck a friend of mine in to see her."

The prince's smile evaporated, and his eyes started glowing. "What friend?"

She knew now that it wasn't a display of jealousy, so the response must have been about him perceiving what she had done as dangerous to his sister.

"Edgar, the guy I took to see her, was the pilot who worked with the gods and me on the mission to rescue you. After all he has done, I thought he deserved to see how well the two of you were doing."

And just like that, the smile was back, but only for a moment, and then he frowned. "You said that gods accompanied you on the missions. Who are they?"

"Aru, Negal, and Dagor. Why?"

The prince nodded. "Aru was one of my visitors. I suspected that he was a god."

"Good." She patted his hand. "Your memory is starting to come back if you can tell gods from immortals."

"It is not easy. They look a lot alike."

"Tell me about it." Jasmine rolled her eyes. "To me, Kian looks like a god. He is so incredibly good-looking."

"I was not sure myself whether he was an immortal or a god," the prince admitted, and again, there was not an iota of jealousy in his tone.

It was a little disappointing.

Jasmine didn't like Edgar's excessive jealousy, but a little bit would mean that the prince was interested in her as more than just a friend.

"Okay." Bridget walked into the room with Julian and Gertrude in tow. "Let's do this."

As Julian and the nurse worked together to quickly and efficiently disconnect the tubes and wires that tethered the prince to the monitoring machines, Jasmine slipped outside so she wouldn't be in their way.

When they were done with that part, they wheeled the bed out into the hallway and maneuvered it to pull it inside the other room.

From the open door, Jasmine saw that they had already moved the princess's bed to the side to make room for the second one, and she wondered if they planned on leaving the prince in his sister's room. He would be overjoyed if they did, but Jasmine preferred to have him all to herself and not to have to worry about his sister hearing them talking or doing other things, even when unconscious.

What other things?

It would take weeks until the prince was well enough for that. Besides, he hadn't shown any romantic interest in her yet.

He's been awake for one day. Get a grip.

Patience had never been Jasmine's strong suit.

The moment his bed was aligned with his sister's and his eyes fell upon her face, the prince's eyes filled with tears, and as he reached with a trembling hand to her, Julian helped him by moving the princess's hand closer and putting his on hers.

"Morelle," he whispered.

Jasmine stood at the doorway, unsure whether he wanted her there. "Morelle," he said louder and turned to look at Jasmine with a grin spreading over his handsome face. "My sister's name is Morelle."

Jasmine clapped her hands. "You remembered her name. That's amazing." She was giddy with happiness for him, and yet her eyes stung with tears.

She squeezed to stand on the other side of his bed and placed a hand on his shoulder, hoping he would find it supportive rather than intrusive.

"Can you try and remember your own name?" Bridget asked.

"Ell-rom. We are each other's mirror image."

Ell-rom, Jasmine repeated in her head. She didn't know what it meant, but it suited the prince much better than Cedric.

"Anything else that you remember?" Bridget asked gently.

"No. Morelle and Ell-rom. Those are our secret names, but I guess we don't need to keep them a secret anymore."

"Why were your names a secret?" Julian asked.

"I do not know." Ell-rom's eyes were focused on his sister's face. "I hope you wake up soon, Morelle, and I hope your memory didn't suffer as much damage as mine."

56

KIAN

Kian glanced at his watch while Onegus delivered his report, hoping the chief hadn't noticed. As usual, he was pressed for time, and even more so now because of his back-and-forth trips to the keep.

But it wasn't as if he could delegate the task of escorting his mother to see her half-brother. He had to do it himself and ensure she didn't reveal every possible secret in her excitement over finding her siblings.

The guy seemed pretty harmless, but Kian wasn't taking chances, especially when his mother was involved.

"William's crew installed two surveillance cameras in the mailroom overnight," Onegus said. "They made sure that no one saw them even enter the building, and the cameras they installed are tiny. The pranksters won't suspect a thing."

"You think it's just pranks?"

Onegus shrugged. "I judge things by the harm done, not by their moral implications, and the stolen items are cosmetics, some clothing items, and a jewelry box. None of the items is worth more than fifty bucks."

"So, our culprit is a female." Kian leaned back in his chair. "A male wouldn't have stolen such items."

Onegus lifted a brow. "Are you sure about that? Maybe a guy is collecting items to gift a female, or he wants to try them on himself. It seems to be in vogue now."

Kian shrugged. "I still remember when men wore wigs, stockings, and heeled shoes, painted blush on their cheeks, and used pomade to make their skin look whiter. Things come and go. This too shall pass."

"I don't know about that." Onegus rubbed a hand over the back of his neck. "Not that I care about who wears what and why, but it seems to me like a big, noisy smokescreen, so people focus on this and not that. You know what I mean?"

"I do, and I'm worried, but I can only deal with so many things at the same time, and right now, we need to find out what's happening under our noses because these small thefts and acts of sabotage could be a smokescreen too, or rather a smoking gun."

Onegus nodded. "William's crew is working on the

malfunctioning shutters. They're checking every unit to determine if it's a design flaw or tampering."

"It can't be a design flaw." Kian sighed. "Too many going bad at the same time."

"My money's on the Kra-ell teenagers," Onegus said bluntly. "They're bored out of their minds. People that age with no structure and no purpose, it's a recipe for trouble."

"What do you suggest we do with them?" Kian asked.

Onegus leaned forward, bracing his elbows on his knees. "Enroll them in the Guardian training program. Everyone sixteen and older who is not pursuing academic education should enroll. Give them something to work toward, a sense of accomplishment, pride, and belonging."

Kian's eyebrows rose in surprise. "You think that's wise? Sixteen is young."

Onegus lifted his hands. "Most of them are not interested in higher education, and fighting is in their blood. The older ones who joined are doing very well. I'm already using them to assist our rescue teams. We put them in tactical gear that hides their alien features and keep them in backup positions so they are not in direct contact with the victims we rescue. Our Guardians feel much safer having them defending their backs."

It might work, provided that the young Kra-ell wanted in. Forcing them would make them more resentful.

"Let's do it. But we need to be smart about this. We need to hype up the force so they will want to join, supervise them closely and have a zero-tolerance policy for any hint of trouble."

The Chief nodded. "I'll speak with Jade. She knows how to keep them in line."

"Apparently not, if they are running around perpetrating petty crimes."

Onegus leaned back in his chair. "Jade has one deputy, Kagra. It was enough when all she needed was to police her tribe, but now she has a whole community, and she's not set up for that. She needs to deputize more people."

Kian smiled. "You are welcome to suggest that to her."

"I will. Looking forward, we could expand our rescue operations once they graduate, which will not take them as long as it takes our people. Shoring up our defenses is also a huge benefit."

"I agree. What about the pay? Do we pay them the same as our people?"

Onegus sighed. "That's somewhat complicated. While in training, they should get paid the same as our trainees, but once they graduate, we might want to introduce a new pay structure that rewards seniority and the types of positions people hold. We don't want to upset our people who have been serving for years, and we don't want to appear as if we are discriminating against the newcomers. There needs to be a balance."

"I will leave it up to you to figure this out. When you have the pay structure ready, bring it to me for review."

"Of course." Onegus rose to his feet. "I'll let you know what William's crew finds out about the shutters."

"Thank you, Onegus."

After the chief left, Kian swiveled his chair toward the window and looked at the peaceful scene outside. The village green was bathed in sunlight, with immortals, Kra-ell, and humans alike passing by.

Who was the culprit?

Immortals showing their displeasure about the changing nature of their village? The Kra-ell fertility rate was higher than the immortals', and there were whispers about them one day taking over.

It was a valid concern, and even though they seemed to coexist peacefully with their hosts, they weren't really integrating. The two groups kept to themselves, with Jade, Phinas, Vanessa, and Mo-red being the exception, not the rule.

Had he made a mistake by inviting the Kra-ell to join their community?

The surveillance cameras and the Guardian training program were all just stopgap measures, temporary solutions to a deeper problem. The real challenge lay in bridging the divide between their peoples and finding a way to coexist while maintaining the balance of power.

After all, the village belonged first and foremost to the clan. It was not fair to expect them to share it, or worse, fear that they would be outnumbered and driven out of their homes one day.

No one had said that, not to him anyway, but if he was thinking that, others were too.

57

MARINA

When the morning rush had finally subsided, leaving behind a welcome lull in the constant bustle of the café, Marina wiped down the tables and the counters and then poured herself a much-needed cup of coffee.

Leaning against the counter, she listened to Wonder as she was humming while rearranging the pastry tray so it wouldn't look so depleted. "I hope the delivery from Jackson arrives before the afternoon gets busy."

"Is it ever late?" Marina asked.

Wonder snorted. "It's Los Angeles. Traffic is unpredictable, and the delivery is done in a roundabout way."

"I was wondering about that. Who brings stuff to the village?"

"Everything is delivered to our downtown location, and one of ours brings it from there. Up until not too long ago, Jackson restocked the café himself, but he got too busy and hired help." She chuckled. "His friend Gordon recently graduated from Oxford with a degree in philosophy, but he makes a living delivering pastries and sandwiches to the village." She smiled. "It's just temporary. He wants to continue his studies."

Marina frowned. "Peter told me that clan members don't need to work if they don't want to and that they get a monthly allowance."

"They do." Wonder pushed to her feet. "I guess Gordon likes to be busy, or he just wants to help out his friend." She glanced at the back of their shop, where Aliya was doing the dishes. "I'm going to help her out."

"I'll do it." Marina put her coffee cup down.

Wonder stopped her with a hand on her shoulder. "You need a break. Rest, drink your coffee, and eat something."

"Thank you." Marina smiled at her gratefully.

She was used to working hard but couldn't compare with the immortals and the Kra-ell. They were machines. Still, despite how crazy it sometimes got, she loved it at the café. The people were so friendly and welcoming, especially the Guardians, who stopped by and chatted with her and Wonder as if they were part of the gang because their mates were on the force.

Hearing footsteps approaching, she put her coffee cup

down and turned around with her professional smile in place.

Seeing who the customer was, the smile slid off her face.

Borga.

What the hell was she doing in the café?

She was a pureblooded Kra-ell, so it wasn't like she was there to order a cappuccino and a pastry.

There could be only one reason, and that was to taunt Marina. For some reason, the female despised her and made it her mission to make Marina's life miserable.

She knew the reason, but it was as unhinged as the female herself was. Kra-ell were not supposed to be possessive or demand exclusivity from their bed partners, but since Borga had given Mo-red a son, she had convinced herself that he belonged to her and gave every female he ever looked at the stink eye.

The thing was, Marina had never been with the pureblooded male. The extent of their interaction had been him smiling at her a couple of times, which, given how severe the Kra-ell usually were, had given Borga ideas.

"Well, well, well," Borga drawled, her voice dripping with disdain. "If it isn't the little blue-haired koraba."

Koraba sounded like the name of an animal from the Kra-ell home planet, which probably had some unfavorable characteristics for Borga to hurl it so derisively at Marina.

Marina affected a neutral expression. "What can I get for you, Borga?"

The female leaned against the counter, her lips curving in a cruel smile. "I need my house cleaned. You are a maid. Figure it out. Or are you too busy servicing your immortal when you are not working in the café for pocket money?"

Behind her, Marina heard Wonder's intake of breath, and tension practically crackled in the air. Hopefully, Wonder would stay out of it and let her handle it herself.

Rising to Borga's bait would only make things worse.

The female thrived on conflict and used her so-called power over those she considered beneath her, whether hybrids or humans. Engaging with her would only feed that twisted need, and Marina wouldn't give her the satisfaction of knowing that she had gotten under her skin.

"I'm sorry, Borga," she said evenly, meeting the female's gaze without flinching. "But I'm afraid I can't help you with that. If you are not here for coffee or pastries, I will have to ask you to step aside so I can assist the next customer in line."

Borga's eyes flashed with anger, her nostrils flaring as she leaned in close. "Don't use that tone with me, human," she hissed. "You might think that you are all that because you are an immortal's plaything, but you are nothing, just a novelty that will wear off sooner or later."

Borga was trying to get a rise out of her, the words designed to cut and wound and leave her feeling small and insignificant, but a small, treacherous part of her couldn't help but wonder if there was a kernel of truth buried beneath the vitriol. After all, what did she have to offer someone like Peter?

"That's enough, Borga," Wonder said, her voice low and menacing. "You need to leave. Now."

Since Borga had spoken to Marina in Kra-ell, her tone alone must have annoyed Wonder enough for her to intervene.

The Kra-ell female sneered, her gaze flicking dismissively over Wonder's face. "Or what? You'll make me? You and what army?"

Even Marina's surprise over Borga's mastery of English couldn't diminish her panic as the two females squared off, their bodies coiled with tension and radiating aggression.

Wonder was a big female, but she was immortal, and as a pureblooded Kra-ell, Borga was much stronger and definitely more vicious.

She didn't want Wonder to get hurt because of her.

"I don't need an army to teach a conceited, rude female her place." Wonder leaned over the counter, staring Borga down.

Aliya sidled over to Wonder. "And if she needs help teaching you some manners, I happen to be an excellent teacher." She put her arm around Wonder's shoulders.

"A hybrid and an immortal defending a worthless human." Borga snorted. "I can hand you both your asses without breaking a sweat."

"You can try," Aliya snarled, her eyes flashing red and her fangs on full display.

Damn, the girl was scary. Marina was glad that Aliya was on her side.

Borga must have thought so too, because she took a step back. "As much as I would have enjoyed tearing you two a new one, we are under compulsion not to harm each other." She spun on her heel, and as she stalked away, she flipped them the finger.

The three of them stood there for a moment, the tension slowly leaching out of the air.

"What's her problem?" Aliya asked.

"She's unhinged." Marina let out a breath. "For some reason, she hates me and enjoys taunting me. I had forgotten about her when I asked to be transferred here."

Wonder's eyes were still blazing with anger as she turned to Marina. "You need to report this to Jade," she said firmly. "This is not acceptable behavior in the village."

Wonder was correct, but Marina was reluctant to make a fuss and draw attention to herself. Borga had been living in the village for a while, while Marina had just arrived. If Borga had behaved well so far, Jade might blame Marina for provoking her.

Besides, Jade was even scarier than Borga.

"It's okay. Eventually, she will tire of picking on me and move on."

"That's not how it works." Wonder sighed. "I don't have a lot of life experience, but even I know that bullies need to be dealt with, or they just get emboldened."

"Why you, though?" Aliya asked. "Borga is unpleasant, but I've never seen her that vicious to anyone."

"Borga is a bad apple, always has been. Not that the other purebloods were much better, but they were mostly just condescending, and she was mean. I was one of the maids assigned to clean the pureblooded females' quarters, so I was forced to interact with her. Maybe she'd gotten it into her head that I caught Mored's eye, or she just enjoyed lording it over me. No one had much in Igor's compound, not even the pureblooded Kra-ell, and because they had so little, the ones whose characters were less than stellar tried to make themselves seem better than others by tormenting the humans."

58

THE PRINCE

Ell-rom blinked, confusion clouding his features as he stared at Bridget. "What do you usually eat?" she repeated, her voice gentle but insistent.

He frowned, searching his fractured memory for some clues, some hint of what his body required for sustenance. But there was only blankness, a void where that knowledge should have been.

After having such a remarkable breakthrough and remembering his and his sister's names, he had hoped more memories would come rushing in, but he had no such luck.

After they had rolled his bed back to his room, he'd fallen asleep again, and when he'd woken up, it was with the same confusion as before.

"I don't know," he admitted. "I can't remember."

Bridget nodded as if she had expected as much. "That's all right," she reassured him, laying a comforting hand on his arm. "We'll figure it out together. I don't think your body can process blood, but that's what the Kra-ell live on, so let's start with that. Does drinking blood appeal to you?"

He felt bile rise in his throat, and his stomach convulsed as if preparing to purge what was inside of it.

"Not at all. I find even the thought of it disgusting."

"How about animal or fowl flesh? Raw or cooked?"

Ell-rom's stomach lurched violently again, a wave of nausea crashing over him. He swallowed hard, fighting the urge to hurl, his face twisting with disgust.

"No," he managed, shaking his head vigorously. "No meat, either."

"That's odd." Bridget frowned. "The gods eat everything." She glanced at Jasmine. "Am I right?"

Jasmine nodded. "We all ate the same things, and there were all kinds of you-know-what in the dishes. I don't want to mention it because Ell-rom looks green."

"I do?" He lifted his hand and looked at it. "I still look slightly gray."

"It was a tease." She patted his knee through the blanket covering him.

The friendly touch shouldn't have aroused him, but he couldn't help it. He didn't know how old he was, but he knew he hadn't been touched much, and definitely not by females other than his sister. He couldn't remember their mother touching him either, but she must have, at least when they were little.

"It makes sense," the senior medic said. "It's not like they could get the you-know-what or cook it in the temple." She looked at him. "How about baked food, fruits, or vegetables?"

Tearing himself away from sinful thoughts, Ell-rom tried to catch a flicker of memory that danced at the edges of his consciousness.

The scent of ripe fruit, sweet and fragrant, the taste of it bursting on his tongue like a small sun. His mouth watered at the thought, a sudden, visceral longing filling him.

"Fruit," he said. "I remember the taste of fruit."

Bridget smiled. "Good. That's a start. I'll bring you some vegetable broth to start, and we'll take it from there."

"Yay!" Jasmine clapped her hands. "You are about to eat real food."

Ell-rom glanced at the clear line that extended from a bag full of liquids to the back of his hand. "What about this? Do we still need it?"

Bridget hesitated. "You are holding down water just fine, so we can take it out, but if we encounter problems feeding you, we might need to put it back in."

He lifted his hand. "I am willing to take the risk."

"Excellent." Bridget looked at him with assessing eyes. "Since you seem eager to get out of bed, I'm inclined to assist you in that. But first, we need to remove everything else, including the other end." She winked. "I'm sure there is no Kra-ell translation for that word."

He knew what she meant, and having such an exchange in front of Jasmine was embarrassing.

"Yes, I am willing to risk that as well."

"Excellent. That means that you will have to use the restroom on your own. The first couple of times, Julian will help you, and I will get you a walker for later."

It was a terrifying prospect, and he didn't know if he was ready, but he was so tired of the bed and the white wall in front of it. He needed to see the sky and breathe fresh air, but until he became mobile and stable, he could not do any of those things.

"I'll help," Jasmine offered. "You can lean on me on the way to the bathroom." He would rather die, but he did not say that.

"Also," Bridget said. "It's time you got a proper shower. After Julian removes all the wires and tubes, he will help wash you."

Ell-rom knew what a shower was because Jasmine used it to clean herself every night. She did not wash her hair every time she used the shower, but she always smelled good when she came out.

He did not want to think about how he smelled. Julian, the male medic, had been wiping him clean with some special kind of towel with cleansing agents, but it wasn't the same as standing under a spray of water and using cleansing products directly on his skin.

Had he had showers where he came from?

He couldn't even remember what kind of bed he slept on, let alone any other comforts.

"Julian will come over to help you," Bridget repeated. "Is that okay?"

"Yes, of course. I'm looking forward to it."

Bridget turned to Jasmine. "I think Ell-rom would like privacy for his first shower."

Jasmine jumped up from her chair as if something had bit her lush bottom. "Yes. I'm leaving right now."

No, he wasn't going to think about her bottom, or her bosom, or her lips… Oh, dear Mother above. He would need some time to calm down before the male medic arrived, or he would die from embarrassment.

Jasmine turned to him and smiled. "I'll come back when Julian tells me it's okay. I'm going to take a walk and stretch my legs."

Still dying on the inside, he nodded.

When Bridget and Jasmine left, Ell-rom released a long breath and turned his thoughts toward all those poor souls who hadn't made it. Perhaps using them to douse the fire coursing through his veins was disrespectful to their memory, but he had nothing else.

He would pray for their forgiveness later.

59

ANNANI

As Annani waited for Kian to join her for lunch, she looked out the sliding doors of her house at the lushly green backyard. The view, together with the sounds and smells coming from the kitchen where Oridu was bustling about, provided a soothing background to her racing thoughts.

How could it be that a half-brother, born on a distant planet and raised under such different circumstances, was so much like her?

They shared a father, but, although Annani had loved Ahn dearly and respected him immensely, he hadn't been ruled by his heart like she was and like the prince seemed to be.

Ahn hadn't been known for his compassion either.

Her father had never been cruel for cruelty's sake, and he had not been a tyrant obsessed with ruling, but he had been ruthless, unforgiving, and steadfast in following the code he had imposed on their people. But then, Annani hadn't inherited her impulsivity and her romanticism from her mother either. She actually shared those traits with her uncle Ekin, who was also the Eternal King's son, but not Queen Ani's, so if they were, in fact, inherited traits, they had to have come from the Eternal King, the only ancestor they had in common. But, Annani sincerely doubted that they had all inherited good hearts from him.

Genetics were complicated, and as much as the gods thought they could control every aspect of creating an intelligent being, some things were the Fates' doing.

As the warm, savory scent of the simmering stew filled the air, Annani started to get impatient for her son's arrival.

She was eager to share lunch with Kian, a rare treat they seldom enjoyed, and then drive together to see her brother again. It wasn't that she didn't like family meals with Syssi and Allegra, but it was nice to get her son all to herself occasionally.

The sound of the doorbell brought a smile to her lips, and as Ogidu opened the door for Kian, she rose to her feet and walked over to greet him.

"You are right on time." She tilted her head for him to kiss her cheek and then the other way so he could kiss the other.

"Something smells good," he said.

"Oridu got excited when I told him you would join us for lunch. He made the vegetable stew you like."

Usually, her butler prepared the stew with beef, but since Kian did not eat animal products, Ogidu had found wonderful substitutes.

Kian's eyes widened. "I have not had that in such a long time."

"Then let us begin the meal without delay." She led him to the dining room table.

After pulling out a chair for her and waiting until she was seated, Kian took the seat to her right.

"I have good news," he said as he unfurled his napkin and draped it over his lap. "Bridget called me this morning to tell me that the prince remembered his and his sister's names."

Annani's heart rate accelerated. She had not expected such fast progress. "This is indeed wonderful news. What are their names?"

"His is Ell-rom, and his sister's is Morelle."

Annani felt tears prick at the corners of her eyes. "Ell-rom and Morelle," she repeated softly, the names feeling both foreign and achingly familiar on her tongue. "My brother and sister. What jogged his memory? Did Bridget say?"

"She did, and she credited Jasmine with the idea that led to it. Ell-rom was desperate to see his sister, so he tried to get out of bed on his own. Naturally, he was in no state to do that, and Bridget caught him in time before he face-planted on the floor. Bridget offered to show him a camera feed of his sister, but the prince was adamant about seeing her himself and holding her hand. When Jasmine saw how distraught he was because he couldn't see his sister, she suggested that they take him to see her by wheeling his bed into her room. Bridget agreed to try it, and somehow, they managed to squeeze his bed next to his sister's so he could reach over and take her hand."

Imagining the reunion, Annani could not hold back the tears falling down her cheeks.

"I wish I had been there to see them together. It must have been such an emotional moment."

"I bet it was," Kian said. "So much so that the prince remembered his sister's name, which in turn brought back his own."

Annani smiled through the tears. "I think the Fates were very wise choosing Jasmine as my brother's mate." She chuckled. "She is so dedicated to him and so resourceful. I hope she will transition and prove that she is a princess at heart."

She waited for Ogidu to serve the stew, toasted bread, and fresh salad. "We do not know anything about her family." Annani leaned back to allow Ogidu to place some stew on her plate. "From what you told me, she is not close to her father, and her mother died when she was young. I would like you to look into that."

Kian nodded. "I'll get someone onto that. If she is to become my aunt, I need to know more about her history."

Annani winced. "An actress who is a Wiccan witch would not have been my first or second or third choice for my brother's mate, but I need to have faith in the Fates."

"She is a lovely young lady." Kian reached for a piece of toast to dip in his stew. "Beautiful, kind, and most importantly, full of joie de vivre. You will like her."

"I would like to meet her. Perhaps today, you will allow her to remain by his side when I visit?"

Kian sighed. "Not yet."

"Why not?"

"First of all, I would rather wait for her to transition. Meeting you will leave such an indelible impression that we will not be able to erase her memory of that, provided that it is needed."

Annani laughed. "After finding an alien pod with twenty stasis chambers inside, eighteen dead Kra-ell, and two live half gods, half Kra-ell royal twins, I do not think meeting me will be the most memorable thing in Jasmine's mind."

For a moment, it seemed like she had won the verbal sparring with her son, but then he got that gleam in his eyes that portended otherwise.

"You might be right about that, but it's also not the right way to introduce her to you. Would you rob Jasmine of the full experience of meeting a goddess for the first time by doing so in a cramped clinic room?"

He got her there.

Or maybe not.

"We can do this in your office in the keep. I will sit at the head of the conference table, looking regal and glowing, and you will bring her in to meet me. I will do my thing, welcoming her to the clan and acting godly, and from there, we can walk together to Ell-rom's room."

60

THE PRINCE

"This is a happy moment," Julian said as he entered the room and closed the door behind him. "It deserves a celebration."

"Yes. I hope so."

Julian smiled. "Close your eyes and count to a hundred. By the time you are done, I will be done too."

It was probably how the medic took care of frightened small children, but Ell-rom was happy to follow the advice.

In a way, he was like a small child, learning the world he had recently awakened to. Everything was strange and unfamiliar, but his sister was in the next room over, and he had Jasmine by his side.

He wasn't alone.

There were also the others who had visited him the day before—Annani, who had been so gracious and promised to take care of him and Morelle. Kian, Jade, and Aru also seemed like good people who did not mean him or his sister harm, and maybe they could all become friends at some point. Perhaps he and Morelle would find a community among these people.

"All done," Julian announced. "You can open your eyes now."

"Thank you. That was good advice. I did not feel most of it."

"I tried to be as gentle as possible, but some things hurt no matter how hard I try." Julian leaned over Ell-rom. "Wrap your arms around my neck. I will count to three, and on three, I will lift you off the bed. Try to help by hoisting yourself up and moving your legs over the side of the bed."

As Ell-rom followed the medic's suggestion, he was glad Jasmine was not there to see the humiliating display of helplessness.

"You are doing very well," Julian said as Ell-rom got his feet on the floor. "Now, try to stand straight and leave only one arm around my neck."

His legs shook, and he hung from Julian's neck, but he managed to make one step and then another. Then, he was at the door to the bathroom, and Julian helped him get inside.

"I don't know if you had toilets where you came from, but this is where you empty your bladder and bowels.

After you are done, the toilet automatically activates and washes everything down. After a bowel movement, you can press this button, and a water spray will clean the area. All that will remain to be done is to wipe the moisture with some paper. I don't expect you to need to do that yet, but you need to empty your bladder." Julian tilted his head. "Do you want to give it a try?"

"I should." Ell-rom smiled nervously. "I don't want that tube inside of me again."

Julian helped him sit down on the toilet. "I'll give you some privacy by turning my back to you, but I don't want to leave you alone here just yet."

It was glorious to relieve himself, to perform that small function on his own, but when it was time to get up, Ell-rom lacked the strength.

Shame and frustration warred within him, but he could not bring himself to ask for Julian's help.

Instead, he sat there and waited until the medic turned around. "All done?" Julian asked cheerfully.

"Yes, thank you. I just can't get up."

"That's perfectly all right." Julian offered him both of his hands. "Let's do this together."

When he was up, the toilet whooshed behind him, startling him.

He looked over his shoulder, watching as the water spiraled inside and a blue light flashed.

"The light sanitizes the bowl," Julian explained. "I've never thought to ask Jade how things like that worked back on Anumati." He guided Ell-rom into the shower stall and helped him sit on a small stool. "It's funny how you never think about things like that until you meet someone who can't remember anything."

The medic removed the garment that covered Ell-rom and tossed it into a bin that stood in a corner. "I've got a pair of loose pants for you and a matching shirt. You will feel so much better in them."

"Thank you." Ell-rom was trying to maintain some dignity by sitting up and not allowing himself to slide down to the floor.

He was so frail, so vulnerable.

As Julian washed Ell-rom with brisk but gentle movements, the medic kept talking in his soothing, conversational tone.

"Do you want me to cut your hair?" he asked after washing it with some fragrant lotion and then rinsing it. "You have those clumps of long hair and a fuzz of new growth, and it doesn't look good. Cutting everything short will look better."

"I trust your judgment." He chuckled weakly. "I haven't looked at myself yet." "You are about to in a few moments." Julian turned the water off, rubbed a soft towel over Ell-rom, and then helped him into a robe made from the same soft fabric as the towel.

Leaving him sitting on the stool in the shower, Julian stepped out and returned with a paper cup and a brush with some white paste on it.

"This is a toothbrush. As the name implies, it's for cleaning your teeth. Don't swallow the paste. After I'm done brushing your teeth, you will rinse it out with water from the cup." He handed it to him.

"I can brush my teeth by myself," Ell-rom said.

Julian looked doubtful, but he gave him the brush. "Go ahead."

It was a challenge, his hands shaking and his grip weak as he tried to maneuver the small brush over his teeth and gums. In the end, Julian had to help him, guiding his hand and steadying his arm until the task was done.

"Okay." The medic grinned at him. "Looking good. Let's get rid of those clumps before I lead you to the mirror."

He must have looked bad if the medic felt the need to fix his hair before letting him see his reflection.

Julian returned with a pair of scissors. "I'm not a barber, so don't expect anything fancy, but I will do my best."

By the time Julian was done and helped Ell-rom up, exhaustion was dragging him down, and as he stood in front of the mirror, he didn't recognize the face staring back at him.

Gaunt and pale, with sunken cheeks and hollow eyes, the male in the mirror looked like a ghost. Ell-rom lifted a hand to his face, tracing the sharp angles of his cheekbones and the sparse tufts of new hair on his scalp.

"I don't know who I am," he whispered, his voice cracking. "I don't recognize myself."

Julian's hand was warm and solid on his shoulder, his arm wrapped around Ell-rom's middle, holding him from falling. "You still have a long journey back to yourself, but you can make it only one step at a time."

As Julian helped him into the fresh clothing he'd brought and then back into bed, Ell-rom clung to those words like a lifeline.

One step at a time.

61

ALENA

The first contraction came out of the blue and hit Alena with the force of a freight train, a searing, twisting pain that radiated from her back and left her breathless. She gasped, one hand flying to her belly with the other groping for Orion's arm.

"It's happening," she managed, her voice tight with strain. "The baby's coming."

With a strangled sound, Orion tore the virtual reality headset off his head and dropped it on the couch. His face drained of color as he stared at her with wide, panicked eyes. "What do we do now? I forgot what I need to do."

They'd been preparing for weeks, and he'd had everything memorized, but panic had a way of erasing sense. Her mate, the fearless warrior, was reduced to a stammering mess at the prospect of impending fatherhood.

It was endearing to see him so unraveled. But she didn't have time to coddle him, not when their child was eager to make its way into the world.

Kid number fourteen would not take as long as kid number one had taken, or even number five. That first contraction had not been a gentle warning. It was a war horn.

It was time.

"Call Merlin," she said, her voice calm and steady now that the pain had subsided. "Tell him that we are on our way to the clinic. I suggest you summon a golf cart because I won't make it there on foot. The baby would come out on the way."

Yeah, that wasn't the best way to approach a male who was already panicking, but she really didn't have time. This baby was going to be out in less than an hour.

Orion nodded, fumbling for his phone with shaking hands. As he dialed, Alena focused on her breathing, on the familiar rhythm of inhale and exhale that had carried her through thirteen previous labors. This was like a comfortable old hat for her, a dance she knew by heart. But for Orion, it was all new, all raw and terrifying in its intensity.

Her delivery bag had been packed since before the cruise, and she kept it by the door so Orion wouldn't have to look for it.

There was nothing to prepare because she'd been ready for weeks, hoping the baby would arrive early. Instead, it was arriving late.

She reached for Orion's hand, lacing her fingers through his and giving them a reassuring squeeze. "It's going to be all right," she murmured, meeting his gaze with a soft smile. "I've done this many times before, remember? Fourteen is my lucky number."

Orion didn't look convinced, but he managed a shaky nod, bringing her hand to his lips and pressing a kiss to her knuckles. "I love you so much," he whispered. "I love you so much, Alena. You're the strongest person I know."

"I love you too." She smiled. "But we better get moving, or this baby will be born on this sofa, with you delivering it."

The last comment did what she'd expected: lighting a fire under Orion's bottom and getting him moving fast.

When they left their house, a Guardian was waiting for them with a golf cart. "Hold on tight." He smiled at Alena. "It's going to be a bumpy ride."

She lifted a hand. "No need to drive like a bat out of hell, Rodney. Slow and safe will get us there on time."

During the drive another contraction hit her harder than the first, and as she white-knuckled the seat and bit on her lip to stop herself from whimpering, Orion continued calling her family to let them know that the baby was coming.

By the time they reached the clinic, she'd had three more contractions. They were coming every two minutes now, which meant she was getting close.

Orion half-carried her inside, his strong arms supporting her weight as Merlin and Hildegard rushed to meet them.

The eccentric doctor was a comforting sight. He hadn't delivered any of her other babies, who had all been born before he had even been born, but she liked him and his unruly shock of white hair and his piercing blue eyes that seemed to see straight into the heart of things.

Orion, on the other hand, wasn't pleased with Merlin. The doctor's eccentricities blinded him to how brilliant and compassionate he was.

The distrust was written all over his face. "When are Bridget and Julian coming back?"

Merlin smiled good-naturedly. "When the twins are back on their feet, I guess. But don't worry. Alena is in good hands. Hildegard and I have delivered plenty of babies over the years, and your mate is a pro at this. She'll be fine."

"You delivered human babies."

Hildegard stifled a chuckle. "There is no difference.

Now stop jabbering and get your wife on the bed. There is no time to waste."

62

THE PRINCE

Ell-rom wasn't sure what woke him up. Jasmine's gasp or the aroma of food. Forcing his eyelids to lift, he looked into her stunned face. "What happened?"

"You are gorgeous."

He frowned. "Your translation device must be malfunctioning. It said that I'm exceedingly good to look at."

"You are." She smoothed a hand over his mostly bald head. "You look so much better without those long strings of hair." She scrunched her nose. "You know what else I've just noticed?"

"What?"

Jasmine must be prone to exaggeration because he had seen himself after Julian had cut off the loose locks, and he still looked like a walking shadow.

"You don't have facial hair," Jasmine said.

"Is that bad?"

"No, it's just strange since all the immortals and gods I know either have beards or shave them off. Maybe it's a Kra-ell trait." She pressed the lever, which he now knew was under the bed, and lifted the back of it. "Bridget tasked me with feeding you."

He glanced at the steaming bowl of fragrant clear liquid in her hands. "What is that?"

"It's called vegetable soup. You are probably wondering where the vegetables are. Right?"

"Yes. I was curious to see what Earth's vegetables look like."

"I wouldn't be surprised if they are the same as on Anumati. After all, everything probably originated from there. But that's beside the point. Because your stomach is just getting used to regular food, you are supposed to consume only clear liquids, so even though the soup was cooked with vegetables, they were taken out." She lifted a spoonful to his lips. "Taste it."

Ell-rom hesitated a moment before opening his mouth and allowing her to put the spoon inside. As the warm, savory liquid slid over his tongue, he was surprised to find it pleasing. It was rich and flavorful, a medley of tastes that he couldn't quite identify but found appetizing, nonetheless.

"Good?" Jasmine asked.

"Yes."

She smiled brightly and brought another spoonful to his mouth. Before long, the bowl was empty, and his stomach felt warm and full.

As if waiting for the exact moment he was done, Bridget walked in. "How does your stomach feel?" she asked. "Any discomfort? Nausea?"

Ell-rom shook his head. "It feels fine. Warm. Good." His eyelids were already growing heavy with exhaustion.

Bridget nodded, stepping back and allowing Jasmine to adjust his blankets and fluff his pillows. "If you can keep that down, we'll try something a bit more substantial later on," she said, her voice fading into the background as sleep began to claim him.

Ell-rom mumbled something in response, but the words were lost as he drifted off, his mind slipping into the waiting embrace of dreams.

He saw himself standing with a goblet of dark, viscous liquid in his hand. He lifted it to his lips, pretending to drink, but as soon as the rim touched his mouth, he felt a wave of revulsion wash over him. Subtly, carefully, he let the liquid dribble back into the cup, the metallic scent of blood filling his nostrils and making his stomach churn.

No one could see what he had done because the veil covered his head, the goblet, and the hand holding it, but the noises his stomach was making were a little harder to hide.

From whom?

He did not know. There was no one around he could see, but he heard a distant murmur of voices.

"Go to your room," his sister whispered urgently next to him. "Slowly. Do not draw any attention to yourself."

She was small, a child still, and covered in robes and veils—a walking tent like the adult priestesses, just smaller.

He assumed that he looked like her. Just another small tent, but he listened to her and retreated as slowly as he could, which was not slow at all because the contents of his stomach refused to stay down.

Finally, when he reached his chamber and closed the door, he ran into the bathroom while tearing the veil off. Sliding into position at the toilet, he retched and heaved, his body rejecting the small amount of blood that had managed to slide down his throat.

A figure loomed over him, a female draped in the black robes of a priestess. "You fool," she snarled, her voice dripping with contempt. "You will get yourself and your sister killed with your foolishness. What did I tell you to do?"

He wiped his mouth with the back of his hand and looked up at her helplessly.

"Tell me! What did I tell you to do?"

"I was supposed to hold the goblet under my veil and just pretend to drink." "And what did you not understand about that simple directive?"

"It was just a drop," he whispered. "I did not mean to drink it. The drop was on the rim."

The priestess crouched next to him, her eyes blazing at him through the veil. "A mistake like that is the difference between life and death, little Holy Brother. You might not care for your life, but I know you care about your sister's."

"It will never happen again, Holy Mother."

Ell-rom jerked awake with a gasp, his heart pounding and his skin slick with sweat.

For a moment, he couldn't remember where he was, but then he recognized the white walls of the clinic and let out a relieved breath.

He was safe here, in this little room with walls that were white but not quite. There were shades of pink and yellow in the white, making the room feel cozy rather than stark.

Or maybe it had nothing to do with the colors but the female sitting in the chair beside his bed, her face soft and peaceful as she read a book with a tiny light illuminating the pages.

When he'd asked her what it was, Jasmine had explained that it was a story written on paper. Humans had special machines that printed many thousands of those things, and people purchased them in stores. She'd said they also had stories on electronic tablets, which he found much more logical, but many still preferred the paper books.

Humans were strange creatures, but he was eager to learn more about them, particularly about her.

Absorbed in her reading, Jasmine did not notice that he was awake, and he was glad that she didn't because he needed a few moments to collect his thoughts.

He was safe, surrounded by people who cared for him and wanted to help him heal. Not kill him and his sister because they were unlike everyone else.

But even as he clung to that thought like a talisman against the darkness, he couldn't shake the sense of unease that lingered, the feeling that something was lurking in the shadows of his past, something dark and dangerous that was more than his inability to tolerate the taste of blood.

What was it about him and his sister that he was not supposed to let anyone see?

63

ALENA

Alena liked having people around her when she was having her babies. It was a joyous occasion, especially for people who didn't get to celebrate births often, and she liked to share her blessings.

It got a little crowded with her mother and Kian there, but she was glad Orion managed to catch them in the parking lot before they left for the keep.

If they had left earlier and had been at the keep when Orion called, her mother wouldn't have made it in time to see the baby born, and she would have regretted it dearly.

Her mother had witnessed all her babies coming into the world, and this last one shouldn't be any different.

Hopefully, it wouldn't be the last, but Alena didn't want to be greedy and anger the Fates who had been so incredibly generous with her.

Also, Orion seemed much calmer now that Annani was there, and Alena hoped her mother wasn't thralling him to take the edge off.

He was probably glad to have someone with plenty of experience helping Alena.

"Breathe." Annani clasped Alena's hand as another contraction hit her hard. "In and out, slow and steady."

"Syssi and Amanda are on their way," Kian said, his face pinched with unnecessary worry. "They're coming from the university, but they'll be here as soon as possible."

Alena laughed, the sound strained and a little breathless. "They probably won't make it," she managed, shaking her head. "This baby is coming out fast."

"Not necessarily," Merlin said as he entered the room. "Your contractions are coming every two minutes, but that doesn't mean the baby will come flying out. It could still be a couple of hours yet."

Alena shook her head. "Wanna bet?"

Merlin chuckled. "Save your energy for pushing," he advised, his voice warm with affection. "I'll give you all a few minutes, and then I need everyone out for a little bit to check how things are progressing." He winked at Alena before stepping out of the room.

As she settled onto the bed, resting between contractions, she glanced at her mate, whose pale face was drawn with worry. He looked like he was about to be sick.

"Hey." She reached for his hand and gave it a gentle tug. "There is absolutely no reason to worry. I'm a demigoddess, remember? Nothing is going to happen to me."

"I know, but I can't stand seeing you in pain. It's killing me. And then I worry about the baby. He's not going to be born immortal even though we are both demigods, and if something goes wrong, all of our powers combined might not be able to save him."

He was wrong about that, but she couldn't tell him what her mother's blood could do, or his father's. If the baby was in trouble, Fates forbid, a small donation from either would bring him back.

That wasn't guaranteed, though. If the baby was stillborn, even a god's blood could not bring him back.

Kian leaned against the wall, holding his phone. "Did you find out the baby's gender and didn't tell anyone?"

"We didn't." Alena winced as another contraction started. "Sari convinced me that statistically it was more likely that I would have a boy this time, so we started referring to the baby as he."

As the pain took her breath away, she couldn't talk anymore; holding on to Orion's hand and panting was all she could do.

When the contraction subsided, Kian was not in the room, and Merlin was back.

"I can give you all kinds of things for the pain, from mild relief to an epidural."

Orion looked at her with hope, but Alena shook her head. "I've delivered thirteen children with nothing to ease the way. I'll do no less for my fourteenth."

Merlin nodded. "I had a feeling that you would say that." He turned to Orion. "I don't mind if you stay, and naturally, the Clan Mother can stay as well, but I need to check the opening."

When Orion swallowed audibly, Alena patted his hand. "Wait outside with Kian, sweetheart. Maybe get some coffee from the café."

He shook his head. "I'm not leaving your side."

"The baby is not coming out yet, and you'll just be in the waiting room. Go."

Her mother pushed to her feet. "Come on, Orion. Let us give Alena some privacy."

When he stood up, she threaded her arm through his. "So, did you two come up with a list of names?" She looked over her shoulder at Alena and winked.

She sent her mother an air kiss.

Merlin smoothed a hand over his long beard as the door closed behind the two. "Maybe the Clan Mother shouldn't have left. Do you want me to call Hildegard to be in here while I perform the examination?"

Alena rolled her eyes. "Don't be silly, Merlin. Just do it."

She could have reminded him that he was her great-grandson, but there was a chance that it would make him even more uncomfortable.

64

ANNANI

The first cry of new life filled the air, a piercing, precious sound that brought tears to Annani's eyes. Her heart was full to bursting as she watched Hildegard wipe the tiny boy clean while Merlin took care of the afterbirth.

Delivering children into the world was messy, difficult, and painful, but no greater joy existed.

"Here you go, Mommy." Hildegard placed the baby on Alena's chest.

"He's perfect," Orion whispered, his cheek next to Alena's as both gazed upon their little miracle.

"Do you want to hold him?" Alena asked her mate. His eyes turned the size of saucers. "I'm too scared."

Annani took a step closer and leaned to touch her latest grandson's tiny cheek. He had a mop of dark hair like his father and cupid-bow lips like his mother.

"Your brother is in the waiting room, biting his nails. Can I invite him in?"

"Of course." Alena smiled. "I want him to be here when we reveal the name we have chosen for our son."

"Maybe we should wait for Amanda and Syssi to get here," Orion said.

Alena winced. "Amanda will be pissed if she misses it. You're right. Let's wait for them to get here."

Merlin opened the door and waved Kian in. "Come. Say hello to your new nephew."

A grin spread over Kian's face. "So, it is a boy after all."

"Of course," Annani said. "We all knew it was going to be a boy."

"Right." He leaned down and kissed her cheek. "Congratulations, grandma."

"Congratulations, uncle."

"I'll be in my office if anyone needs me," Merlin said. "I'll send Syssi and Amanda in when they get here."

As the door closed behind the doctor and Kian shifted his gaze to his new nephew, his eyes softened, and his smile turned tender. "Congratulations, Alena, Orion. So, does this strapping baby boy have a name?"

"He does," Alena said. "But we decided to wait for Amanda and Syssi to get here before we name him. You know how upset Amanda will be that she wasn't here when he was born."

"Yeah, she will." Kian pulled out the one chair that was in the room for Annani. "Please, sit down, Mother."

Annani did not argue. It was not that she was tired, but with everyone towering over her, she was more comfortable sitting down.

The door swung open, and her daughters, one by birth and the other by marriage, walked in, both looking rushed and sweaty as if they'd run the entire way.

"Oh, Alena, he's beautiful," Amanda gushed.

"Adorable," Syssi whispered.

"Where is Allegra?" Kian demanded.

"With Merlin." Syssi walked up to him and kissed his cheek. "Evie, too. The guy is in heaven, holding one on each knee."

"Do you trust him with them?"

Syssi gave him a scolding look. "What kind of question is that? Of course, I trust him."

Smiling, Annani shifted her gaze to Orion, who still looked shell-shocked.

"Do you want me to help hold him?" Hildegard asked the new father.

He nodded, but even though it did not look convincing, Hildegard lifted the baby off Alena's chest and put him in his father's arms.

Orion's face was a mask of wonder and terror, and he looked like he might faint at any moment.

Kian chuckled, putting a steadying hand on the new father's elbow. "Breathe, Orion. He is a beautiful, healthy baby boy."

Orion nodded jerkily, his gaze never leaving the perfect face of his son. He took a few stumbling steps forward, his arms cradling the infant like he was made of spun glass, and then he went down to one knee in front of Annani.

"Clan Mother," he said hoarsely, his voice cracking with emotion as he held the baby out to Annani. "Meet your grandson, Evander Tellesious."

Annani's heart swelled with love as she took the child into her arms, marveling at his solid weight, the impossibly soft brush of his skin against hers. "Evander," she repeated. "A beautiful name for a beautiful boy."

Looking at the tiny face, she drank in every detail of her grandson's face, committing each tiny feature to memory. The slope of his nose, the bow of his lips, the wispy curl of hair that clung to his scalp. He was perfect, a miracle in miniature, and Annani already loved him fiercely.

She dipped her head and brushed a kiss on the silky soft cheek. "There is nothing better in the universe."

Orion was still kneeling in front of her, his hands twitching as if he longed to take the baby back and cradle him close to his chest.

Annani smiled, shifting Evander in her arms and giving his father a reassuring nod. "Do not worry, Orion. I have held hundreds of newborns in my time, and I have not dropped one yet. Your son is safe with me." She stood up with the baby securely held against her bosom.

Orion pushed to his feet as well and hovered nearby as Annani walked over to her daughter's side.

Alena looked radiant, her face flushed with the glow of new motherhood, her eyes bright with joy and love. She held out her arms as Annani approached.

"He is perfect." Annani agreed, carefully transferring Evander into his mother's waiting embrace. "Just like his mother." She kissed her daughter's forehead. "I am so proud of you, my Alena."

Her daughter just smiled, as she always did when she thought Annani was being overly dramatic or too much of a diva. That quiet acceptance was one of Alena's greatest strengths.

The baby settled against his mother's chest, yawned adorably, and fell asleep. "Such a good little boy," Amanda said. "So calm."

Alena stroked his little back. "All my babies were like that."

"That's because you are calm." Syssi leaned against Kian's arm. "You project it. By the way, did you tell Allegra what you were naming the baby?"

Alena shook her head. "We told no one. Why?"

"She insisted that the baby's name was going to be E.T."

"Like mother like daughter." Kian wrapped his arm around Syssi's shoulders. "Allegra is already predicting the future."

As Amanda and Alena murmured in agreement, Annani looked around at her family and noticed that Hildegard had left the room at some point. Still, that did not mean that she could talk freely because there was a camera in the room, and even though she doubted Merlin would pry intentionally, he might take a look to ensure that mother and baby were doing okay.

"I have news," she said quietly, not to disturb little Evander. "Bridget called this morning to tell us that the prince remembered his and his sister's names. That is a very good sign that his memory is coming back."

"What are the names?" Alena asked.

"The prince's name is Ell-rom, and his sister is Morelle."

Alena's face lit up. "That's wonderful news, Mother. I think it's symbolic that he recalled their names on the day Evander was born and named."

"Indeed." Annani nodded. "That is why I decided not to wait to tell my brother I am his sister."

As she had expected, Kian was not happy. "It's too early, Mother. Let's wait for him to regain more of his memories so we can assess his intentions."

Annani pinned her son with a hard look. "The more I tell him, the more I reveal, the faster he will regain his memories, and the quicker we will learn his true nature. I do not have patience, and I do not want to wait to make Ell-rom and Morelle part of my family. The only concession I am still willing to make for the sake of your insistence on security is to wear the earpieces, but once I am convinced that my brother does not harbor ill intentions toward me, I will remove them."

She leaned down to press a final, lingering kiss to Evander's forehead, breathing in the sweet, milky scent of him.

"It is a blessed day for our family as we welcome Evander, Ell-rom, and Morelle into our clan."

65

MARINA

The morning sun slanted through the kitchen windows, bathing everything in a warm, golden glow. Marina stood at the counter, her hands wrapped around a steaming mug of coffee, and tried to ignore the knot of tension that had taken residence in her gut.

Beside her, Peter moved with easy grace, cracking eggs into a bowl with one hand and whisking them with a fork with another. Thinly sliced onion and mushroom pieces were sizzling in a pan, waiting to be folded into the omelet he was working on.

"This one is going to be a masterpiece." Peter put another pan on the stovetop and turned on the burner.

"It sure smells like it." She leaned up and kissed the underside of his jaw. "You are spoiling me."

He grinned. "I love spoiling you, so stop complaining." He dropped a generous portion of butter into the pan.

"I'm not complaining. I'm just stating a fact. You didn't even let me make toast."

If she let him cook for her daily, she could kiss her slim figure goodbye. The guy loved his butter.

"Today is my turn to make breakfast." He poured the egg mixture into the pan. "Sit down and enjoy."

"Yes, sir."

She walked over to the dining table and sat down. Alfie had gone to the gym, so it was just the two of them, and Marina should have been enjoying the homey atmosphere. Still, she couldn't shake the memory of the previous day's confrontation with Borga and the cruel, taunting words that had dripped like venom from the Kra-ell female's lips.

She'd tried not to let it get under her skin, but it was hard. Back in the compound, Borga had been at the top of the so-called food chain and Marina at the bottom, but here in the village they were supposed to be equal, and Marina hadn't expected to be subjected to that crap, nor was she willing to just roll over and let Borga stomp all over her.

She wanted to fight back, but she didn't know how.

"You're quiet this morning," Peter said as he slid a plate of a delicious-looking omelet and toast in front of her. "Everything okay?"

Marina sighed, setting her mug down and running a

hand through her hair. "Not really," she admitted. "I had a run-in with Borga yesterday at the café."

Peter frowned. "Borga? Pavel's mother?"

Marina nodded. "She came into the café and tried hard to get under my skin. She used to taunt me in the compound, too, but I wasn't mentally ready for it in the village, and it did get under my skin."

Peter's eyes blazed with inner light. "What did she say?"

Marina shrugged. "She threw around comments about wanting me to clean her house and then also about our relationship. She had the nerve to bring you into it and suggest I was just using you to get ahead."

Peter's jaw clenched, his eyes flashing with anger. "Nasty person."

"She is, but she's just saying what others are thinking. I was a maid all my adult life, first in the compound, then in Safe Haven, and even on the Silver Swan. I've been a barista for less than a week." Marina picked at the omelet with her fork. "People also wonder what you could possibly see in someone like me."

Peter reached across the table and took her hand. "I don't care what anyone else thinks. I love you, and I want you in my life. Nothing and no one can change that. Not that I think anyone other than Borga has a problem with you. Even my mother has warmed to us being together, and she asks about you every time I call."

A lump formed in her throat. "I love you too."

Peter's mother probably wanted to hear him say they had broken up, but Marina kept that to herself. It was good that the woman was in Scotland, and she didn't have to deal with her every day.

His lips quirked in a smile. "Borga and anyone else who has a problem with us being together can go to hell. They are not worth your energy."

Forcing a smile, Marina nodded. "You're right."

Peter grinned. "That's my girl." He leaned in to press a kiss to her lips. "I'll talk to Kagra about Borga. She will put her in her place."

Marina didn't want him talking to his ex, not about Borga or anything else. "I'd rather put this episode behind me and pretend it never happened."

Peter leaned back in his chair. "I don't think that's smart. Borga didn't make trouble before, and suddenly she's allowing herself to be rude to a community member right as a slew of things start happening that have never happened before."

"Like what?"

"Theft. Packages are being stolen from the mailroom, shutters are malfunctioning, and yesterday, one of the trash incinerators broke down. Those things are built to last forever. There is no way it malfunctioned without someone doing something deliberately to sabotage it."

"I don't think the incidents are connected to Borga, but I'm not a Guardian. You have experience with stuff like that."

"Not really," he admitted. "This is the first time we've had things stolen in the village. No one even bothers locking their doors, and unless things start going missing from inside homes, they'll continue leaving them unlocked. But before I call Kagra, let's finish breakfast."

Talking about Borga and Kagra was enough for Marina to lose her appetite, but she made an effort to take a few more forkfuls before pushing the plate away.

"Okay. Let's do it." Peter reached for his phone, his fingers flying over the screen as he texted Kagra.

Once he was done and hit send, the reply didn't take long to arrive. "She's on her way. She wants to get all the details straight from you." Marina swallowed.

She hadn't seen Kagra since their community had been divided between Safe Haven and the village, but that wasn't why she was apprehensive about meeting the female.

What if she also made derisory comments about her former boyfriend shacking up with a human?

When a few minutes later, a knock sounded at the door, Marina tensed. Peter gave her hand a reassuring squeeze before rising to answer it.

"Good morning." Kagra walked in like she owned the place. "Long time no see, Marina." She nodded at her. "Looking good."

Did she mean that Marina looked good, or was she referring to Peter's house being in a much better state than it had been when the two of them were together?

Marina kept it clean and organized, so that could be what Kagra had meant. "Good morning." She forced a smile. "Please, take a seat." She motioned to the couch. "Can I get you some coffee?"

The purebloods could drink coffee and tea as long as it didn't have added cream or sugar.

"No, thank you." Kagra sat down. "We all have jobs we need to get to. Tell me what happened with Borga."

"It's not a big deal, but Peter thinks it might be connected to other things happening in the village, and that's why he texted you." She continued telling her about the encounter and her past interactions with Borga.

Kagra nodded. "Borga is a character. She needs to be reminded of her place occasionally, and then she behaves for a while." Chuckling, Kagra stretched her long legs and crossed her booted feet at the ankles. "She's like a hormonal human, no offense, Marina."

"As if the Kra-ell are so even-keeled," Marina murmured. "'Between the big egos, the power plays, and the petty jealousies, you are much worse than humans."

Marina would have never dared say that to a Kra-ell while still in the compound, but she felt fearless with Peter at her side.

Kagra barked out a laugh. "Every word you said is true. Still, Borga has her good and bad sides like everyone else, and she is usually not that vicious."

"For some reason, she is to me."

"I don't doubt that." Kagra turned to Peter. "What's your take on this?"

"You know my take. I wouldn't have called you here if I thought there was nothing to it. But what bothers me is that none of the Kra-ell or humans should be able to pull off the recent wave of thefts and the small acts of sabotage. You were all subjected to a powerful compulsion that should prevent you from harming the clan and the village."

Kagra pursed her lips. "Many of the Kra-ell and the humans in the compound spent their entire lives under Igor's compulsion, and they learned to take advantage of every possible loophole that allowed them to maintain some semblance of free will." She leaned forward, her eyes boring into Peter's with an intensity that made Marina's skin crawl. "Borga, or whoever else is committing those small acts of rebellion, might have convinced themselves they are harmless pranks and as such, don't fall under the umbrella of Toven's compulsion."

Marina felt a chill run down her spine. The thought of Borga or any of the other Kra-ell being able to defy the compulsion that bound them by mislabeling their actions as pranks was terrifying. Countless acts of small cruelty could be defined as pranks by the perpetrators while being much more than that to the victims.

Kagra uncrossed her feet. "We should tell Kian." She shifted her gaze to Marina. "Call your supervisors and tell them that you will be late. I'll check with Kian when he can see us."

66

KIAN

Kian put the phone down and turned his chair to look out the window at the village below.

From his vantage point on the second floor, he could see the bustling activity of the café and even hear the laughter and shouts of Kra-ell children playing on the playground. The small pond glittered in the sunlight, its surface rippling with the gentle breeze that stirred the leaves of the trees.

It was a peaceful scene, a tableau of harmony and contentment that should have filled Kian with a sense of pride and satisfaction. After all, he had worked so hard to achieve this—a community where immortals, former Doomers, Kra-ell, and humans could coexist in mutual respect and understanding. But it was an illusion, and dark currents were circling underneath the surface.

The recent string of thefts and acts of sabotage, and then Borga's unprovoked attack on Marina, were all troubling signs of unrest that he knew better than to ignore.

It was like dismissing a slight whiff of smoke when what was causing it was an inferno raging undetected underground.

For the sake of the children, his daughter, his newborn nephew, and all the others, he needed to make this place a sanctuary again, and if harsh steps needed to be taken, so be it. His people, his clan, always came first.

That was why he had called Jade and Onegus and asked them to join the meeting with Kagra, Peter, and Marina. They had to get to the bottom of this and do it fast before the smoke became suffocating and the fire consumed his village.

When his guests arrived a few moments later, he guided them to the conference table.

"Borga is not the main instigator behind this," Kagra said without preamble. "I'm sure of it. But I'm also sure she knows who the leader is, who else is involved with the saboteurs, and what they hope to achieve."

Jade's eyes flashed with anger. "I can get her to talk."

Kian did not doubt that, but there were better ways of handling the situation. Lifting his hand, he got everyone's attention. "Let's not get ahead of ourselves. Borga may or may not have operated on her own, but until we know what's going on, I would rather not tip our hand." Remembering that some of the people present might not know the idiom, he added, "We don't want them to know we are on to them, so they don't go into hiding. I want to do it discreetly."

Jade crossed her arms over her chest. "I can throw Borga in the brig just for being rude to Marina. I'm curious who will come to speak on her behalf."

Kian nodded. "That's a possibility, or just put a bug on her and find everything you need to know."

"Which is?" Jade asked.

"I want to find out who the other players are and what their agenda is."

Jade scoffed, her lip curling in a sneer. "What does it matter? Their grievances are irrelevant. There is no excuse for breaking the law and endangering everyone in the village." Her eyes were blazing with anger. "How are they even doing that? They shouldn't be capable of sabotage."

Kian sighed, rubbing a hand over his face in frustration. "We assume the Kra-ell are responsible, but maybe they are not. It occurred to me that some of the clan members might not be happy about the village's latest changes, and they are showing their discontent."

Jade frowned. "You told me everyone got to vote, and the decision was unanimous."

"People succumb to peer pressure," Onegus said. "They might not want to look like the bigots who refuse to invite a group of alien refugees. It's also possible that they believed things would work out better between the two groups, but contact between the groups is minimal. Except for you, Phinas, Vanessa, and Mo-red, even friendships between Kra-ell and clan members are rare or nonexistent." He flashed his charming smile. "Maybe we should organize parties so everyone will get to hang out together, and barriers will get broken."

That suggestion had been raised before, but it had never materialized. The younger immortals and Kra-ell had tried to bond over music and form a band, but even that had fizzled out. People tended to stick to the familiar and the comfortable, and forming friendships with members of a significantly different tribe was not easy. It needed work and the will to do it.

Kian sighed. "You know my opinion about all that kumbaya. Seems good in theory but seldom works in practice."

Onegus didn't seem discouraged. "Just give the assignment to Amanda, and it will be done."

"That's not a bad idea," Kian said. "But we need to solve this mystery first. Who's doing it, why, and how."

Onegus leaned back in his chair. "If they are Kra-ell or humans, that would require impressive creative thinking on their part to excuse malfunctioning shutters as a prank. Light at night gives the village away and renders our sophisticated camouflaging measures ineffective. Everyone knows that."

Kagra nodded. "I was thinking about that on the way here. It's possible that the saboteurs convinced themselves that they are doing it for the greater good, for the benefit of the community."

Kian frowned. "How could that be for the benefit of the community?"

Kagra shrugged, a bitter smile tugging at the corners of her mouth. "They might think separating the Kra-ell from the clan would be better for everyone. I know that some think we'd be better off on our own."

"That's ridiculous," Marina said. "We're stronger together. I mean, you are stronger together. Humans are inconsequential to both groups in that context." Kian nodded. "Marina is right." He turned to Jade and Kagra. "Find out whether Borga is working with others or is a lone player, and at the same time, snoop around for clues about the saboteurs. Once you have the information, report back to me, and we will decide how to proceed."

Jade looked like she wanted to argue, her jaw clenching with barely contained frustration. But after a long moment, she nodded. "We'll do it your way, Kian. But if this backfires, and Borga and her cronies cause more serious damage, don't blame me, and remember that I wanted to put her in the brig."

67

ANNANI

Annani stood before the mirror and surveyed her reflection. The dark blue silk of her gown shimmered in the soft light of her bedroom, the rich color bringing out the vibrant red of her hip-length hair and the fluid fabric skimming over her figure.

It was just another day dress, but it was her favorite. She never wore anything constricting, and silk was her preferred fabric because it was gentle on her skin and breathable, so at first glance there was no difference in her appearance today compared to any other day. But she had taken extra care for the grand reveal.

Ell-rom had already met her, so this wouldn't be his first impression of her, but it would be the first time she would face him as his sister rather than the Clan Mother.

It was a big deal, as the young ones liked to say. She had spent so long without any family other than the one she had created herself, and thinking that she was all alone, the only one of her kind, had been difficult. Discovering that Areana lived had been a tremendous joy, but her sister was out of reach for all intents and purposes, imprisoned by Navuh. Then the Fates brought her childhood best friend, Wonder, as she preferred to be called, back to her. As if that was not enough of a boon, Toven returned to her as well, and Annani was immensely grateful for having her cousin in her life.

Now, the Fates had guided two more siblings to her.

She had also discovered that there were trillions of beings like her on a distant planet, and yet she was still one of a kind because she was the only legitimate heir to Anumati's throne.

Annani smiled at her reflection. "There was a good reason for all these years of acting like a diva after all."

She had assumed that her penchant for theatrics was just a way to amuse herself and her family. After all, she had never abused her status and had only used it to make things special. Ceremonies needed some pomp and grandeur to be entertaining and memorable.

Evidently it was part of her DNA, her unique genetics. She was born to be a queen.

The problem was that she preferred to be a ceremonial figure rather than engage in actual ruling. If she ever took over the Anumati throne, she would create a council that would be democratically elected and be the de facto governing body of the planet and, by extension, the galaxy.

Oh, well, she should not dwell on such heavy topics on the day she was going to welcome her brother into the family.

Sighing, Annani turned around and walked over to the jewelry section of her closet.

Most of the pieces stored in the velvet-covered drawers were modern acquisitions, some custom-made for her by renowned artists and others store-bought. But those seemed inappropriate for today.

Opening the one drawer with her most precious possessions, she pulled out a lapis lazuli bracelet. It was priceless not because the stones were precious or the silver binding was costly, but because it was an antique. For her, though, the value came from the memories attached to the item. It was the first gift Khiann had ever given her when he was still pretending to be her tutor.

Even now, so many centuries after his untimely death, the sight of it brought tears to her eyes and a bittersweet ache to her chest.

She slipped it onto her wrist, the cool metal warming quickly against her skin.

When the doorbell rang in the living room, she turned around and stepped out of the bedroom to greet her son.

"Hello, Mother." Kian dipped his head to kiss her cheek. "You look lovely today. That color suits you."

"Thank you." She kissed him back. "I am ready to see my brother again."

Kian winced. "Are you sure I cannot convince you to wait? At least until Morelle wakes up as well. Wouldn't it be better to tell them the good news together?"

Smiling, she patted his arm. "That was an excellent argument, but I do not wish to wait." She moved her hand to her chest. "I feel that I need to tell him now, and I trust my instincts."

Kian nodded. "I won't argue with that. Your gut feelings are rarely wrong."

She gave him an amused haughty look. "Almost? Were they ever wrong?"

"I can't recall right now, but I'm sure you've not always been right."

"If you cannot think of an example, I must have been right every time." She strode toward the front door. "Did you bring the golf cart?"

"Of course, Mother." He opened the door for her. "I'm thinking of buying one that has air conditioning." He helped her up and walked around to the other side to sit behind the wheel. "It usually doesn't get hot enough in the village, so it's not a necessity, but occasionally we get very hot days." He smiled as he pulled into the path. "Imagine it was one of those days, and you were sweating on the way to an important meeting. You would be annoyed."

Annani knew what he was trying to do, and she appreciated the effort, but it was unnecessary.

She was not apprehensive about revealing who she was to Ell-rom and did not need to be distracted. She was excited, yes, but not nervous.

"I would not sweat during the five minutes it takes to drive the golf cart from my house to the pavilion, even on the hottest days, but it might benefit someone, and it is not a great expense, so go ahead. You do not need my permission to get it."

Kian smiled. "I am not asking for your permission, just for your advice."

Annani adjusted the folds of her skirt. "You are a very good son, Kian, but you were never very obedient."

He arched a brow. "When was I ever disobedient?"

She laughed. "Unlike you, who cannot remember even one occasion of my gut steering me wrong, I remember each of your many acts of defiance."

68

KIAN

"I took Allegra to see Evander yesterday," Kian said as Anandur started the engine and pulled the SUV out of its parking spot. "Or E.T., as she named him. I was surprised at how emotional she got. She was so quiet when Alena held her together with little Evan, just staring at him until Alena told her that she could touch him. She brushed a finger over his hand and looked at Alena to make sure that it was okay. When Alena complimented her for being so gentle, she finally smiled, put her head on her aunt's chest, and just kept looking at the baby."

His mother smiled softly. "That is the wonder of new life, Kian, of creation. Even a little girl who is still a baby can feel the magic."

From the front seat, Anandur chuckled, his eyes twinkling with mirth in the rearview mirror. "Just wait until Evander is old enough to start causing trouble. Then we'll see how magical he seems. But that's nothing compared to Allegra. That little girl of yours is a rebel at heart. One look at her eyes, and it's obvious that she will be a major troublemaker."

Kian laughed. "Thank the merciful Fates we've got a few years before we need to worry about that."

"So, you don't deny it?" Anandur asked.

"No, I agree. My mother accused me of not being an obedient son, and she gave me several examples to prove her point. I don't expect my daughter to be any different."

Annani chuckled. "I cannot really blame you. You have gotten that from me. I was not an obedient daughter either."

"Thank the merciful Fates for that." Kian patted her hand. "Imagine where we would be if you followed your father's commands to the letter."

She nodded. "It is not good to be overly obedient. It is much better to think and evaluate than to follow blindly. People can do terrible things when they cease thinking critically and independently. The result is them usually turning into a mindless herd when pacified. Becoming a dangerous mob is only a spark away."

"There is always an instigator," Anandur said.

Kian sighed. "Speaking of trouble and instigators, I must confess that I have been keeping some things from you."

She usually knew everything that was going on, so his news probably wouldn't surprise her.

His mother frowned. "What is happening?" Maybe she didn't know.

Kian sighed, running his hand through his hair. "There've been a few minor acts of sabotage and thefts. Also, one of the pureblooded Kra-ell was very rude to the new human in the village. On their own, these are not events that would merit a mention, but the pattern I'm starting to see indicates discontent."

His mother nodded. "The village is going through demographic changes, and you cannot expect everything to go smoothly or settle without some friction. People need time to adjust to a new reality."

He hesitated, his gaze sliding away from his mother's. "I'm starting to wonder if inviting the Kra-ell and some of the humans from their compound to live with us was a mistake. We don't have the same culture or the same values, and we are immortal while they are not. That might make them envious and resentful. On the other hand, they have many more children than the clan members have, and that could bring resentment from the other side."

His mother was quiet for a long moment. "You are correct that there are differences, but they are not that big that we cannot coexist. It is not like what is happening in the human world where religious wars still rage in this day and age." She sighed. "I hoped that era was done with and that we had entered a new era of enlightenment, never to return to that darkness, but as usual, humans make a step forward, grow complacent, and then let evil drag them two steps backward. I am so tired of that never-ending cycle." She turned to look out the window. "I keep wondering what part Ellrom and Morelle will play in our future."

Kian nodded. "Bringing the twins into the fold introduces yet another factor into an already delicate balance. I worry that it might be too much for our community."

To his surprise, Annani laughed, a beautiful sound that held no trace of reproach or judgment. "Oh, Kian," she said, shaking her head with a fond smile. "There have always been voices of dissent, my son. You have just chosen to forget about them. Our community survived then, and it will survive now."

Kian knew what she was referring to, and she was right. Not everyone was happy about him leading the American arm of the clan, and Sari the one in Scotland, despite the stellar job they were doing. Some just did not want Annani's children ruling over them.

They wanted a full democracy.

Perhaps he should give it to them. After all, if he held an election today, the vast majority would vote for him.

His mother leaned back in her seat, her gaze growing distant as she lost herself in memory. "Do you remember Alex?" she asked, her voice tinged with a hint of old anger. "I still cannot believe one of ours could commit such crimes, but he did. I guess every society has its share of sociopaths. Amanda considered him a friend because he was charming and perfected his act. But only a sociopath could kidnap young women and sell them for profit while blaming the unfair clan leadership system for his evil deeds." She turned a pair of glowing eyes at him. "When he was caught, he expressed no remorse."

"That's because he was indeed a sociopath, as you have aptly noted. What did trafficking unsuspecting, naive college girls have to do with the clan's leadership? Nothing. It was just an attempt to put a political spin on his evil deeds."

His mother snorted. "He was right about one thing, though. The clan is not a democracy. It is a family. And like any family, there will always be bad apples, those who seek to sow discord and strife for their own gain."

"Rotten apples," Anandur murmured. "If you don't catch them, they will spoil the whole bushel."

"Then we have to catch them," Kian said. "Pretending that they don't exist will not save the bushel." He turned to his mother. "On another subject, what do you want to do about Jasmine? We can keep her out of the room when you talk to Ell-rom, or we can get the introductions out of the way and let her stay. It's up to you."

Annani didn't answer right away. "Jasmine might be Ell-rom's mate, so even if we keep her out of the room, he will tell her everything later. She is there for him around the clock, and I am sure that a bond between them already exists even though they have not been intimate yet."

Kian groaned. "I need to get into her head and make sure she is who she claims to be."

"Edna probed her," Anandur said. "There is no need for that. Just imagine what will happen when Ell-rom is back to his full power and discovers that you violated his mate's privacy by peeking into her mind."

He had a point.

"I will ask her permission first," Kian said.

That seemed to satisfy Anandur. "Good. That way, she can't complain to him later."

His mother smiled. "As we have discussed before, we shall welcome Jasmine into the clan with all the usual pomp and ceremony, and I would rather you did not spoil her welcome by asking to look inside her mind. I trust Edna's intuition or the probe, as you call her talent."

His mother was right, and the truth was that he didn't get any negative vibes from Jasmine. "Where would you like to do that?" he asked.

"I will wait for Jasmine in your office at the keep, and you will bring her to me."

Kian hesitated. "I've thought about it, and I'm not sure it's wise. Jasmine is not a clan member yet, Mother. We don't even know for certain that she's a Dormant, although the odds seem to be in her favor."

Annani's eyes sparkled with a knowing light. "Finding the missing pod was a great feat of supernatural ability, which indicates that Jasmine is a Dormant. Besides, the Fates have spoken loud and clear. The threads of Ellrom and Jasmine's life were woven into the Fates' tapestry. They are destined for each other." She leaned forward and took Kian's hand. "The end of their journey is already known, my son. They need only to take the right steps to get there."

Kian chuckled. "Isn't that true of everything in life?"

"Ah." Anandur looked at them through the rearview mirror. "But the joy is in the journey. All the twists and turns and unexpected detours make the destination all the sweeter."

69

JASMINE

Jasmine flipped through the magazine pages, looking at the photos of glamorous people and not reading any of the articles.

There was no point.

The magazine was at least two years old, and everything written in it was no longer true. Heck, it had been untrue even then. Hollywood couples hooked up to promote their movies, not because they were in love, and once the movie was over, they usually went their separate ways.

Once upon a time, she had fantasized about being a part of that world, but it wasn't in the cards.

Jasmine chuckled. In her case, that was a literal description. Her tarot had never promised her a great acting career.

Looking up at Ell-rom, she watched his chest's steady rise and fall. Even that was getting stronger. At first, his breathing had been barely discernible, but now it was deep and resonant.

He slept a lot, which Bridget claimed was precisely what his body needed, and Jasmine had lost track of how long she had been sitting next to his bed.

Minutes blurred into hours, hours into days, and the outside world faded into insignificance as she focused all her attention on her prince.

At the sound of the door opening, she turned to check who was coming in and smiled at Julian. "Hi. Is it time for check-ups?"

Julian shook his head. "Kian wants to see you in his office."

A ball of dread nestled in Jasmine's gut. Was Kian dismissing her? Was he ordering her to leave Ell-rom's side?

"Do you know why? Is something wrong?" She rose to her feet and stretched out the kinks in her neck and shoulders.

"It's nothing bad." A reassuring smile tugged at the corners of Julian's mouth. "He just needs to talk to you."

Casting another glance at Ell-rom, she sighed and followed Julian out of the room. "I don't like leaving him alone for long."

"It's not going to take long," Julian reassured her.

As they walked, Jasmine ran her fingers through her hair, trying to tame it a little so she would look semi-presentable to Kian.

Watching her efforts, Julian chuckled. "Do you want to stop by a restroom before we go in? You look a little disheveled."

"I don't have a brush with me, so there is really no point." Jasmine doubled her efforts, combing the strands with her fingers and twisting them to form large curls.

As they approached the door to Kian's office, she felt a surge of nervousness, making her palms grow damp and her heart race. She paused and turned to Julian. "Is there going to be someone other than Kian in there?"

A glimmer of amusement sparked in Julian's eyes. "You're very astute, but I'm afraid I can't tell you. It's a surprise."

He didn't seem worried, so perhaps it was something to look forward to. "A good one, I hope?"

Julian's smile widened. "The best," he assured her, his voice ringing with a quiet certainty that made Jasmine's breath catch.

As the doctor opened the door and gestured for her to go in, Jasmine took a final fortifying breath and took a step forward.

Her eyes widened, and her breath left her lungs in a sharp, stunned gasp. A glowing angel was seated on a chair in front of a large conference table.

It wasn't a trick of the light because the room was not very well illuminated, and the glow emanated only from her exposed skin.

She was small, almost impossibly so, with a delicate, ethereal beauty that seemed to radiate from within. Her hair was a rich, vibrant red, falling in soft waves down her back and over her shoulders. Her eyes were a piercing, luminous blue, filled with wisdom and knowing that seemed to stretch back through the ages.

She was a goddess.

Jasmine had seen male gods. She had traveled with them to Tibet, but they were nothing like the one sitting before her.

This female was in a class of her own.

She emanated power and benevolence and had an aura of timelessness and majesty that made Jasmine's knees buckle, and her heart skip a beat.

Without thinking, she sank into a deep, reverent curtsy, her head bowing low.

She had never felt so small, insignificant, as she did at that moment, standing before a being of such immense, unfathomable power.

"Rise, child," the female spoke. Her voice was simultaneously commanding and soft, kind, musical, and filled with a warmth that seemed to wrap around Jasmine like a gentle embrace. "There is no need for such formality."

Jasmine lifted her head, eyes wide and uncertain as they met the goddess's steady, unwavering gaze. She swallowed hard, her throat suddenly dry as she searched for something to say and found nothing.

"I am the Clan Mother," the goddess said in that musical voice of hers.

"Clan Mother?" Jasmine repeated, her voice little more than a whisper of sound. "Are you Kian's mother?"

The goddess nodded, a glimmer of pride and affection shining in her eyes as she glanced at her son. "I am also the mother of Alena, Sari, and Amanda. Most of the immortals you met on the cruise are my grandchildren, great-grandchildren, and so on, stretching back through the centuries."

The goddess rose to her feet in a fluid, graceful motion. She was even smaller standing up, her head barely reaching Jasmine's shoulder, but there was no mistaking the power that radiated from her in palpable waves.

"Come, child." She took Jasmine's hand. "Let's visit Ellrom together." It felt surreal to walk holding hands with a goddess.

She did not doubt that the Clan Mother could crush her hand with ease or maybe even reduce her to dust and ashes with a single thought. But there was no threat in her touch, no hint of malice or danger in the gentle pressure of her fingers—only warmth.

As they approached the prince's room, the Clan Mother paused and turned to face Jasmine. "You may stay in the room while I talk with Ell-rom. He would appreciate you being there for him."

70

ANNANI

As Annani stepped into her brother's room, the earpieces nestled snugly in her ears were a concession she had made to appease Kian but also a necessity.

She did not speak the Kra-ell language, and the devices translated Ell-rom's words in real time for her. If he asked what they were for, she could answer that they facilitated translation, which would not be a lie.

It just would not be the entire truth.

Oh, well. Life was full of compromises, and Annani had learned to live with that.

"Clan Mother." Ell-rom dipped his head respectfully, shifted his gaze to Kian, and repeated the gesture. Lastly, he smiled at Jasmine without saying a thing.

"Good afternoon, Ell-rom," Annani said. "I am happy to see you improving so quickly."

He looked so much better than the last time she had seen him. His skin no longer looked gray and lifeless; his face was no longer gaunt and hollow. There was a hint of color in his cheeks and a spark of life in his eyes. Julian or Bridget had trimmed the hair that had hung in limp clumps off his skull, and even though he was nearly bald, he looked very handsome.

"Thank you, Clan Mother. I feel so much better after proper cleansing and a meal." He made as if to rise, his arms trembling with the effort of pushing himself to a sitting position.

Annani held up a hand. "Please stop," she chided. "I am overjoyed that you are feeling better, but I do not want you to exert yourself. You do not need to prove anything to me."

He groaned in frustration. "I made it to the bathroom earlier. I can stand."

"I am sure you can, but perhaps you have overexerted yourself, and you need to gather your strength before making another attempt." Annani sat down on the chair closest to the bed.

Looking nervous, Jasmine waited until Kian sat down before taking her seat. Ell-rom seemed so deflated as he reclined against the stack of pillows that Annani scrambled for something to say to cheer him up.

Perhaps seeing a picture of his grandnephew would do the trick.

Reaching into a hidden pocket in her gown, she withdrew her phone. "I planned to visit you yesterday, but I could not because of a surprise visit by this little guy." She rose and held up the phone with Evander's picture on the screen. "This is the newest addition to my family. Evander Tellesious, son of my daughter Alena and my son-in-law Orion."

Beside her, Kian hissed, no doubt worried that she was getting too close to the prince and that he could yank the earpieces out and compel her, but Annani ignored him.

She trusted her brother.

Ell-rom's eyes widened, a look of wonder and joy flooding his face. "Congratulations. May he be blessed by the Mother of All Life and grow into a mighty warrior."

Annani stifled a wince. It seemed that Ell-rom was remembering more about the Kra-ell warlike culture.

She did not want little Evander to grow up to be a warrior. Her clan needed more scientists.

"I would rather that little Evander chose a different path for himself, but thank you for the blessing."

Ell-rom's eyes misted with tears. "You have a beautiful family."

Annani's heart swelled at the longing in his tone. "They are your family, too." She returned the phone to the secret pocket, sat back down, and waited for the words to sink in.

He dipped his head. "Thank you for welcoming my sister and me into your community, Clan Mother."

He had misunderstood her meaning.

Annani sighed. "I did not mean that figuratively. We are related by blood, Ell-rom. You and I share a father. I am your and Morelle's half-sister."

On Kian's other side, Jasmine gasped softly.

Ell-rom's eyes widened, a look of shock flashing across his face. "How is that possible?"

"It is a long story, and I will tell you everything." She sighed. "It would be easier to explain if you remembered your life before boarding the settler ship, but perhaps my tale will help you remember."

He nodded. "Thank you, Clan Mother."

"Please, call me Annani."

He looked horrified. "I cannot take such liberties with the leader of the clan."

Annani's lips twitched. "Do you address your twin sister as princess or as Morelle?"

Ell-rom blinked, a look of confusion flitting across his face. "Of course, I would call her by her name. She is my blood—" He trailed off, his eyes widening as understanding dawned, the puzzle pieces suddenly snapping into place.

"I am your blood too, Ell-rom," she said softly, her voice thick with emotion.

Ell-rom stared at her, his eyes wide and disbelieving, his mouth opening and closing soundlessly as he struggled to find the words.

She reached out, her hand finding his and clasping it tightly. "It is a lot to take in, but it is all good. You and Morelle are not alone here on Earth. You have a large family to call your own."

Ell-rom swallowed hard, his throat working as he fought to keep his composure. "I don't know what to say," he whispered. "We are so different. We don't even look alike." He sounded ashamed for some reason.

Annani's heart clenched, a fierce, protective love surging through her veins. "Oh, my dear Ell-rom. You are perfect, exactly as you are. A child of two worlds, a bridge between the gods and the Kra-ell. You are more than the sum of your parts." She rose to her feet and brushed her fingers over his cheek. "Our father was a dreamer, a visionary who dared to dream of a world where everyone was judged and treated based on the merits of their character and nothing else. For a while, your mother shared his dream."

71

THE PRINCE

Ell-rom stared at Annani, his mind reeling with the revelation that she had just dropped on him like a bombshell. Could it be true?

He had felt an affinity toward her, had seen something familiar in her impossibly beautiful face, and now she was telling him that the reason for that was that they were related.

The same god had fathered them.

He and Morelle were not alone anymore. They had a family. A big one.

Even though he couldn't remember his life before waking up in this room, Ell-rom knew that he and his sister had been mostly alone. The dreams and tidbits of memories that had surfaced so far indicated that they had lived in profound isolation.

"Do you believe me?" Annani looked into his eyes with hope shining in hers.

He lifted his hand, intending to cup her cheek, but put it over his heart at the last moment.

Annani might be his sister, but they were strangers, and her son would not like Ell-rom touching his mother. The guy was tense and ready to pounce, and his bodyguards loomed dangerously from where they were standing against the wall by the door.

"I felt the connection in here." He tapped his chest. "And your face looked familiar. I thought that maybe you looked like my sister, but now I realize that the resemblance I have noticed is to both Morelle and me. It's subtle, but it is there." He swallowed. "It is so frustrating not to remember my past. If I knew my history, I would probably be able to deduce how we could have the same father."

Annani smiled, a soft, patient curve of her lips that held a world of understanding. "It is a long and complicated story; much of it is speculation." She sat back down, and he had to turn on his side to look down at her face. "My father did not tell me about his past on Anumati. The exiled gods did not share their history with their children; I can only guess the reasons. They might have been ashamed of their home world and its injustices, or maybe they wanted their children and the humans they ruled over to believe that all gods were benevolent and followed the same moral code as the one adopted and enforced by the gods on Earth." She shrugged her slim shoulders. "Or they might have been ashamed of being exiles. Regrettably, all the founders of the colony on Earth are gone, so we cannot ask them."

"What happened to them?" Ell-rom asked.

"Mass assassination—an act of terror. One of the gods did not like being ruled by our father and established his stronghold away from the other gods. Our father was willing to negotiate with him to maintain peace, which was a mistake. That god committed the heinous crime of killing a fellow god and was sentenced to entombment by the council of gods. To avoid that fate, he dropped a bomb over the assembly that killed all the gods. He was caught in the blast and died as well." She sighed. "Mind you, I was not there because I escaped, so the only thing I know for a fact is the aftermath. I can only hypothesize how it happened. The version I told you was the most likely one until recently, but after we found Jade and the Kra-ell people, we learned things that might indicate another party might be responsible for that abominable act of terrorism. Not only the gods died in the nuclear blast. The entire region was devastated, and everything living within a radius of hundreds of miles died. It took decades for the region to recuperate."

Ell-rom had an uneasy feeling in the pit of his stomach when he asked, "Who is the other possible party?"

Annani smiled sadly. "Our grandfather, the Eternal King. But I am getting ahead of myself. You need first to understand why the gods were exiled to Earth. As I mentioned, I did not know their history until I learned about Anumati from Jade and the three gods who came to look for the missing Kra-ell settlers."

His sister paused and turned to the tall redheaded guard standing by the door. "I am getting parched from all the talking. Can you please call the security office and have someone bring us refreshments from the café?"

As the guard asked everyone what they wanted to order, Ell-rom thought about what Annani had said about their father and his and Morelle's mother. Our father was a dreamer, a visionary who dared to dream of a world where everyone was judged and treated based on the merits of their character and nothing else. For a while, your mother shared his dream.

Had his mother been a rebel? But she was the queen? Who had she rebelled against?

"What about you?" Annani asked. "What would you like from the café?"

The question caught Ell-rom by surprise. "I do not know what I am allowed to have. The medic said that I can only have clear liquids."

"Herbal tea, then," Annani told the guard.

The guard did not have a teardrop, and he responded in the language they spoke on Earth, but his tone was friendly and respectful, not fearful or reverent.

Seeing how Annani treated the guy warmed Ell-rom's heart. He might not remember much or have a lot of life experience, but the interaction between Annani and the guard spoke volumes about the kind of person she was.

72

THE PRINCE

Ell-rom wasn't surprised that Annani did not wait for the drinks to be delivered to continue her story.

She seemed eager to share it with him.

"Our father, Ahn, was the Eternal King's only legitimate heir and a rebel. He led a group of young gods who dared to challenge the status quo and fight for the rights of the Kra-ell. Your mother, who was the crown princess at the time, worked closely with the resistance, which was how they met and either fell in love or lust."

Annani laughed, the sound so beautiful that it sent tingles down his arms. "Who knows? Maybe it was just another act of rebellion for them. They are not here to tell us one way or another, and neither left a diary behind. Whatever the nature of their relationship was, you and your sister are the testament that they were together for a brief moment in time."

"It's so romantic," Jasmine murmured, probably unaware that everyone could hear her.

"Indeed." Annani smiled at her. "I bet it would have made a great love story."

Jasmine shook her head. "Love stories need to have happy endings, and theirs didn't."

Annani's face fell. "No, it did not. What Ahn and your mother did was forbidden. Perhaps they dreamt of a future where they could be together openly, and their love would be celebrated rather than condemned, but the resistance was crushed. The rebellion's leaders were exiled to Earth, and others were probably exiled to even less hospitable planets. Your mother became the queen, and Ahn left, not knowing that he had fathered her twin children."

Ell-rom felt a chill run down his spine. "I am glad that the rebels were exiled and not executed. I guess the king did not have the heart to kill his own son."

Annani's lips twisted in a bitter smile, a flash of anger sparking in her eyes. "Trust me, Ell-rom. The king did not do that because he loved his son. The Eternal King loves only one thing, and that is his throne. He had a public image to uphold, and appearing merciful and forgiving toward his rebellious children was a political move. The exile was only the first step in his plan, though. I think that he planned on eliminating them from day one."

"Why?" Ell-rom asked. "Why would he want to kill his heir?"

"Because Ahn was a threat," she said flatly. "As his name implies, the Eternal King does not need an heir because he is eternal. A legitimate heir to the throne, who happened to be popular among the young gods, could challenge the king's rule, and so he had to be removed, first by being cut off from his power base and his supporters, and then killed." She shook her head, a hint of disgust creeping into her tone. "It was a masterstroke. The king trumped up charges of war crimes against Ahn and then severed all communications with Earth to prevent Ahn from contesting them and blamed the communications blackout on Ahn. He claimed that our father had destroyed the satellites because he did not want to face the questions and accusations coming his way."

Ell-rom felt a surge of anger, a pulsing fury that burned hot in his chest. "That's absurd," he sputtered. "How could anyone believe such nonsense?"

Annani shrugged. "Most people believe what they are told by their leaders, and the Eternal King is a master manipulator. He is a skilled propagandist who uses mass compulsion to drive his message home, so to speak."

Ell-rom frowned. "Compulsion? What is that?"

Kian leaned forward and looked at him with suspicion in his eyes. "What does it sound like to you?"

"Compelling people is using some kind of leverage to make them do things they would not normally do."

"Give me an example," Kian demanded.

It took Ell-rom a long moment to think of something that would fit the word. "If I know something that you do not, and I know that you will be upset when you hear it, I would rather not tell you, but if it is important to prevent something bad from happening, I will feel compelled to warn you."

Beaming, Annani patted his hand. "That was an excellent example, but that is not the type of compulsion the king uses. He has an innate ability to enter people's minds and force them to accept what he tells them as truth and to follow his instructions. It is a very rare gift, or curse, depending on how you look at it, and those who wield it are very dangerous because most people cannot defend themselves against it. The Eternal King is probably the most powerful compeller in existence, so much so that he can compel people while broadcasting his speeches on the Anumatian media." She looked at him with a slight tilt of her head that made her seem contemplative. "The Kra-ell queens are usually strong compellers as well.

"You and your sister should have inherited the trait."

He shook his head. "I wouldn't know the first thing

about it. Perhaps when more of my memories return, I will."

"Interesting." Annani pursed her lips. "It is possible that you were not taught how to use it. I inherited the talent from my father, but I did not like forcing people to do things they do not want to do, so I did not practice it." She turned to smile at her son. "Later in life, I was convinced to use my ability for good."

Ell-rom was about to ask in what way she had used compulsion for good when a knock sounded on the door. The tall guard opened it, and someone handed him two trays filled with cups.

"Coffee and tea are here," he announced.

"Wonderful." Annani accepted one of the cups from him and motioned for him to continue to the others. "Let us take a short break."

73

ANNANI

Annani put her half-empty coffee cup on the floor. "That was a timely refresher."

"Indeed." Ell-rom cradled his paper teacup in his hands. "This is a delicious drink. What is it called?"

"Jasmine white tea," Jasmine said.

He smiled. "With you as its namesake, it is no wonder it is exceptional."

Jasmine chuckled nervously. "You flatter me, Prince Ell-rom."

"Just Ell-rom and it is not flattery when it is the truth."

Annani stifled a smile. Her brother was definitely taken with Jasmine, and she was with him. It was always such a pleasure to observe love blossoming. That and babies were the best life had to offer.

"Are you ready to hear the rest of the story?" Annani asked.

"Yes, please," he said.

"After the Eternal King destroyed the communication satellites, he declared Earth a forbidden planet. He had it expunged from all the official records and maps, and as far as the Anumatian civilization was concerned, it ceased to exist."

Ell-rom frowned. "Why go to such lengths? Why not just kill Ahn outright?"

"He could not." Annani paused, thinking of how to continue without revealing her connection with her grandmother. "From what Aru told me, the queen, Ahn's mother, holds great power herself. She is the daughter of one of the most prominent industrial families, and she represents all the other houses. It was important for the king to convince her and the rest of the Anumatian citizenry that he was a loving and merciful father and was doing his best under grave circumstances."

In a way, telling her brother the story and explaining the Eternal King's motives was crystallizing things for Annani.

"To exile his rebellious son and his closest supporters to a forbidden planet was a brilliantly evil move, which should not surprise anyone given the Eternal King's long rule over Anumati and his ability to maintain the reputation of a great and benevolent ruler. I hate to sound so admiring of that monster, but there is no denying his genius. Instead of eliminating Ahn by killing him and making himself look bad, the king destroyed Ahn's reputation and made him practically disappear. Then, when enough time had passed, and most gods had forgotten about Ahn, he also arranged for his assassination. Mortdh, the god who I blamed for the murder of my people, could have been a convenient scapegoat. By the way, he was also the Eternal King's grandson, the son of one of the king's many illegitimate children."

Ell-rom frowned. "But if Earth was deleted from all the records, how could the king send assassins to eliminate the rebels?"

Kian snorted. "That was all propaganda for public consumption. Earth was erased from all the civilian records, but the king and his military retained the information, and patrol ships were sent occasionally to check on Earth and its inhabitants. The king wasn't taking any chances. He wanted his son dead, and he got it done."

Ell-rom sighed. "It is strange to grieve for a father I have never known. I wonder if our mother told us about him."

"Probably not," Kian said. "She was doing everything in her power to shield you. It would not have been wise to tell you."

Annani tilted her head. "Maybe she told you right before sending you to him. I think that was her plan. She wanted you to be with your father so he could protect you."

Now that it seemed the twins were not as powerful as they had suspected, that option made even more sense. They were no match for Ahn, who had indeed been powerful, and they had not been sent to undermine him or replace him. They were sent to him for protection.

"I wish my mind wasn't so blank," Ell-rom murmured. "This is so frustrating." He took a deep breath. "How long did the exiled gods live on Earth before they were assassinated?"

"About two thousand years. They were not the first gods to arrive on Earth, though. Gods have been mining gold on the planet for hundreds of thousands of years. But before our father and his supporters' permanent settlement on the planet, the gods' involvement with humans had been much more limited. The gods needed obedient workers, and they created them by manipulating the genetics of early humanoids. They deemed them a commodity, not people. When Ahn arrived on Earth, he set out to elevate humans by providing them with the tools of an advanced civilization. He introduced a writing system and a code of law that was moral and just. His brother Ekin, a gifted scientist and engineer, taught the humans agricultural and shipping methods. Things were going well until

Mortdh, Ekin's son, decided he was better suited to rule the gods and started causing trouble for Ahn and the other gods."

"What about your mother?" Ell-rom asked. "Who was she? How did they meet?"

Annani smiled. "My mother was a clever and cunning goddess. She knew in her heart that Ahn was her fated mate, but she was still too young to pursue him. She could have waited, but she was afraid that he would wed another before she was of age, so she trapped him and seduced him, and he had no choice but to make her his official wife. Despite their first encounter's less-than-perfect circumstances, they were deeply in love and very happy together."

74

THE PRINCE

Ell-rom had so many questions.

When the assassins killed the exiles, what happened to the gold mining operations and the other gods that had been on Earth before their arrival?

How had Annani alone survived while all the other gods had perished? Perhaps she wasn't the only one, and other gods had survived as well?

He was about to voice his questions when he noticed Kian glaring at his mother. Why was he angry at her?

What had she said that he objected to?

Going over her story in his mind, the realization dawned on him like a crack of lightning. After Ahn's death, Annani, Ahn's only daughter from his official mate, became the only legitimate heir to the Anumati throne, which put her in great danger.

That was why Kian was so angry. He did not want her to reveal her status.

But who would Ell-rom tell? It wasn't as if he posed any threat to Annani or anyone else. He was a helpless male who had miraculously survived in stasis for far longer than should have been possible.

He wanted to tell Kian that he had nothing to worry about, but the anger and suspicion that flashed in his nephew's eyes gave him pause.

Wariness and mistrust radiated from Kian in palpable waves. He did not trust and did not welcome Ell-rom into their community with the same open arms as his mother.

Ell-rom did not blame Kian for his animosity. Annani, Kian's beloved mother, was a possible challenger to the Eternal King's throne, which put her in grave danger.

He, of course, would stand with Annani and defend his sister even if his loyalty came at the price of making an enemy of the most powerful being in the known universe.

So be it.

He and Morelle had been saved thanks to Annani's determination to find them. She had earned their loyalty.

Besides, what she offered them was priceless.

Annani offered them a family, a community that accepted him and Morelle as they were without passing judgment or discriminating against them, while on their home planet they were considered abominations and would have been killed if discovered.

He could not comprehend a world in which people believed that it was okay to murder others just for being different. The ugliness, the cruelty, and the barbarism of such beliefs were abhorrent and unnatural. He was proud of his parents for starting a rebellion and trying to change that.

He was also proud of Annani and what she had accomplished practically on her own.

He had to wonder, though. Was Annani so happy to have found him and Morelle because she had lost her family in the assassination? Or did she think that they could assist her against the Eternal King?

Ell-rom did not know if he and his twin could help in any way, but he would do what he could, and hopefully, so would Morelle.

The truth was that he did not know how his sister would react. Was she like him? Motivated by the same things he was? Why couldn't he remember even that?

"I am so sorry for all you have lost," Ell-rom said at last. "Did you have any siblings?"

"I did, and I do. My older sister Areana also survived."

Ell-rom released a relieved breath. "So, you are not the heir."

She smiled. "I am. Areana's mother was a goddess my father had a short dalliance with. She was not his official wife. She is very dear to me, but regrettably, she is not around. She mated my archenemy."

His eyes nearly popped out of his head. "How could she do a thing like that? And who is that enemy? Is he another god who survived?"

Unexpectedly, Annani laughed. "Those are excellent questions, Ell-rom, but that is not the story I want to tell you. Are you not curious about what happened to your ship and why it was delayed for seven thousand years?"

"Jade and Kian told me the settler ship had malfunctioned, probably because it was sabotaged. But I'm more interested in hearing about you and your enemies. I thought I only had to worry about the Eternal King, but now you are telling me that you have a local enemy and that your sister is mated to him."

Annani nodded. "I will give you the shortest version I can. The long version can wait for another time."

He nodded. "I will accept whatever you are willing to offer."

"You are so agreeable, Ell-rom." She put her hand on his and gave it a light squeeze. "Mortdh, the god we believed killed all the other gods, was my intended.

Ahn thought he could appease and maintain peace by promising him my hand. Mortdh was much older than me, had countless concubines and scores of children, and did not care about me. I knew that once we were wed, he would get rid of me as soon as I gave him a child. None of his children were gods. They were all immortals. Naturally, I did not want to mate Mortdh, and when I found my truelove mate, it was my right to dissolve the engagement because to deny true love was to anger the Fates, and not even Ahn or Mortdh would dare do that. As an alternative, Ahn offered Mortdh my sister Areana, who was a widow. Mortdh reluctantly accepted her, but he did not want her. He left his son Navuh to escort her to his stronghold in the north. That was why she was away from the assembly when Mortdh bombed it and died along with the other gods.

"Navuh is just an immortal, but he is more powerful than many gods, and by the Fates' will, he and Areana are truelove mates. Nevertheless, he harbors great hatred for me, blaming me for his father's death and that of all the other gods. He also disapproves of my role in continuing Ahn's work and encouraging humans to do better. He and his army of immortal minions would see humanity enslaved, and me and my clan eradicated."

75

ANNANI

Annani observed Ell-rom's response and the warring emotions playing across his face.

"What Mortdh did was not your fault, and it was not even he who killed the gods, so you should not blame yourself. Navuh is not right in the head for blaming you even if he does not know about the Eternal King and his assassins."

Relief washed over Annani. She knew that Ell-rom was right and that the demise of the gods was not her fault, even if Mortdh had been the one to drop the bomb. It was survivor's guilt, and logically she rejected it, but in her heart, doubt lingered.

"Thank you. In my mind, I know that you are right, but my heart is harder to convince."

Beside her, Kian shifted uneasily, his jaw clenched and his eyes wary as he watched her brother with suspicion and concern.

Annani ignored him.

Ell-rom was not a threat. She felt it in her heart and her gut.

"Let us go back to why your mother feared for your lives and snuck you onto the settler ship."

Ell-rom frowned. "Wasn't it because Morelle and I are hybrids? If we had been discovered, we would have been killed, and so would she. That was what Jade told me."

"That is true, but there is more." She took a deep breath. "The Eternal King feared you. The belief was that a product of god and Kra-ell would be an abomination, which could mean a hideous creature or one so powerful that it could be a threat to the king. He wanted to eliminate you the same way he wanted to eliminate your father, just for different reasons."

"I don't have any special powers; I don't think I do."

Annani nodded. "You are still weak from the stasis, so we need to wait and see about that. It is also possible that Morelle is the more powerful of the two of you. Your Kra-ell genes might make her so."

He nodded. "It is possible, but I don't remember much about her. She was protective of me, that's the one memory I have of her." He sighed. "I guess our mother did not know that the Eternal King planned to kill our father. Otherwise, she wouldn't have sent us to him."

"I do not know for certain if that was her plan. But if I were in her place, that is what I would have done. I would have sent my children to the one person I knew would protect them. Ahn was progressive, and he did not believe in all that abomination nonsense. He was much more open to interracial relationships. After all, he allowed gods to take human partners. That is how immortals were born."

"Was it common practice to send Kra-ell settlers to other planets?" Ell-rom asked.

"Pressures were growing on Anumati about the Kra-ell multiplying much faster than the gods. After the rebellion ended and the King of the gods and the Queen of the Kra-ell negotiated a truce, an agreement was reached that the Kra-ell would start colonizing other planets. That was long before Earth was declared a forbidden planet and expunged from the records. A settler ship was sent to Earth, and the queen smuggled you on board, hoping your father would take you in and protect you. Then something happened, and the ship was lost in space, and communications with it were lost."

Annani couldn't tell Ell-rom who was responsible for the ship's sabotage.

Their grandmother's part in the plot still needed to remain a secret.

Next to her, Kian released a breath as if he feared that

she would tell Ell-rom about her communications with the queen of Anumati.

She cast him a quick glance and shook her head at him. He should know that she would never do a thing like that. She would not betray Aru's trust and endanger his sister even if the risk was nearly nonexistent.

"By the time the ship arrived, your mother was long gone." Annani squeezed her brother's hand. "The Kra-ell are long-lived but not immortal. They have a lifespan of around a thousand Earth years."

Annani didn't add that the queen hadn't gotten to live to that old age. She had suffered an accident that was most likely also an assassination.

Ell-rom swallowed. "I wish I could remember her. I dreamt about her, but it was just a few snippets in time. I got the impression that she cared about us but also that she was remote."

"She was the queen." Annani gave him a reassuring smile. "According to Jade, the Kra-ell do not believe in coddling their children. Although observing them living in our village, I would say this is only partially true. They are affectionate with the little ones but also strict." She sighed. "On Anumati, where tribal wars used to claim the lives of many young males, mothers needed to distance themselves from their children, and those Kra-ell social norms persisted even after the tribal wars were outlawed. Here on Earth, where their offspring are most likely to live to old age, there is no need to adopt such strict practices."

Ell-rom nodded. "That's good to know. What about Ahn? What kind of a father was he?"

"He was the ruler of the gods and had to project a certain persona. He also needed to raise me to be strong so I could one day become a ruler. But he still showed me love even though he was not the type to hug or kiss freely. He was a good male. Brave, disciplined, and dedicated to his people."

76

JASMINE

Jasmine listened to the goddess in stunned silence, her mind reeling with the weight of all she had just heard. The tale Annani had woven, the history of the gods and the Kra-ell, of the Eternal King and his boundless ruthlessness, which he had so masterfully hidden behind a convincing act of benevolence and the love of a father for his son.

In a way, it was such a human tale that she had no problem understanding the players and their motives, but the vastness of it made it hard to wrap her head around it.

She felt small and insignificant in the face of such cosmic forces and ancient conflicts. What was she, a mere human, in the grand scheme of things? It was such a tangled web of politics, evil schemes, and subterfuge.

So far, Ell-rom had been handling everything the goddess had told him remarkably well, but Jasmine could see that he was growing tired.

Annani must have realized that he was reaching his limit as well because she stopped talking and rose to her feet. "You look exhausted, Ell-rom." She kissed his cheek. "I will return tomorrow, and we will talk some more."

Ell-rom nodded, his eyelids heavy with fatigue even as he fought to keep them open. "I'm looking forward to it. Thank you for being so honest with me."

"Of course." She leaned to brush a kiss over his forehead. "I will stop by Morelle's room on my way out and kiss her cheek as well." Annani's eyes had a sheen of moisture that glittered in the room's soft light. "Rest, brother of mine."

He held on to his sister's hand. "Tomorrow, would you tell me about Areana? Our other sister?"

"I will. Areana is the sweetest person I know, and she has done much good in her life, but she deserves more than a couple of sentences uttered in passing. I will tell you more about her tomorrow."

He nodded. "I have three sisters. It is hard to believe."

Chuckling, Kian rose to his feet. "As someone who also has three sisters, I can tell you that it is not a walk in the park. My sisters are all wonderful people, but I can't help but worry about them all of the time."

Ell-rom smiled tiredly. "That is a lot of responsibility."

"That's right." Kian patted his shoulder and turned to follow his mother. "Goodbye, Jasmine," he said as he left the room.

"Goodbye. Thank you for letting me be here for all of this."

"You are welcome." He closed the door behind him.

With a sigh, she walked over to the bed and smiled at Ell-rom. "How are you feeling?" She took his hand and twined their fingers together, her thumb tracing soothing circles over his knuckles.

He let out a shuddering breath, his eyes fluttering closed for a moment. "Overwhelmed, confused, and grateful. Annani gave me a tremendous gift. She gave me a family and a community."

Jasmine nodded, a lump forming in her throat at the wonder in his tone. "It's a lot to take in."

He was silent for a long moment, his eyes searching her face as if looking for some sign, some hint of the thoughts and feelings that swirled like a maelstrom beneath the surface. "Tell me about how you found me."

He had taken her by surprise, and she hesitated. "You are so tired. Do you want to hear about it now? After all you have learned?"

He nodded. "I need to fill in the missing pieces in this picture."

"Okay," she said. "But only if you promise to rest. Don't force yourself to stay awake. If you fall asleep, I'll continue the story when you are awake."

As he nodded and closed his eyes, she hoisted herself on the bed and sat beside him. "It all started with the tarot cards my mother left for me."

"What do you mean left for you?"

Jasmine sighed. "She died when I was a little girl. She left me a jewelry box with the tarot hidden in a secret compartment. My father disapproved of them, so she hid them where I could find them."

"Why didn't he approve?"

Jasmine chuckled. "If I tell you my entire life story, we will never get to the part of why and how I found you."

He turned on his side and looked at her. "I want to hear your life story."

"And you will, but not right now, back to the tarot. I learned how to read them and got good at it. Since about a year ago, I started getting the same cards over and over again. The cards promised me that I would meet a prince."

She told him of Alberto the scumbag, and the ill-fated vacation that had led her into the clutches of the cartel. And she told him about Margo, the woman who had saved her life and had brought her into the fold of Annani's clan.

Ell-rom listened silently, his eyes never leaving her face as she spoke. She could see the emotions playing across his features: anger, sorrow, gratitude, and wonder.

She somehow managed to tell him about the scrying stick and the trip to Tibet without mentioning her relationship with Edgar, but she knew she would need to tell him sooner or later.

Just not right now.

Ell-rom already had a hard time processing all that he had learned today, and adding a former boyfriend who was a clan member might be the last straw, so to speak.

When she told him about hiking through the Himalayan mountains and the Chinese military base, his eyes began to drift closed, and then his breathing slowed and evened out into the gentle rhythm of sleep.

For a long moment, she sat on the bed and gazed at his handsome face, her hand still clasped in his, and her heart full to bursting.

She was in love with this male and desperately needed him to love her back.

77

THE PRINCE

Ell-rom lay against the pillows, contemplating all that he had learned and all that he still did not know and had not gotten around to asking.

Like, what time of day was it?

How long had it been since he had awakened for the first time in this bed?

So much had happened every time he opened his eyes that it felt like each awakening was a new day.

Regardless of the actual passage of time, a lot had happened since his first awakening.

He knew his own name now, his sister's name, and today, Annani had told him that she was their sister and that the two of them had a welcoming family and a community waiting for them when they got better.

Ell-rom was so glad he'd gotten to see Morelle with his own eyes. She was still painfully thin and pale, and most of her hair was missing, but she was beautiful to look at, warm to the touch, and, most importantly, getting better.

He owed it all to Jasmine.

If not for her, he and his sister would have perished, their bodies withering away to dust in the sealed stasis chambers.

The thought made his stomach churn and his heart ache for the others who had not been so fortunate, the ones their mother had chosen to accompany them on their journey to their father. He was sure she hadn't chosen randomly and that each of those Kra-ell had been selected for a reason, but even if they had not been, he still mourned their deaths.

Ell-rom found it frustrating that his faulty mind had forgotten basic knowledge, like the physiological differences between the Kra-ell and the gods.

Why could gods enter stasis unaided while the Kra-ell could not? Why were gods immortal while the Kra-ell were only long-lived?

Why did the Kra-ell consume only blood for sustenance while the gods could eat a variety of things but not blood?

That was only a tiny sample, and he was sure there were many more differences. Je-Kara, or Jade as she preferred to be called now, could explain everything to him, but he didn't want to talk to her. He knew Jade thought him weak and overly emotional. She had no respect for him.

He preferred for those memories to return on their own, even if he had to wait for them a little longer.

"Good morning." Jasmine rose to her feet. "How are you feeling?"

"Good. Is it morning, though? How long has it been since Annani left?"

"It's late afternoon, and you slept about four hours since she left." She smiled. "It was a very exciting visit, and you learned a lot. You hung on the goddess's every word until you lost the fight with your eyelids. No wonder that you slept for so long."

Ell-rom let out a breath. "It's so confusing not even knowing the passage of time down here."

"You can always ask me." She took his hand.

"I have so many more questions that no one can answer. Was I a learned male before I was put on the settler ship? Are Kra-ell priests taught about science and technology?"

"Perhaps Jade knows the answers to those questions. She served in the queen's guard."

He did not want to tell Jasmine why he preferred not to speak to Jade.

"She might not know my particular circumstances. She

only saw me from afar. I do not know who I was as a person."

Jasmine smiled. "I don't know who you were before, but I know who you are now. You are kind, loving, loyal, and compassionate."

"Are those good things? Jade thought that I was acting like a little boy. She did not know I could hear her murmuring behind Kian's back."

"Ugh. That's nasty." Jasmine's eyes glinted with anger. "She's lucky that I didn't hear her, or I would have put her in her place, no matter how intimidating she is."

The ferociousness with which Jasmine defended his honor warmed his heart. "Thank you. It means a lot to me that you don't share her opinion, but her words hurt because they are at least partially true."

Jasmine's eyes blazed with anger. "They are not. Do not listen to her." She put a warm hand on his cheek. "Love, kindness, compassion, and loyalty are wonderful qualities. Jade is a soldier who thinks that all civilians are soft."

"Maybe she is right?"

"She is not. It takes strength to show compassion, courage to love, and a good moral compass to be loyal." She leaned closer, her breath fanning over his face. "I want to kiss you so badly. May I?"

The request caught him unprepared, stunned even. His breath caught in his throat, and his pulse quickened with a sudden, fierce anticipation. He wanted to answer with an enthusiastic yes, but all he managed was a slight nod.

"Good answer." Jasmine leaned forward and captured his lips with her own.

At first, the kiss was soft and tentative, but when he moaned and wrapped his palm around the back of her neck, she deepened the kiss, her mouth hot and hungry with a desire that equaled his.

The kiss washed over him like a wild storm, transforming him from the outside in or the inside out, he wasn't sure.

He responded instinctively, his lips parting to welcome her and his fingers tightening around the back of her neck to pull her closer to him, closer and deeper into the heat and the hunger of their embrace.

As the world fell away, there was nothing but the two of them, lost in the fire and the fury of their passion.

He knew that he would never be the same after this kiss because he had found something precious, something rare and beautiful and infinitely valuable.

Hope.

Fate.

He and Jasmine were destined to be together.

In her arms, Ell-rom had found a sanctuary from the

raging storm, and he knew, with a certainty that defied explanation, that he would never let her go.

COMING UP NEXT
The Children of the Gods Book 86
DARK AWAKENING: NEW WORLD

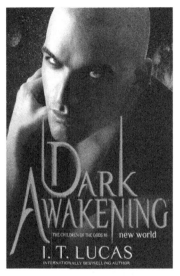

To read the first three chapters, JOIN the VIP club at ITLUCAS.COM. To find out what's included in your free membership, flip to the last page.

"Your destiny awaits across the stars," Ell-rom's mother told him. "The seer foretold your future. You will live, and you will thrive, and you will be safe."

The seer's prophecy has come true. Ell-rom and his sister are safe, surrounded by people who care for them and want to help them heal, which is in stark contrast to where they came from. On Anumati, they were considered abominations because of their mixed heritage. As half gods and half Kra-ell, they would have been eradicated if ever discovered.

But even as he clings to that thought like a talisman against the darkness, he can't shake the lingering sense of unease, the feeling that something lurked in the shadows of his past, something dark and dangerous that is much worse than his inability to tolerate the taste of blood.

What is it about him and his sister that he is not supposed to let anyone see?

Coming up next in the
PERFECT MATCH SERIES

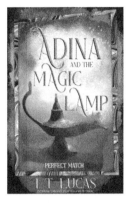

To read the first three chapters, JOIN the VIP club at ITLUCAS.COM. To find out what's included in your free membership, flip to the last page.

ADINA AND THE MAGIC LAMP

In this post-apocalyptic virtual reimagining of Aladdin, James, the enigmatic prince, and Adina, the fearless thief, navigate the treacherous streets of Londabad, a city that echoes London and Ahmedabad and fuses magic and technology. In the face of danger, the chemistry between them ignites, and the lines between prince and thief, royalty and commoner blur.

JOIN THE VIP CLUB
To find out what's included in your free membership, flip to the last page.

NOTE

Dear reader,

I hope my stories have added a little joy to your day. If you have a moment to add some to mine, you can help spread the word about the Children Of The Gods series by telling your friends and penning a review. Your recommendations are the most powerful way to inspire new readers to explore the series.

Thank you,

Isabell

Also by I. T. Lucas

THE CHILDREN OF THE GODS ORIGINS
1: Goddess's Choice
2: Goddess's Hope

THE CHILDREN OF THE GODS
Dark Stranger
1: Dark Stranger The Dream
2: Dark Stranger Revealed
3: Dark Stranger Immortal

Dark Enemy
4: Dark Enemy Taken
5: Dark Enemy Captive
6: Dark Enemy Redeemed

Kri & Michael's Story
6.5: My Dark Amazon

Dark Warrior
7: Dark Warrior Mine
8: Dark Warrior's Promise
9: Dark Warrior's Destiny
10: Dark Warrior's Legacy

Dark Guardian
11: Dark Guardian Found
12: Dark Guardian Craved
13: Dark Guardian's Mate

ALSO BY I. T. LUCAS

DARK **A**NGEL
14: Dark Angel's Obsession
15: Dark Angel's Seduction
16: Dark Angel's Surrender

DARK **O**PERATIVE
17: Dark Operative: A Shadow of Death
18: Dark Operative: A Glimmer of Hope
19: Dark Operative: The Dawn of Love

DARK **S**URVIVOR
20: Dark Survivor Awakened
21: Dark Survivor Echoes of Love
22: Dark Survivor Reunited

DARK **W**IDOW
23: Dark Widow's Secret
24: Dark Widow's Curse
25: Dark Widow's Blessing

DARK **D**REAM
26: Dark Dream's Temptation
27: Dark Dream's Unraveling
28: Dark Dream's Trap

DARK **P**RINCE
29: Dark Prince's Enigma
30: Dark Prince's Dilemma
31: Dark Prince's Agenda

Dark Queen
32: Dark Queen's Quest
33: Dark Queen's Knight
34: Dark Queen's Army

Dark Spy
35: Dark Spy Conscripted
36: Dark Spy's Mission
37: Dark Spy's Resolution

Dark Overlord
38: Dark Overlord New Horizon
39: Dark Overlord's Wife
40: Dark Overlord's Clan

Dark Choices
41: Dark Choices The Quandary
42: Dark Choices Paradigm Shift
43: Dark Choices The Accord

Dark Secrets
44: Dark Secrets Resurgence
45: Dark Secrets Unveiled
46: Dark Secrets Absolved

Dark Haven
47: Dark Haven Illusion
48: Dark Haven Unmasked
49: Dark Haven Found

ALSO BY I. T. LUCAS

DARK POWER
50: DARK POWER UNTAMED
51: DARK POWER UNLEASHED
52: DARK POWER CONVERGENCE

DARK MEMORIES
53: DARK MEMORIES SUBMERGED
54: DARK MEMORIES EMERGE
55: DARK MEMORIES RESTORED

DARK HUNTER
56: DARK HUNTER'S QUERY
57: DARK HUNTER'S PREY
58: DARK HUNTER'S BOON

DARK GOD
59: DARK GOD'S AVATAR
60: DARK GOD'S REVIVISCENCE
61: DARK GOD DESTINIES CONVERGE

DARK WHISPERS
62: DARK WHISPERS FROM THE PAST
63: DARK WHISPERS FROM AFAR
64: DARK WHISPERS FROM BEYOND

DARK GAMBIT
65: DARK GAMBIT THE PAWN
66: DARK GAMBIT THE PLAY
67: DARK GAMBIT RELIANCE

DARK ALLIANCE

ALSO BY I. T. LUCAS

68: Dark Alliance Kindred Souls
69: Dark Alliance Turbulent Waters
70: Dark Alliance Perfect Storm

Dark Healing
71: Dark Healing Blind Justice
72: Dark Healing Blind Trust
73: Dark healing Blind Curve

Dark Encounters
74: Dark Encounters of the Close Kind
75: Dark Encounters of the Unexpected Kind
76: Dark Encounters of the Fated Kind

Dark Voyage
77: Dark Voyage Matters of the Heart
78: <u>Dark Voyage Matters of the Mind</u>
79: <u>Dark Voyage Matters of the Soul</u>

Dark Horizon
80: Dark Horizon New Dawn
81: Dark Horizon Eclipse of the Heart
82: Dark Horizon The Witching Hour

Dark Witch
83: Dark Witch: Entangled Fates
84: Dark Witch: Twin Destinies
85: Dark Witch: Resurrection

Dark Awakening
86: Dark Awakening: New World

ALSO BY I. T. LUCAS

PERFECT MATCH

Vampire's Consort
King's Chosen
Captain's Conquest
The Thief Who Loved Me
My Merman Prince
The Dragon King
My Werewolf Romeo
The Channeler's Companion
The Valkyrie & The Witch
Adina and the Magic Lamp

TRANSLATIONS

DIE ERBEN DER GÖTTER
Dark Stranger
1- Dark Stranger Der Traum
2- Dark Stranger Die Offenbarung
3- Dark Stranger Unsterblich

Dark Enemy
4- Dark Enemy Entführt
5- Dark Enemy Gefangen
6- Dark Enemy Erlöst

Dark Warrior

ALSO BY I. T. LUCAS

7- Dark Warrior Meine Sehnsucht
8- Dark Warrior – Dein Versprechen
9- Dark Warrior - Unser Schicksal
10-Dark Warrior-Unser Vermächtnis

LOS HIJOS DE LOS DIOSES

EL OSCURO DESCONOCIDO
1: EL OSCURO DESCONOCIDO EL SUEÑO
2: EL OSCURO DESCONOCIDO REVELADO
3: EL OSCURO DESCONOCIDO INMORTAL
EL OSCURO ENEMIGO
4- EL OSCURO ENEMIGO CAPTURADO
5 - EL OSCURO ENEMIGO CAUTIVO
6- EL OSCURO ENEMIGO REDIMIDO

LES ENFANTS DES DIEUX
DARK STRANGER
1- Dark Stranger Le rêve
2- Dark Stranger La révélation
3- Dark Stranger L'immortelle

The Children of the Gods Series Sets

ALSO BY I. T. LUCAS

BOOKS 1-3: DARK STRANGER TRILOGY—INCLUDES A BONUS SHORT STORY: **THE FATES TAKE A VACATION**

BOOKS 4-6: DARK ENEMY TRILOGY —INCLUDES A BONUS SHORT STORY—**THE FATES' POST-WEDDING CELEBRATION**

BOOKS 7-10: DARK WARRIOR TETRALOGY
BOOKS 11-13: DARK GUARDIAN TRILOGY
BOOKS 14-16: DARK ANGEL TRILOGY
BOOKS 17-19: DARK OPERATIVE TRILOGY
BOOKS 20-22: DARK SURVIVOR TRILOGY
BOOKS 23-25: DARK WIDOW TRILOGY
BOOKS 26-28: DARK DREAM TRILOGY
BOOKS 29-31: DARK PRINCE TRILOGY
BOOKS 32-34: DARK QUEEN TRILOGY
BOOKS 35-37: DARK SPY TRILOGY
BOOKS 38-40: DARK OVERLORD TRILOGY
BOOKS 41-43: DARK CHOICES TRILOGY
BOOKS 44-46: DARK SECRETS TRILOGY
BOOKS 47-49: DARK HAVEN TRILOGY
BOOKS 50-52: DARK POWER TRILOGY
BOOKS 53-55: DARK MEMORIES TRILOGY
BOOKS 56-58: DARK HUNTER TRILOGY
BOOKS 59-61: DARK GOD TRILOGY
BOOKS 62-64: DARK WHISPERS TRILOGY
BOOKS 65-67: DARK GAMBIT TRILOGY
BOOKS 68-70: DARK ALLIANCE TRILOGY
BOOKS 71-73: DARK HEALING TRILOGY
BOOKS 74-76: DARK ENCOUNTERS TRILOGY
BOOKS 77-79: DARK VOYAGE TRILOGY

ALSO BY I. T. LUCAS

BOOKS 80-81: DARK HORIZON TRILOGY

MEGA SETS
THE CHILDREN OF THE GODS: BOOKS 1-6
INCLUDES CHARACTER LISTS
THE CHILDREN OF THE GODS: BOOKS 6.5-10

PERFECT MATCH BUNDLE 1

CHECK OUT THE SPECIALS ON
ITLUCAS.COM
(https://itlucas.com/specials)

**FOR EXCLUSIVE PEEKS AT UPCOMING RELEASES &
A FREE I. T. LUCAS COMPANION BOOK**

JOIN MY *VIP CLUB* AND GAIN ACCESS TO THE VIP PORTAL AT ITLUCAS.COM

TO JOIN, GO TO:
http://eepurl.com/blMTpD

Find out more details about what's included with your free membership on the book's last page.

ALSO BY I. T. LUCAS

TRY THE CHILDREN OF THE GODS SERIES ON <u>AUDIBLE</u>

2 FREE audiobooks with your new Audible subscription!

FOR EXCLUSIVE PEEKS AT UPCOMING RELEASES & A FREE I. T. LUCAS COMPANION BOOK

Join my *VIP Club* and gain access to the VIP portal at itlucas.com
To Join, go to:
http://eepurl.com/blMTpD

INCLUDED IN YOUR FREE MEMBERSHIP:

YOUR VIP PORTAL

- Read preview chapters of upcoming releases.
- Listen to Goddess's Choice narration by Charles Lawrence
- Exclusive content offered only to my VIPs.

FREE I.T. LUCAS COMPANION INCLUDES:

- Goddess's Choice Part 1
- Perfect Match: Vampire's Consort (A standalone Novella)
- Interview Q & A
- Character Charts

If you're already a subscriber and you are not getting my emails, your provider is sending them to your junk folder, and you are missing out on

IMPORTANT UPDATES. TO FIX THAT, ADD isabell@itlucas.com TO YOUR EMAIL CONTACTS OR YOUR EMAIL VIP LIST.

**Check out the specials at
https://www.itlucas.com/specials**

Made in the USA
Coppell, TX
14 July 2024

34593875R00252